WINGS OF MERCY

THE LAST PHOENIX: BOOK SEVEN

STEPHANIE MIRRO

TANNHAUSER PRESS

ALSO BY STEPHANIE MIRRO

THE LAST PHOENIX
Wings of Fire
Wings of Death
Wings of Winter
Wings of Magic
Wings of Life
Wings of Deceit
Wings of Mercy

IMMORTAL RELICS
Curse of the Vampire
Fury of the Gods
Revenge of the Witch
Rise of the Demons

COLLECTIONS
The Outsiders: An Hourlings Anthology
Rejected Mates: A Paranormal Romance and Urban
Fantasy Collection

Dedication

For you.
Because you stuck with Veronica to the very end. Fingers crossed our girl makes it out alive.

CHAPTER 1

Saturday Evening

I laughed at myself for ever thinking war discussions were easy. How naïve that line of thinking was. Then again, how was I supposed to know any better?

The only war I'd ever prepared for was against Galina, and back then—a whopping six weeks ago—I had little say in matters and less knowledge than I had now. I longed for the days when I was simply Veronica Neill, barista by day and master acquirer by night.

"I cannot find it in myself to believe the queen is involved," Adam LaRue, the archangel of Miami's DEA branch, repeated for the umpteenth time. I lost count hours ago. Despite his words, the archangel's bright blue eyes betrayed his doubt, and his pristine white feathers fluttered as he leaned back in his chair.

We sat in a conference room within the Death Enforcement Agency's headquarters in downtown Miami. Adam had given us one of the largest rooms, which had become our war council operations center, similar to the one back in Haven. But instead of hand-drawn maps on rolls of parchment, the DEA used fancy, expensive pieces of technology.

Glass panels resembling transparent whiteboards extended from the ceiling and rested against the long back wall. On one, maps of Miami identified the few portals into the Otherworld as bright yellow dots, while several other panels displayed topographic details of the fae realm.

A small wet bar took up a corner, and it had been well-used today, maybe for the first time. Windows took up one wall, allowing us to monitor any disturbances in the hallway.

Today, seven of us took up space at the oval table that comfortably allowed a dozen, with plenty of room for people to stand and move about. Except everyone else was busy with other preparations or resting, something I was very jealous of at the moment.

Regardless, I did my best to pay attention over the last few hours as Adam, Pietr, and the *drakony* alpha Imos discussed the impending war against the fae man Colin Ó Broin. If it came down to it, maybe all the fae. We didn't know how many were involved in Colin's plans yet.

"Queen Fiadh has always been loyal to the DEA," the archangel added as if he hadn't mentioned that several times already.

The fae queen and Adam had a long history, governing

their own realms for centuries, if not longer. Technically, Adam only oversaw the southeastern corner of the United States. Still, his reach was likely similar in size, considering how much larger our realm was than hers.

Because she oversaw the entire Otherworld, Queen Fiadh held a higher title than the archangel. Her word was as good as her gods' and goddesses'. Adam wasn't a king, and he had to obey his god's law above all else.

Anyway, Thane, Ivan, and Lena chimed into the conversation as well, though the four of us agreed the others were the true war experts. As the hours dragged on, it didn't matter that we all came from different backgrounds and species. War was war.

Except following the back-and-forth conversations between warriors who'd trained for this type of scenario from birth was like trying to read a book with tiny handwritten print when you're dyslexic. And I knew how challenging that was from personal experience.

The only thing keeping me awake now was my coffee with our takeout dinner.

Did I mention my brain was turning to mush?

"Or perhaps that's only what Fiadh wanted you to think," Thane said beside me.

His thick black hair was tousled from running his hand through it all day, and his ocean-blue irises appeared almost black thanks to the dark circles under his eyes. He'd been going nonstop since waking up to find me missing four days ago, not that any of us had gotten much rest lately.

"Until we know the depth of the fae's deceit," he continued, "we can't say one or another. We must plan for the worst."

My mate might not have trained for war like Pietr, Imos, or even Adam, but he had plenty of experience negotiating with and studying Community members during his five years as a reaper. If he thought there was a chance, no matter how slight, that the queen sided with Colin—or commanded him to carry out these terrible acts—then I would take his word for it.

My phone buzzed in my pocket, and I pulled it out, welcoming the distraction. It was just an email advertisement for a gym, but it reminded me I needed to check on Kit. I'd texted my best friend hours ago, shortly after we arrived in the human world and after a brief trip to my penthouse for a proper shower and change of clothes.

I loved my bestie, but I had priorities.

Besides, Thane had said she was fine.

I'd used one of my backup phones since I'd long since lost my real one in Mirdrakona, but Kit had all my numbers. Staying silent for so long wasn't like her, and considering she was likely still at her mother's house—aka the Devil's—her silence was even more nerve-wracking.

I typed out another message, "Girl, you can't possibly be so busy you can't message back. Come to the DEA ASAP before I do something crazy."

There. That threat should do it.

After all, I had a history of crazy.

"You're sure he's returned to the Otherworld?" Pietr asked, drawing my attention back to the conversation.

As captain of my royal phoenix guard, Pietr was a strategic mastermind. He also had the most mesmerizing eyes. His irises swirled between all the colors of the rainbow, a unique trait he shared with his mother, Inessa.

She and her dragon mate Tundreg had helped me stop the war in Mirdrakona only a few short days ago. A war Colin started to distract everyone from what he was doing in the Otherworld.

Add in Pietr's long blond hair and matching beard set against a deep brown complexion, and it was no wonder he'd captured my interest when I stumbled into Mirognya. His well-defined muscles and leather musk hadn't helped.

Thankfully, Thane understood my predicament. He had been on his way to angelic ascension and was not available for romantic anything, or so we thought. Fates—or maybe the gods—had other plans, and we had solidified our mating bond since then. Many times over.

There would always be handsome men in my life, but there was only one who had captured my heart and soul.

"We have angels stationed at every portal," the archangel answered Pietr with a nod. "Colin was last seen entering his own realm and has not returned. He claimed the queen called him back."

"Coward," Lena mumbled from her chair on my other side.

Narrowing her bright blue eyes, she ran a whetstone along her sword's blade to sharpen it and keep her hands busy. Her black dreadlocks had been half pulled back with a clip, keeping the thick strands out of her olive-toned face.

After I killed the usurper Galina, Lena became my personal bodyguard, and the warrior woman was as entertaining as she was fierce. Without her, I wouldn't have gotten through the vampires' Blood Trials, and Thane would have died.

"I may not like the guy, but I wouldn't have thought

Colin capable of all this," Thane said, rubbing his scruff-covered face, his eyelids hooded from exhaustion. "I wouldn't have mentioned anything about the fae's involvement in front of him if I had."

Even though the reason for his scruff sucked, it gave him a ruggedly sexy look I could get used to.

The door opened, and a younger-looking grim reaper pushed a large trash can on wheels inside. He moved to the kitchenette and cleaned up the leftover food and drinks from our afternoon discussions.

I wondered whether the job bothered him. Dying and waking up to find yourself a janitor couldn't be much fun. At least this kind of cleanup didn't often happen since reapers and angels didn't need food or water, and they rarely had visitors stay this long.

Who knows, maybe he enjoyed getting to listen in. I sure would, even if it bored me. I was nosy like that.

"Do not blame yourself. I had suspicions but no concrete evidence, or I would have brought you in sooner." Adam tilted his head to the side. "Although, I must point out that you do not work for me anymore."

Thane chuckled. "You know I'm always willing to help."

I yawned, which caused a chain reaction from most of those gathered. If I wasn't so tired, I would have laughed. "I don't mean to be the party pooper, but can we reconvene in the morning?"

As much as I wanted to murder the manipulative fae fuck responsible for orchestrating everything terrible that had happened in my life, I also knew things were somewhat stable at the moment. Colin wasn't even in this realm right now, and I needed to be on my A-game when I faced him and killed him.

Gods, that was going to be such a glorious moment.

The others looked as tired as I felt and agreed to stop for the night. Adam had offered our *drakony* guests rooms within the DEA's building until he secured another location.

If we couldn't capture Colin in the human realm, we intended to bring most of the dragons and a bunch of phoenix warriors with us to the Otherworld. In that case, we would need a much bigger space to house everyone.

The dragons' weirdly dilated eyes and overly tall bodies weren't easy to hide from humans without magic. We needed to conserve all that we had unless absolutely necessary.

"Imos, before you go, I wanted to get your thoughts on something," Thane said, remaining in his seat.

"Of course." The dragonman's skin was a darker brown than Pietr's, but Imos had hair as black as Thane's. Sitting almost a foot taller than either of the other two men, his golden irises regarded my mate patiently from across the table.

Thane explained what had happened on the battlefield in Mirdrakona when black scales like the dragons' appeared on his skin and protected him. We didn't know what it meant or how to control the ability.

Imos's expression turned thoughtful. "I'd not heard of that happening outside a mated bond, but the tsarina does not have enough *drakon* blood to shift in such a way."

"Could it be from the dragonstone?" I asked.

He tilted his head as he considered it. "It's possible, though I admit I hadn't thought a human would be capable of inheriting those qualities."

"Well, he's more than just human," I pointed out. "He's a realm walker and mated to a phoenix."

Imos smiled, an expression he'd finally mastered. When we first met, he and the other dragons had just woken up from a few decades-long slumber and were adjusting to muscle movement again. That or he hadn't smiled much before.

"And mated to a royal phoenix, at that," he said. "I suppose I could be wrong. Perhaps the combination of the stone and your *drakony* blood passed through the mate bond and created this ability."

Thane leaned forward, resting his forearms on the table. Eagerness lit up his face. "My main reason for asking is to learn to control it. So far, it's only appeared during battle."

Beneath the table, I slid my hand over his thigh and between his legs, brushing against him. Immediately, he stiffened, and I had to hold back a laugh.

The scales had shown up during other climactic moments than just battle. If they hadn't appeared, I would have killed him during one of my many fiery orgasms.

Imos dipped his head. "I will ask Tundreg to assist you tomorrow."

Perfect. Out of anyone here, the blind dragonman with seer-like abilities was sure to have answers or some ideas. One less thing to worry about.

If only he'd gotten that chance sooner.

CHAPTER 2

Sunday Morning

After the excitement of returning home to my extremely expensive pillowtop mattress and silk sheets had subsided, I'd fallen into a deep but troubled sleep. Even as I got dressed the following day, nightmares haunted my thoughts and followed my steps.

Something terrible loomed on the horizon, and not just the impending war. Everywhere I turned, monsters lurked in the shadows, waiting to strike. I hated this uncertainty of not knowing who I could trust, worried I'd make the wrong choice and someone I loved would die.

Sure, I once thought of Colin as a bad guy after seeing him with William at the stadium. But when Adam cleared his name, I hadn't doubted Colin's loyalty. Certainly not like this.

I'd even dated the guy, which was harder to swallow.

Thane and I met Lena and Ivan in my penthouse living room, and we used Thane's realm walking ability to jump into the DEA's conference room where we'd met the night before. Imos and Tundreg were already there, filling their plates with fresh fruit, breakfast pastries, and coffee set out on the bar top.

The blue-winged angel Nathan and Pietr were already seated and deep in discussions. Pietr had declined my offer to stay at my penthouse, claiming a need to be close if Colin showed up at the DEA. He'd also said he didn't want to sleep on my couch—Lena and Ivan shared my guest room— even though it was super comfy for naps.

I was pretty sure his reasoning stemmed from seeing Thane and me together, even if the phoenix man and I had moved past any romantic involvement and awkwardness.

Sleeping arrangements aside, at least I had company with my sour attitude. Everyone was grumpy after rough nights of sleep all around. Everyone except Ivan.

"If your snores keep me awake one more night, you're sleeping on the couch," Lena threatened him with a growl.

The always chipper young phoenix grinned. His twinkling green eyes reminded me even more of my little brother. Though, unlike Maddox, Ivan's eyelashes were nearly translucent. His shoulder-length hair was the same shade as a raging fire, and his caramel-colored skin spoke to his love of the sun.

"Just wear those weird squishy things Veronica gave you." He bit into an apple with a loud crunch.

I poured coffee from the carafe into my cup and chuckled. That was an accurate description for earplugs if I ever heard one. I took my seat between Thane and Lena and sipped on my black coffee.

Whatever bright and sweet blend they'd brewed today was heaven, which was good because I would need an entire pot to get through the day.

Lena scoffed. "Like I could ever wear those while Veronica exists."

"What do I have to do with it?" I asked over my cup, blowing on the hot brew gently. A slight citrus scent wafted off of it and made my mouth water.

"I can't risk sleeping through the chaos you create."

I shrugged. That was fair. Most recently, I had slipped away in the middle of the night to hunt down Jackson Reed, the man who killed my little brother, only to wind up stranded in Mirognya and captured by dragons.

Dazhbog must really have a lot of faith in me.

Adam, Luka, and another man walked in. The alpha of the Miami werewolf pack was as handsome as ever. His eyes were a darker amber than the dragons', and because of his Latino ethnicity, his skin was more of a russet brown than Imos's dark brown.

Like most men present, he was big and beefy, but one of a handful who'd made Lena's jaw drop when she first met him.

I vaguely remembered the shorter man beside Luka as his beta. He wasn't handsome, and unfortunately for him, the effect was worse while standing next to the alpha and archangel, especially considering the broken nose that hadn't been set correctly.

Although I doubted that he cared about his looks, not with his status as beta. Now that Luka had his mate, this guy had the pick of the litter.

Adam gave a quick round of introductions between the dragons and wolves. Outside of pack meetings, having two alphas in the same room was unique, even if they were two different species.

Imos and Luka eyed each other as they shook hands, but their friendly expressions made it clear they were both more intrigued than threatened.

"I told Adam on the way in that my pack is ready and waiting to provide whatever support you need," Luka said as he pulled back a chair and sat.

His beta snagged a chocolate croissant before leaning against the wall and taking a bite.

I smiled. "Thank you."

"Don't thank me yet. We've got another problem developing with the rogue shifter clan, so my attention will be split until action is required." Luka motioned to his beta. "I brought Francisco to stand in when I cannot."

His mouth full, Francisco raised his pastry in acknowledgment.

"What's the issue there?" Thane asked, his eyebrows drawn together.

Unease trickled through our soul link, a fantastic perk we'd discovered after solidifying our bond. We could feel each other's emotions, especially the stronger they got.

"A member of another pack got word of a meeting between their leader Rico and a vampire."

I groaned. Not vampires again. All they ever seemed to do was cause trouble.

"Do they have a new Master of Miami?" I asked.

Vampires had a more complex hierarchy than most Community species, the highest of which was a king and queen who presided over a continent. Master Vampires were a step below them and oversaw large metropolitan areas like Miami. Sometimes whole states.

"Yes, but I would not count on their support," Adam said.

I snorted. "Oh, I definitely don't count on it. I actually think it might be best not to include them at all."

"Wouldn't they see it as a slight?" Ivan asked, then shoveled another fork full of melon into his mouth. Thanks to my involvement in the Blood Trials, he'd become a bit of an expert on all things vampire.

Adam shook his head. "Not after what happened with Emilia. We must remain cautious with them until they or we can prove no other vampire is involved."

Emilia, as in the Master Vampiress who had worked with Colin and Galina to overthrow my parents' Mirfeniksan throne, then tried to get me unfairly killed in the Trials. She'd gotten what was coming to her.

Because the DEA had a rule against their involvement in otherworldly affairs, we couldn't count on any other agency branches coming to our aid. Adam was risking his job by making an exception. We would have to make do with the Miami Community, minus the vampires of course.

"What about other witches?" Lena asked as she set down her empty mug. She'd devoured her fruit and croissant before Ivan had, which I was sure she'd rub in his face soon. "What did you call their groups? Covens?"

A sinking sensation dropped into my stomach. I still hadn't heard from Kit. She might be preoccupied with her visit to her mother's, but going this long without a reply wasn't like her. Even when she was mad at me, she always replied.

Had something gone wrong at Octavia's?

CHAPTER 3

Sunday Morning

My heart pounded as I looked over the stream of unanswered messages I'd sent to Kit and Angela the day before. "Adam, did Kit get a new phone while I was away?"

The archangel frowned. "I do not believe so."

Rising panic wrenched at my insides, making it challenging to sit still. I excused myself and stepped outside the conference room, Lena and Thane on my heels.

The hallway continued to my left and opened into a generous office space for cubicles and desks. Fluorescent lights shone above our heads, reflecting off the white linoleum floor.

I called Kit and Angela's phones, but both went straight to voicemail. Dread churned within my stomach, and I lowered the phone, my hand shaking. "Nothing."

Thane wrapped his arms around me, comforting me with his warmth. "She told me she was okay, and we have to trust that she is."

As much as I loved his positivity and wanted to agree, I knew something wasn't right. I wiggled out of his grasp and shook my head. "Something's wrong. I can feel it. We need to go to Octavia's."

Lena groaned, but I shot her a stern look before she could argue. "I'm not being impulsive. I've texted and called her *and* Angela since yesterday with zero response. Adam hasn't heard from her, and Thane only got a text that she was okay. No one has actually talked to her."

Frowning, Thane rubbed his chin. "It is unusual for her not to respond for so long."

He would know, too. They worked together for a month while I hid from the necromancers in Arizona and when I disappeared to Mirognya. Both times.

Man, I had a record.

"Let me tell Adam we're going to check on her." Thane stepped toward the conference room door, his arm raised to open it.

Blinding light exploded around us, followed by a deafening boom that shook the floor and nearly knocked me off my feet. A fast wind swept down the hallway, tugging at my clothes and hair and threatening to topple me over along with the shaking floor.

Raising my arm to cover my face from the wind and light, I reached for the wall to steady myself.

What in Dazhbog's name was happening?

Just as I called on my inner fire, the wind and light ceased abruptly, as if they'd never occurred. Lowering my arm, I blinked away the spots in my vision.

Dense fog surrounded me, and somehow I knew I wasn't in the DEA building anymore. A chill crept over my body, goosebumps rising in its wake.

"Hello?" I took a cautious step forward, squinting into the fog.

The grey mist swirled around my legs and dissipated, revealing a sidewalk in downtown Miami. A full moon shone brightly in the clear night sky between two towering buildings, and several couples walked by, holding hands or locking arms.

My thoughts were fuzzy and sluggish like I'd just woken up from too short of a nap. A quick glance showed I had dressed in high heels and a short black dress, and I held a black clutch in one hand. I frowned.

Where had I been going?

My phone buzzed, and I read the message from Kit, "Have fun on your date."

Oh, that was it. I was heading to Azul Restaurant with Thane. Spinning around, I didn't see my mate anywhere, and I didn't even know why I had stopped. I shrugged and kept walking, smiling as I thought of the night to come.

An unlit alley opened on my right, and a snarl came from deep within the shadows. Pinpricks skittered across my scalp as I recognized the sound. Flipping on my avian vision, I approached the alley.

My lungs seized with fear. Bathed in a red glow from their heat signatures, Thane and Maddox knelt at the end of the alley, bound and gagged as they stared up at the man facing them. Their eyes were wide with fear.

The other man turned to me and grinned, his white fangs glinting even in the shadows. His brown hair brushed against his chin, and his dark eyes focused on mine.

Xavier.

My blood ran cold. I reached into my clutch and grabbed the stake I knew would be there. After my first encounter with the Master Vampire who'd tried to capture me, I never left home without one.

Moving faster than I could blink, Xavier's teeth were at Maddox's throat, ready to rip him to shreds. In his other hand, he held a gun to Thane's temple.

"You've got a choice to make, little bird," the vampire said, his voice dripping with honey. It was all a lie, a facade. There was nothing sweet about this monster. "Your brother or your lover."

My heart lurched. That wasn't a choice I could make. No one could. Maddox was my little brother, my blood, and I loved him more than life. I couldn't lose him.

But Thane was my everything, my heart and soul.

I needed them both.

I gripped the stake tighter. "Let them go, and I'll make your death quick."

Xavier's eyes gleamed. "Dealer's choice then." He opened his mouth and sank his fangs deep into Maddox's neck, ripping through tendons and muscle. My brother's eyes widened more while he screamed in agony behind his gag.

I lunged forward, but I was too late.

A bullet exploded from Xavier's gun and drove into

Thane's head, traveling straight out the other side, embedding blood and bits of brain matter in the alley's wall. My mate toppled to the side and fell, his eyes lifeless.

My legs froze in place, every part of me going numb. I could do nothing but stand and watch in horror as Xavier fed on my brother's dying body. When Maddox was as still as Thane, the vampire looked up and smiled, his chin coated with crimson.

"You're mine, little bird."

Once again, thick fog swirled around me and stole the light. Finally able to move my quivering legs, I screamed out my rage and agony and stumbled forward, raising the stake.

Except they had vanished.

The world had disappeared, nothing but grey mist swirling around me.

Falling to my knees, I squeezed my eyes shut as grief washed over me, a tidal wave of pain ready to destroy everything in its path. I wrapped my trembling arms around my middle, sobbing.

Had I really just lost my little brother and my soulmate?

My eyebrows drew together, and I opened my eyes.

Wait…

Maddox had died three years ago. I remembered the agonizing grief vividly, and I wiped away my tears, confusion settling in.

The fog parted, and I was back in my penthouse, kneeling on the dining room floor. I stood and blinked against bright morning light streaming in from the tall windows. A crashing noise snapped my attention to the side.

Sitting on my L-shaped couch, Maddox laughed and cheered, raising his game controller in the air like a trophy.

Beside him, Thane grumbled and slumped back against the cushion. I flicked my gaze to the TV, where a race car had crashed. They were playing video games together.

My heart pounded against my ribs, almost painful in its intensity.

What the fuck was going on?

"Such a sweet sight, isn't it?" Xavier's voice whispered behind me.

I spun to face the Master Vampire. "What are you doing here?"

In the morning light, deep red highlights sparkled within his brown hair. His dark brown eyes burned red, a sign of his telepathic communication with his minions.

From all corners of the penthouse, newer vampires scrambled into view, climbing down the walls and creeping forward. Their emaciated, still-rotten bodies and long claws scraping against the floor made them a thing born from nightmares.

They were on my brother and Thane in an instant, pinning them down on the living room rug. As bloodthirsty vampires hissed around them, terror-filled Maddox and Thane's faces, and their gazes pleaded with me.

I cried out, raising my hands to stop the bloodsuckers hurting them.

Xavier's lips were at my throat, and his unnaturally powerful arms held me tight to his chest. His hard arousal pressed against my back, and bile splashed up my esophagus. I swallowed against the burn, keenly aware of his fangs so close to my skin.

"Which one will it be?" His warm breath fluttered the hairs on my neck.

Something wasn't right, and I didn't mean how ridiculous it was that vampires still breathed.

No, this was the second time he'd asked me that, and he'd killed them both the last time. I closed my eyes, struggling to remember anything before that horrible moment.

I'd been walking to a date with Thane, but what happened before?

Fog. Confusion…

Fear.

I grabbed onto that strand and yanked my mind toward it, willing the memory to surface. I had felt afraid, but of what?

Xavier's fangs brushed against my skin, distracting me and shooting a shiver down my spine. And not the good kind of shiver.

Think, Veronica.

I pushed aside the present and dove into the past until tendrils of memories slunk forward. Lena and Thane had been with me, standing in a hallway—the DEA's hallway. A phone in my hand showed Kit's picture and a string of texts from me with no reply, followed by a bright light and a boom.

Like a broken dam, the remaining memories returned in a flood, and I snapped my eyes open. "This isn't real."

The Master Vampire chuckled and pressed his fangs into my neck until I winced.

It sure as hell felt real.

"You must choose who you'll save," he said, his voice light and teasing. "Your mate or your brother."

That was a choice I could never make. "Me."

Behind me, he stilled. "What?"

"Take me and let them go," I said.

"You would give yourself to me? For life?" His words slithered down my spine, winding around my heart and squeezing. "Centuries under my control?"

There was nothing I wouldn't do for either of them, no matter what it cost me.

"Yes."

"Done." His dark chuckle rumbled through his chest and against my back. As his fangs pierced my skin like butter and sank deep, stinging pain radiated outward from my neck. I cried out as he sucked my blood, my *life*, from my body.

Fighting against the attack, my inner flame rose fast and furious until I shoved it back down, quenching the fire. I had chosen this willingly to let them live. The pain lessened with each tug at my neck, subsiding into a dull, yet weirdly pleasurable, ache, and my life force dimmed.

My body grew limp and tired, my head rolling back to rest on his shoulder, my eyelids fluttering with heaviness. I met Maddox's sorrow-filled gaze and smiled sadly.

I wanted to tell him how proud of him I was for everything he'd done before his life ended much too soon. Like Thane, he was everything to me.

I love you so much, forever and always, Maddie. As I whispered the nickname he'd pretended to hate, I exhaled my last breath, and my vision went dark.

Smooth, cold flooring formed beneath my hands and knees. I took a long, shuddering breath and opened my eyes.

Through a curtain of white-blonde hair, I saw the DEA's linoleum floor beneath me. My limbs shook from the terror of losing my loved ones to Xavier, who was dead—

allegedly. My brain knew it hadn't been real, but my body still needed to catch up.

I scrambled to my feet, my pulse racing from whatever had just happened. Thane stood by the conference room door, unmoving, his hand outstretched for the handle. Lena stood frozen beside me with her arms crossed.

Lightly, I touched her arm. "Lena!"

She didn't move, still as a statue and firmly rooted in place. Her eyes stared straight ahead, no recognition flaring to life. Whatever she saw, it wasn't me, and it wasn't here.

I stepped in front of Thane, studying his unmoving face. "What's happening?"

No response, not a blink or a peep or a twitch. Not that I expected him to, considering his fixed stance, but I hoped my voice would break whatever spell he was under. The same magic that had me trapped only a moment before.

My eyebrows drew together, and I glanced inside the conference room through the wall of windows. Everyone, including Adam, sat immobilized, stuck midway through whatever they'd been doing before the spell hit.

This had to be a spell. Nothing else could explain what was happening. I ran down the hallway, peeking my head inside offices, finding reapers and angels exactly as the others were. I scanned the reapers' faces in the middle of the rows of cubicles, hoping someone would move or blink.

Anything that would give me a sign.

A deafening boom shook the building, scattering paperwork and toppling books from shelves. I grabbed the corner of a desk to avoid going down myself. More explosions and colorful sparks lit up the sky outside an open office window.

I rushed to it and looked out. Two floors down in the courtyard, a line of mages faced the DEA building, casting spells at the eight-story structure. Several pairs of pointed ears peeked through satin-like hair, and my jaw dropped.

These weren't just any mages—they were *fae* mages. An oval portal swirled behind them, ready to whisk them away to safety. Or worse, send even more through if they cracked the DEA's defenses.

Holy fuck.

The DEA was under attack. They hadn't broken through the angelic shields yet, but their nightmarish spell kept anyone inside from interfering. A deep chill gripped my bones despite the sheen of sweat coating my forehead.

If the whole building was under this spell, then no one knew besides me.

I raced back to the conference room and ducked under Thane's arm to push open the door.

"Adam! You have to snap out of it." I ran to the archangel and shook him, to no avail. I even tried slapping him, knowing he'd forgive me. His cheek turned red, but his gaze stared sightlessly at a map displayed on the wall screen.

I racked my brain. I needed Kit and her unbelievably strong magic, even bound as it was, but that wasn't an option until I freed Thane or Ivan. She was too far away.

Succumbing to the need to pace, I thought through the issue. When the spell went off, I found myself living in a nightmare. My worst nightmare, the one that actually haunted my sleep at night, then it repeated itself when I failed to make a choice.

But seriously, no one could make that choice.

Eyeing Thane, I chewed my lip.

Except…

The spell broke when I did something unexpected. Instead of making an impossible choice, I gave myself to Xavier and let him drain me. I sacrificed myself.

That had to be it. Snapping my fingers, I stopped pacing. My sacrifice must have ended the spell.

I stepped in front of Thane again and took his stiff face in my hands. "Whatever you're seeing, it isn't real." I urged my words to reach deep inside his core through our soul link, hoping to push through the nightmare. "Don't fight it. Just let go."

The building trembled again as another massive spell blasted against the outside, and debris rained down from the ceiling tiles. I covered my head with my arms, grimacing as the others got hit.

I had no idea how long the DEA's defenses would last against their magic, but I needed to get help—now.

But who else besides Adam or Kit could end this spell?

My gaze wandered over Thane's face. Maybe I didn't need to end the spell entirely. He hadn't heard me as far as I could tell, which meant I needed to get into his mind.

I needed Tony.

CHAPTER 4

Sunday Morning

Wasting no time, I shifted into falcon form and swooped over the cubicles, racing for the open window. I zipped through it as another spell slammed against the office building. Several windows shattered from the force, sprinkling glass across the sidewalks.

Humans avoided the immediate area thanks to the DEA's repellant spells, but if the building fell, so would the repellant. They'd be in for quite the surprise when a ruined building popped up out of nowhere. Not to mention witnessing real magic and fae.

I had no way of knowing whether the mages wanted to tear it down or just get in, but collapsing it could be collateral damage.

As I soared through the sky at breakneck speed, colors and shapes ran together. I aimed for the piano shop where Tony worked as both salesman and Gatekeeper for *el Mercado Sombra*—the Shadow Market—and prayed he was there.

After landing in an alley, I shifted back to human form and ran to the shop. The bell above the piano shop door rang angrily as I rushed in, out of breath and panting.

"Well, well. Look what the gods dragged in." Tony's rich, baritone voice reached me before he appeared from behind the curtain blocking the back room.

When I last saw the shop owner before his extended vacation, he was still healing from Xavier's near-fatal attack. The physical effects of the Master Vampire's bite were long gone thanks to Community healers. However, emotionally, the wound had still been raw.

I shuddered, remembering the nightmarish spell I'd just endured of Xavier at Maddox's neck.

Today, Tony looked exactly like his old self again. His bald, black head shone as it reflected the shop's lighting. He smiled, forming crinkles all over his rich, coffee bean-colored face, and his darker brown eyes twinkled behind thin wire spectacles.

A geometric print button-down shirt covered his round belly, and the fabric provided a pop of color to the otherwise black and white store. Few people ordered pink or yellow pianos, which was a damn shame if you asked me.

He opened his big arms for a hug, and I rushed into them, wishing this was an actual reunion.

"How you doing, baby girl?" he asked against my hair as he squeezed me. Before I could answer, he stiffened. "Tell me what happened."

Tony was a telepath, a rare type of Community member that earned him the title of Gatekeeper. No one could enter the Shadow Market through his shop without him knowing their true intent.

Despite his request, I didn't actually have to tell him anything. He plucked the disastrous clusterfuck from my thoughts.

Releasing me, he stepped back. His brown face had lost some color. "I'm not sure I can help, but you know I'm gonna try. Let's go."

My eyes warmed with emotion, but I held back my tears. This wasn't the time to get all blubbery. "Thanks, Tony."

I followed him to the back and past the velvet curtain that hid the Shadow Market. Expecting to end up on the winding market street, I blinked as we entered the shop's storage room that most humans would see.

He motioned me toward the back door. "I may be old, but I've still got more than one trick up my sleeve."

Stopping before the door, he rapped his knuckles against it three times. A lock clicked and he turned the knob, pulling the door open and revealing a hallway beyond where I had expected an alley or sidewalk.

As I stepped through, my mouth dropped open. "I'd call that more than a trick, Tony."

We stood in the DEA building, in a long hallway bordered by office doors, and things had gotten worse.

Complete ceiling sections had collapsed, and the fluorescent lights overhead flickered on and off.

"This way." I jogged toward the stairwell. A number six sign showed our floor, and Thane and the others were on level three.

Despite his perceived age, Tony had no trouble keeping pace with me as we practically flew down the steps. It wouldn't surprise me if he was a few centuries older than I guessed, if not more. As usual, age meant little in our world.

As we left the stairwell on the third floor, the world heaved. The ground rolled beneath our feet, loosening linoleum tiles into random patterns. I fell to my knees hard, wincing as I hit the floor. Holding onto a wall, Tony kept himself upright.

"They're almost through," he said through gritted teeth.

Fuck!

Whether he could read their thoughts from here or knew the DEA's defensive magic, we had to hurry. I ignored the shooting pain in my knees and leaped to my feet, racing toward the conference room.

Lena had toppled over onto her side, still frozen in the same hands-on-hips pose, and Thane's shoulder leaned against the doorframe, keeping him from falling. A layer of drywall dust and chunks of plaster covered them both.

Tony approached my mate, resting his hands on Thane's head, and closed his eyes.

I could only guess how long Tony would need, or even if he would succeed in time.

Or at all.

Taking Thane's hand, I lowered my chin and prayed.

Thane

My throat was raw from yelling, from screaming for this nightmare to end. I couldn't endure any more, yet I knew I must. I would never give up.

Kneeling on the ground with my scythe beside me, I panted and wiped sweat and blood from my brow. It didn't do much good—more of both would cover me soon enough.

Veronica's spectral laughter danced away, deeper into the fog.

I groaned. Not again.

As the dense fog receded, the scene changed. Colin stood beside a six-foot-tall gilded cage, within which Veronica cowered. Terror transformed her dirt-smudged face until it was almost unrecognizable, and a worn, oversized t-shirt barely covered her body.

Seeing me appear, she gripped the bars, her knuckles cracked and bloodied. Her quick breaths created puffs in the frost-filled air. "Thane, help me!"

Colin turned his head and grinned at me, his blue-green eyes gleaming with triumph. "You're not strong enough to stop me."

I picked up my scythe and pushed myself to my feet, my legs shaky. "Maybe not, but I have to try."

"Mr. Munro," a deep voice called out from within the swirling fog that clung to the edges of reality.

I whirled, scythe in hand, not knowing whether I faced a friend...

Or a new foe.

Waving away the fog, Tony stepped into view. The Gatekeeper was the last person I expected to see.

I frowned. "What are you doing here?"

Colin surged toward the cage, shaping a spell in his hands. He flung his mutated magic at Veronica. As had happened time and time again, the fae man knew I wouldn't let anything happen to her.

I raised my scythe to intercept the spell.

The fae's shadowy magic stopped just outside the cage, and Colin's body went rigid.

"Veronica sent me," the telepath said, his eyebrows pulled together in a look of intense concentration.

I glanced back at Veronica, whose face contorted in a silent scream. She didn't move. "What do you mean? What did you do?"

Tony approached, gesturing to Colin and Veronica. "None of this is real. Fae mages attacked the DEA. You're all held hostage in what I presume to be your worst nightmares."

The DEA was under attack?

I kept my scythe raised. "If that's true, how do I know you're real? Is this another trick?"

Tony peered at me over the rim of his glasses, his brown eyes gazing intensely. "What are you afraid of happening here?"

"Losing her."

His gaze flicked toward Veronica. "Then you need to let her go."

That was like asking me to stop breathing. I ground my teeth together. "Never."

"The only way to break the spell is to sacrifice the thing you hold most dear."

Something about his words drew forth an inkling of memory, though it was too hazy to recall. Licking my lips, I hesitated. "You said Veronica sent you? She's okay?"

Tony's deep chuckle reverberated through the fog-filled landscape. "Okay, yes, but also panicking, and we know that never ends well. In her nightmare, she gave up her freedom and her life to save you and Maddox."

I clenched my scythe tighter. Freedom was something Veronica treasured above almost everything else. She might act impulsively, and at times those acts might come across as selfish, but deep down, everything she did was for those she loved.

I lowered the scythe. "Okay."

As Tony released his telepathic hold on the scene, Colin's spell slipped through the cage's bars and slammed into Veronica.

Colin's eyes widened, his face contorting in horror, and he raised his hands as if to stop the spell. "No!"

Except he was too late.

I cringed as the shadows wrapped around my mate, consuming her body as she writhed in pain and agony. Her blood-curdling screams ripped into my heart and tore my soul asunder. It was a sound I would never forget. I sank to my knees and watched her die, completely helpless.

"It's not your fault," Tony murmured behind me, placing his hand on my shoulder. "Remember, this isn't real."

It might not be real now, but this same scene and all the nightmares I'd endured—not just here but over the last few weeks—could happen someday. This same powerless feeling pervaded my thoughts and emotions.

Every. Single. Day.

I might not be as weak as a regular human, but without my reaper abilities, I could barely protect myself, let alone my mate. Learning to control my dragon scales would help me in a bind, but it would never be enough to save her life.

I would never be enough.

To make matters worse, she was royalty. A queen in a matriarchal society. Her family had ruled Mirognya for generations, and she was giving it up. She claimed she had no interest in the title or job, but the gods themselves were involved.

Was I holding her back from her true potential?

More importantly, how could I expect to protect a woman chosen by the gods?

Or was I always destined to lose her?

CHAPTER 5

Sunday Morning

Tony dropped his hands from Thane's face and stepped back. Thane's frozen limbs released a moment later, and he stumbled forward into the doorframe, knocking his forehead against it.

"Oh, thank the gods." I threw my arms around his neck, breathing in his familiar scent.

His arms wound around my waist and held me tight as he took deep, shuddering breaths. His heart pounded against his chest and into mine, and terror mixed with sorrow swept through our soul link.

Whatever he'd faced had rocked him to the core.

"I thought I would lose you," he whispered against my hair, his voice shaky. "Over and over."

I leaned back just enough for our foreheads to touch and met his deep blue gaze. "Never. I'm way too stubborn for that."

His cheek twitched, but a full smile didn't form. He was still shaken, and I didn't blame him—my nightmares had been intense and felt so real.

The building groaned and heaved as another wave of magic attempted to break the defensive barrier. Glass shattered somewhere down the hallway.

Our time was almost up.

"Tony, we need to get Adam free," Thane said, snapping into his get-it-done mode I loved so much. He entered the conference room, and I followed him and Tony inside.

Like he'd done with Thane, Tony stood near Adam and placed his hands on either side of the angel's head.

A few heart-pounding beats later, Adam's chair clattered backward as the archangel stood. His expression was dark and stormy, and for the first time since we'd met, his rage felt like a brand on my soul.

I shuddered to imagine what horrors fueled an archangel's worst nightmares.

A shimmering white light enveloped his body as he uttered a command in a language I didn't recognize. A burst of energy surged through the archangel, and the light exploded outward from his body.

It sliced across the room, passing through each of us with a warm tingly sensation that made the fine hairs on my skin rise. The kinetic force continued outward and disappeared down the hall. Holy light in all its glory.

Pietr leaped to his feet, his hand going for his sword, while Imos's scaled black skin rippled with an oncoming shift. A growl rumbled deep in his throat as he assessed the room. Shifting into his dragon form would be disastrous, which he also seemed to understand.

From outside the door, Lena shouted some colorful Yazyk phrases before dashing in, sword in hand. Her gaze landed on me, and she sagged against the wall in apparent relief.

As the nightmare spell's last hold broke, more shouts and yells echoed down the hall.

Reapers and angels came running, and Adam barked out orders to lock down the DEA and prepare for a potential siege. His eyes unfocused, and a moment later, he shook his head, his jaw clenched tight with anger.

"The mages retreated through the portal," he nearly shouted, banging his fist on the table. "They are too cowardly to face us at our full strength."

I had *never* seen the archangel lose his cool like this before, and I also never wanted to be on the receiving end of his anger.

He heaved a sigh and turned to Tony, hand outstretched. "Thank you, old friend. You are as reliable as ever."

The Gatekeeper eyed the angel over the rim of his glasses as they shook hands. "If I'm old, I don't even wanna know what that makes you."

Adam smiled, though it wilted quickly.

Tony lifted his hand in farewell. "Since my work here is done, I'll be on my way."

Everyone thanked him for his help and wished him well, and I jumped up to give him another tight squeeze. Had he not been able to access Thane's mind, then I might have lost my mate forever. I owed Tony my life.

Reading my thoughts, the Gatekeeper shook his head and kissed my forehead. "No favors between us, baby girl. Just take care of yourself."

Too many emotions tumbled through my mind, threatening to release in a torrent of tears. As he left, I settled for sniffling and returned to my seat.

"We need to find the super weapon, the one that neutralizes any type of magic," Ivan said in a nasal voice as he held a bloody napkin to his nose. The poor kid's face had slammed into the table when the spell lifted.

"How do you know about this weapon?" Nathan asked, surprising most of us. The blue-winged angel rarely spoke, and to be honest, I forgot he was there most of the time.

Today, he wore a button-down, collared shirt like the other angels, and he'd pulled his shoulder-length dark brown hair back into a man bun. His matching brown eyes regarded Ivan with interest.

"It's what brought me to the human world," Ivan explained around the napkin. "To fight Galina. But now we can use it against Colin."

"So this super weapon actually exists?" I asked the angels. I'd promised Ivan I would help him find it, but I wasn't sure the thing existed until now.

Adam and Nathan exchanged a cautious look before Nathan answered. "Yes, but using it is risky. In the wrong hands, it would unleash chaos upon the world."

Nothing I hadn't dealt with before.

"First, we need to make sure Kit and Angela are safe." Thane took my hand. "We'll be back."

Lena looped her arm through Thane's. "Not without me."

"Or me." Ivan jumped to his feet and tossed the bloody napkin into the trash can. Blood still streaked under his nose, but looks were the least of our worries. He took my free hand.

I wasn't going to argue. Depending on how we found Kit, we might need all the help we could get.

Adam gave a brief nod. "I welcome her help, and we may need her mother's as well."

Asking Octavia to assist the DEA was like begging the devil to take your soul. I crinkled my nose. No thanks.

The world disappeared around us, and a heartbeat later, solid ground reformed beneath our feet. The white columns of Octavia's two-story Virginia mansion loomed in front of us, and hovering grey clouds weren't helping my impression of the place.

I strode to the front doors and wasted no time trying the handles. Proper etiquette wasn't my concern right now, nor had it ever been. Both doors opened, which was as good a welcome as any.

"Kit!" I called out. "Where are you?" My words echoed down the long, empty hallways leading to the separate wings of the house.

"Let's split into pairs to search." Thane's footsteps tapped against the black-and-white checkered tile floor. "Ivan, you go with V."

I blinked at him, not expecting or wanting him to leave my side.

Catching my look, he sighed. "I hate leaving you, but his phoenix abilities are superior to mine."

The lingering sorrow and guilt in our soul link after the nightmares made more sense now. Even though I disagreed with his plan, I didn't argue because he wasn't entirely wrong about their abilities.

His dragon scales might protect *him*—if they activated at all. Thanks to the mage attack, he hadn't had a chance to work with Tundreg on controlling them yet, but his scales wouldn't do much to protect me unless he acted as my shield.

However, I was no damsel in distress, and I had more than enough firepower on my own. Maybe I should be the one protecting him.

"We'll head left." He nodded Lena in that direction and they took off.

Ivan and I jogged down the right wing, our footsteps echoing down the hall. We checked every door. Most were locked, but no one answered when we knocked. I'd come back and pick them or blast them open later if necessary.

The few unlocked doors turned up empty rooms, and the drawing room where I'd first met Octavia was no different.

After taking a back staircase meant for the staff, we quickly searched the second level with the same results. Although it might have been a good sign that they weren't here—maybe they were out shopping or something—the emptier the house remained, the more my gut tightened and my scalp prickled.

Instinct was telling me something was wrong.

Very wrong.

Plus, there was no way Octavia would have taken her old butler and vampire maid out shopping.

At the top of the main staircase, I looked back the way we'd just come and frowned. Something was off about the hall's layout.

This house was as symmetrical as they came, but more doors stood on one side. A large closet might explain the discrepancy, except I had a hard time believing Octavia would be okay with that.

Before I took a step back to investigate, Thane and Lena rejoined us. Their expressions reflected mine.

"Did you see anyone at all?" I asked, still eyeing the hallway.

Thane shook his head. "I expected to find Shirley or Walter in the kitchen or laundry area, but no such luck. This place is a ghost town."

Moving light caught my eye out the arched second-floor window overlooking the backyard. A greenhouse as big as a two-car garage stood against the tree line, and lights were on inside, casting flickering shadows as someone moved around.

I pointed. "There. Let's go."

Thunder rumbled overhead as we hurried down the stairs and out the back door. The grass was wet and slick from an earlier storm, and a woman's voice hummed a tune from within the greenhouse.

As we neared the door, Lena held up a hand and drew her sword. Although my nerves were just about shot after the nightmare spell and attack on the DEA, I stayed back while she crept ahead and cracked the door open to peek inside. She waved us forward and opened the door all the way.

Thane and Ivan strode in first and took up defensive stances on each side of me, and Lena took up the rear.

Rows of tables holding blooming flowers—everything from tulips to roses and many more I didn't recognize—spread out before us, their colorful petals arranged in rainbow order from left to right. Familiar fragrances mixed with the unknown, creating a unique blend that tickled my nose. The mixture was both pleasant and oddly disorienting.

Wearing a semi-casual look of designer jeans and a light pink sweater that likely cost a few hundred dollars, Octavia ambled down a row toward us. She inspected each yellow-flowered plant with pruning shears in hand.

Grey strands streaked through her sleek black hair, which fell straight to her shoulders. Her espresso foam skin color matched Kit's perfectly and infuriated my best friend—she didn't want to share anything with this woman. It surprised me she hadn't changed her last name by now.

There was no chance in hell Octavia hadn't seen or heard us enter, but she continued her inspection as if nothing had changed.

I eyed her shears, wondering if she knew how to wield them as well as her magic. Considering how powerful her magic was, I didn't want to find out.

"How nice of you to stop by." Octavia clipped a thorny, flowerless branch from a rosebush and tossed the branch to the side. "Though most people call first."

"Where's Kit?" I asked, scanning the rest of the greenhouse. No one else was with her.

Octavia clucked her tongue and snipped off a browning leaf, which fluttered to the ground. "Surely your mother taught you better manners than that." She turned her face toward me. As her dark brown eyes bored into mine, magic sizzled around her as an obvious threat.

She might be scary, but I'd faced scarier.

Most likely scarier, anyway.

I met her gaze straight on. "I'm sure my mom tried. Now answer my question."

The corners of her lips turned upward into a wintry smile, and she returned her attention to the yellow flowers. "She's helping me tend to the garden."

"You mean you're forcing her to help you." I'd only known Kit for a fraction of her life, but gardening had never been among her interests. Not even close.

Octavia examined a few wilting leaves and clipped off another branch, which joined the trail at her feet. "I can assure you, Katherine's quite happy working here."

As if on cue, my best friend entered through the greenhouse's open back door, pushing a wheelbarrow full of potting soil. My mouth dropped open, but my reaction wasn't from the manual labor.

Kit's black hair, which she had worn in braids almost daily for the past five years that I'd known her, had been released, fanning out around her head in a natural fro. A red bandana kept her hair back from her face.

When she looked up and saw us, her brown eyes widened. She halted mid-step, and dirt spilled over the wheelbarrow's edge.

With her back to Kit, there was no way Octavia could have seen the spill. Yet she sighed like she had eyes on the back of her head. "Take the remaining soil to the empty row, then clean up your mess."

Kit's cheeks tinted pink. "Yes, mother." Without another glance in my direction, she wheeled the dirt to where her mother had indicated and headed for the back door.

Something was definitely wrong here.

"Kit!" I rushed across the greenhouse and grabbed her arm. "I've been calling and texting you. What the hell is going on?"

Her lips pulled up into a bright smile, a look I'd never seen on her before. Her eyes met mine, and I swear they were pleading with me. "Oh, hey. Sorry about that. I've been busy helping my mother. You should go."

She dropped her gaze and continued through the door, leaving me there with my mouth hanging open.

The Kit I knew would have slapped me upside the head for my impulsive behavior regarding Jackson Reed, then dragged me into a fierce hug. She didn't even ask what had happened or how I got back.

"Where's Angela?" Thane asked Octavia while I stood stupefied.

She gave a quick laugh. "The dear girl had too much wine last night. I'm afraid she's still sleeping, but we'll tell her you visited. If you'll excuse us, we have work to do."

Resuming her pruning, she hummed her song from earlier.

On the surface, everything appeared perfect. Kit had thanked her mom, fulfilling the blood oath I'd accidentally sworn. They kissed and made up and apparently forgave each other.

Except there was no fucking way Kit would ever forgive her mother for the childhood abuse she'd endured, and she sure as fuck wouldn't be helping her with gardening.

Over a row of yellow flowers, I met Thane's worried gaze. Ivan and Lena exchanged nervous glances behind him, and my stomach clenched painfully.

Something was very, very wrong with this loving family picture.

CHAPTER 6

Sunday Morning

I balled my hands into fists. I wasn't leaving without more answers.

Kit returned with a broom and dustpan. She walked right past me as if I wasn't there and started sweeping up the potting soil that had spilled.

I followed her and leaned in close. "Kit, talk to me. Are you okay?"

She smiled up at me again, that weird friendly smile that didn't reach her eyes. It was totally unlike her and gave me the creeps. "I'm great! We've just been busy. I haven't even looked at my phone."

I blinked at her as she returned to sweeping. This was the woman who had renounced her family for over fifty years, who had warned me about dire consequences when I visited Octavia before the Blood Trials. The woman who lived and breathed tech and would die with her phone or laptop in her hand.

The woman who'd been terrified of visiting this place, convinced her mother would try to control her.

Goosebumps spread across my skin like wildfire, raising hairs everywhere. I licked my dry lips. "I'm glad you're having such a good time here, but we could really use your help back home."

Kit stood the broom upright and laughed, though it was a strained sound. "You'll have to figure this one out without me, I'm afraid. This task can't wait." Her gaze flicked toward Octavia, and she lifted her shoulder in a casual shrug. "You may have to go nuclear again."

Oh, fuck.

That was our coded phrase meaning shit had hit the fan, and it was time to blow the place to smithereens.

Okay, so it wasn't a super coded message when put that way, but Kit signaled that she was in trouble and needed my help. I just had no idea what was wrong or what Octavia was doing.

I nodded, not wanting to draw attention to the brief lull in our conversation. "Yeah, that's always an option. Where's Angela?"

"Like my mother said, she's in the house sleeping." Kit picked up the dustpan and headed for a large trash can.

I frowned. I was missing something. "But the house is empty."

Octavia slammed the shears down on the table of flowers. Her gaze locked on me, promising a nasty storm. "You have overstayed your welcome, Veronica. It's time for you and your friends to go."

I planted my hands on my hips. "I'm not going anywhere without *all* my friends. That includes Kit and Angela."

"Hey, Lena," Kit called out near the trash can. She wiped her arm across her forehead, streaking dirt through her sweat, and pointed at the greenhouse's front door. "Can you and Ivan bring in a few bags of potting soil? They're just outside."

Lena glanced at me warily, her hand gripping her sword's hilt.

"Your help will speed things up," Kit added with a forced smile.

I didn't want Octavia to know that *I* knew what was going on, kind of, so I nodded at Lena. The sooner we got Kit out from under her mother's control, the better.

Except the moment Lena and Ivan stepped outside, Octavia flicked her hand. The thick wooden door slammed shut, and a red light flared around the frame.

I could hear Lena and Ivan's muffled yells on the other side, and the handle jiggled but refused to budge. Flames erupted around the frame through the surrounding glass, but the door held firm, protected by the witch's magic. Resounding thuds beat against the wood.

I unfurled my fiery wings, wrapping them around my front just as Octavia cast another spell. Her wind magic crashed against my wings, fluttering the flames, but didn't burst through.

Thane's scythe flashed as the blade caught the light, and he rushed toward Octavia. A green-tinged spell spiraled toward him, this time coming from Kit.

A ragged gasp tore from my mouth as vine-like tendrils wrapped around my mate's arms and legs, but he sliced through them with ease. The remnants slid off his black scales, and relief settled over my shoulders.

Oh, thank the gods. He might not have known how to control his new ability yet, but the scales were ready to protect him, regardless.

Drawing on my inner flame, I gathered fire in my hands and threw it at Octavia. She caught the fireball with both hands and squeezed until the flames extinguished.

Well, now I knew she controlled both the air and fire elements.

But could she control all five like Kit could?

I didn't want to find out.

Sprinklers and drip lines all over the greenhouse sprang to life. Their spouts turned into mini-geysers and pointed in my direction. The bitch was trying to put my fire out while proving she also controlled water.

Good thing my fire didn't work like that, but I had no problem pretending it did. Maybe I could tire her out. Letting my flames flicker in and out, I drew two knives.

Thane had turned his full attention on Kit, deflecting the spells she cast at him while trying to reason with her.

I pushed them from my mind, trusting that they'd both do their best not to kill each other. Hoping and praying for that, anyway.

As I refocused on Octavia, my flames blazed back to life, engulfing my body in an inferno despite the ongoing streams of water. Whatever she was doing to Kit would end today.

Time to play.

I dashed in fast, jabbing at Octavia with two knives before spinning away from her counterattack. Unlike the rest of us, she didn't wield a weapon other than magic, and she probably didn't need to.

Searing pain slashed down my arm as a thorny rose branch swiped at me. I hissed through my teeth and swiped at the plant, severing the stem from the rest of the bush. The plant emitted a shrill scream, and I ducked in alarm.

Despite the sliced stem, the plant didn't stop coming, and it wasn't alone.

Plants across the greenhouse advanced, their stems and branches growing longer and sturdier as they reached for Thane and me. The sound of their growth was unnerving, a creaking, popping noise that sent shivers down my back.

Air, fire, water, and now earth. Since there was a good chance she was also controlling Kit through the soul element, then this witch could harness all five, just like her daughter.

It also meant we might be fucked.

The greenhouse's concrete floor cracked and groaned, splitting in chunks as gnarled, dirt-stained tree roots forced their way through the openings. With each flick of Kit's wrist, rocks rose from the cracks and hurtled toward Thane. They bounced off his scales with loud pings, and he winced after each hit.

Thick roots slithered along the floor, aiming for my feet. I hopped away as I slashed and chopped, hoping to stop them by cutting them down. Vines stretched toward me from potted plants, and my hops became a dance as I twirled back toward Octavia.

I needed to cut the head off this snake.

Tears streamed down Kit's face as a steady stream of stones battered Thane. "I'm sorry. I can't stop her."

Gritting his teeth, Thane deflected each rock with his blade or arm. Suddenly, the shiny black scales protecting his body retracted into his skin, rendering him vulnerable to attack—physical and magical.

Somehow sensing the vulnerability, thorny branches lashed out. They encircled his ankles, winding their way up his legs and body and digging into his skin. He slashed down with his scythe, separating vines from their roots.

The plants squealed in agony, their inhumane screams sending chills down my back. But they kept growing, wrapping themselves around his arms and throat before he could sever their hold. Blood dripped down the rope-like vines as their thorns dug deeper into his skin.

Thane struggled against the tight hold, grimacing as the spellbound plants raised him into the air.

As I chopped up another root and closed within knife-striking distance, Octavia let out a dark chuckle. "Checkmate. Surrender, or watch him die."

Unlike my worst nightmare, this was real life. This was actually happening in front of me.

Except this witch still didn't know who she was dealing with.

I spread my wings farther, the hungry flames licking the nearest vines and roots until they squealed and recoiled. "Dazhbog, the god of the sun and creator of my kind, entrusted me with a sacred duty. Consider this a warning that messing with me will have divine consequences for you."

She lifted her chin and smirked. "Your gods have no power in this realm."

"That's not entirely true." I never would have survived this long if they didn't have power here. I smiled in a way that made people nervous—Octavia included. "Are you working with Colin Ó Broin? Is that what this is about?"

"That pathetic fae necromancer?" she sneered. "I couldn't care less about what he's planning. Like the rest of you, he's a fool."

Bummer. I had hoped we could ruin some grand part of his plan by taking her down.

"Fool or not, if you kill my flame's chosen mate, I will raze this greenhouse to the ground," I said plainly, "with all of us inside."

She narrowed her eyes. "Doing so would kill the woman you claim is your best friend."

Behind Octavia, I gazed at Kit, and my smile faltered. "To stop you? Yes, I would."

With tears streaming down her cheeks, my best friend closed her eyes and nodded, a sad smile on her lips.

Octavia chuckled, and malice glinted in her eyes. "I highly doubt that."

The vines squeezed tighter around Thane, the thorns digging deeper into his skin. He groaned in pain. "Do it, Veronica."

Like I would actually kill him or Kit. He should know me better by now. Tony wasn't the only one who had more than one trick up his sleeve, and she'd called my bluff.

Time to bring out the big guns.

I took a deep breath and called forth my ancestral magic, that extra fire burning deep within me. The voices of my mother and grandmothers, going back generations, swirled around me. Their flames united with mine as their souls rose from a deep slumber, ready to strike our enemy down.

When I was about to burst from the amount of energy coursing through my veins and limbs, I opened my mouth and released the falcon screech, pouring everything I had into it. Visible sound waves pulsed outward from my body and drove through anything standing in their path.

Tables overturned, pots shattered and flew in all directions. The glass panes of the greenhouse exploded outward, raining glass over the surrounding yard.

Octavia stood her ground, forming a wind shield around herself. But the plants clutching Thane lost their hold as the force of my screech ripped them away from their pots. He dropped to the ground, collapsing in a heap.

As my screech's last pulse faded, Lena and Ivan leaped through the windows' broken glass and moved in front of Thane and me, ready to defend us against the witches' magic. A fire wall erupted around Ivan and Thane, and he knelt to check on my mate.

Thane's chest rose and fell, but I couldn't tell how deep his wounds were.

Another wall of fire soared in front of Lena and me as ice spears pierced the flames and melted.

My best friend lowered her hands with a sob.

"Snap out of it, Kit!" I yelled.

Lena marched toward Octavia, gripping her sword in both hands. She chopped at the air shield, her blade clanging against it without success.

"I know what I have to do," Kit said in a steady voice. As she raised her arms and chanted, glass shards trembled against the concrete floor and rose all around us. Her sad gaze met mine. "It's the only way to break her hold over me. Find Angela and set her free. She's in the house."

Octavia's head whipped toward her daughter, her eyes widening.

Dozens of glass shards spun their sharpest points toward Kit and sped through the air like bullets. They struck hard, embedding deep within her body in too many places to count. Gasping, she stumbled back from the force and fell to her knees, blood dripping from each wound.

"No!" I bolted through the fire shield to catch my best friend before she collapsed. I held her to me as I knelt, ignoring the sharp jabs of glass. A sob caught in my throat. "Why did you do that? We would have taken her down."

Her breaths were raspy and wet, and foaming blood spilled from her mouth. Glass must have pierced a lung. Maybe both. "Tell Angie I'll see her soon."

She exhaled and went still, her brown eyes staring, her body lifeless.

CHAPTER 7

Sunday Morning

Thane

I groaned and rolled onto my side, my hand sliding through something sticky—the greenhouse floor was slick with my blood. I didn't know why my scales had retracted, but I needed to get that shit figured out. Fast.

At the very least, I was thankful my healing ability had increased since using the dragonstone, and my wounds were already closing.

Those thorns were nasty.

"Katherine?" Octavia's rising pitch drew my attention.

I hauled myself to my feet using a table's edge and searched for Veronica. My mate knelt on the ground next to a heap of turned-over plants, tears streaming down her agonized face. She held Kit's limp form in her arms, rocking her gently.

Blood soaked them both, and my heart leaped into my throat before I realized most of it wasn't Veronica's blood. Our bond was strong but filled with soul-crushing grief.

Which meant…

Oh no.

Octavia stumbled toward them with her hand outstretched. Her face was stricken and devoid of color. Lena growled as she stepped in front of the woman, holding the point of her blade at Octavia's throat until a drop of blood appeared.

"Let me see my daughter," the witch demanded, though her voice trembled and her gaze remained on Kit.

"Take another step, and the only thing you'll see is Ognebog's forge." Lena's eyes flashed mercilessly, and she gripped her sword's hilt with both hands, ready to run the other woman through with the slightest provocation.

"Lena, no," I said, raising a shaky hand toward her. "The DEA will handle this."

Her shoulders heaved up and down as she breathed heavily, but she obeyed.

For now.

I pulled out my phone and dialed Adam. After briefly explaining the situation, I asked that he send a team to extract Octavia for breaking Community laws. Controlling another Community member was a grievous offense and would see the witch in iron for decades, if not longer.

Tightening her hold on Kit's lifeless form, Veronica slipped her other arm under Kit's knees and stood. She lifted her gaze to Octavia's. Tears streamed down her cheeks, and a violent storm flashed in her violet irises.

Octavia raised a hand to her quivering lips as she looked at her daughter's body. "Why would she do this?"

"Because she'd rather die than be your puppet," Veronica said, her tone harsh and full of venom.

Octavia winced as if the words gouged into her, inflicting physical pain.

I wished they had.

Brushing past Octavia who'd dropped her head in apparent defeat, Veronica stepped toward me, her hardened exterior about to crumble from the overwhelming emotions surging through our soul link.

I wrapped my arms around her and Kit, supporting the weight even though she was more than capable of carrying her friend on her own.

Had I still been a reaper, I could have collected Kit's soul and sent her on her way to everlasting peace. Hell, I probably could have stopped both witches without too much effort.

As a reaper.

Instead, I was forced to watch my mate's heart break and wait for someone else to do the job. Not only was I powerless to protect her, but I also couldn't do much to ease her pain.

I fought to keep my feelings of failure from leaking through our bond. She didn't need to deal with my doubt right now.

"I'm so sorry, Veronica." There was nothing else I

could say. Nothing that would make her pain go away. I grieved, but my pain was nothing compared to Veronica's.

She stared at her best friend's face. "I've never heard her use the nickname Angie before. We need to find her."

The sound of rustling wings preceded an arrival. Six angels landed directly on the greenhouse floor, courtesy of the blown-out windows. A handful of reapers stepped out of teleportation circles and surrounded Octavia, who wisely didn't resist.

A red-headed angel approached us. It was Jessa, who had watched over Veronica for years after her parents' death. She placed a hand on Veronica's arm. "Please set her down."

I stepped back so that Veronica could kneel and lay her friend on the ground. Jessa reached into a pouch attached to her waist and withdrew a glowing gold orb—a soul. My jaw went slack with sudden understanding, but Veronica blinked at the angel in confusion.

"Kit came to me before she left," Jessa explained as she knelt on the other side of Kit's body. "She guessed that her mother might try something like this and asked that I store her soul until she returned. Just in case."

My mouth ran dry. Had Jessa misplaced the soul—as unlikely as that scenario was—Kit's soul would've faded until she ceased to exist. A terrible risk to take, and only because her mother craved control.

I frowned. "If you had her soul, how did Octavia control her?"

"We left a sliver of her soul within her, just enough for her mother to use." She focused her blue-green gaze on Kit's face. "I tried to talk her out of it, but she wouldn't budge. For once, I'm glad someone didn't listen to me."

Jessa winked at Veronica, whose wide eyes showed she might have been in shock. The angel placed the golden orb on Kit's chest, where it sank beneath her shirt, spreading into her skin.

The witch's body emitted a yellowish glow as the soul restored her life. Hovering her palms above Kit's stomach, Jessa applied her divine magic to push the glass shards out and close the wounds.

Kit's eyes flew open, and she grabbed at her chest with a giant gasp.

Veronica's mouth dropped open a moment before she threw herself across Kit. "Sweet Mokosh, I thought I lost you." She sobbed, her body shaking with each breath. "You're not allowed to die before me. We both know I can't handle it."

Relief loosened my tensed muscles, and I released a deep breath. Kit had quickly become a close friend over the last few weeks; losing her so soon wasn't something I'd envisioned happening.

Grumbling beneath Veronica, Kit pushed her away and sat up. "Let me breathe, woman. It's not every day I die and come back to life."

Lena held out her hands and helped both women to their feet, her eyes glistening with tears. "You're almost as much of a *durak* as this one." She tilted her head toward Veronica.

Kit scoffed as she brushed loose dirt and leaves from her jeans and t-shirt. "Not even close to V's level."

"Welcome back," I said, grinning at her eye roll. She hated being the center of attention.

Bound in iron chains and flanked by two reapers,

Octavia approached her daughter. Her face had regained some color, but her skin was taut with emotion. "You would rather die than be with your mother?"

Kit stared at the woman, a coldness seeping into her steely gaze. "I don't have a mother." She turned her back on Octavia.

A reaper hauled the woman away and into a waiting teleportation circle. With any luck, Adam would ensure she never saw the light of day again. She would never see her daughter again; that was for damn sure.

Veronica pulled Jessa into a tight hug. "Thank you, thank you, thank you! It's also so good to see you."

The angel laughed and patted Veronica on the back. "You're welcome. Does anyone else need my services?"

"Angela might," Kit said, her expression growing fearful.

Jessa addressed the other angels and reapers, "Go on ahead of us. They'll provide their statements in good time. I'll make sure of it."

With a quick wave of her hand, Kit swept the glass sprinkled around the door away. As the agents left, she led us through the still-intact wooden door, into the main house, and to the second floor.

As we headed down the hallway Ivan and Veronica had searched, I drew my eyebrows together in confusion when she slowed and stopped at a blank space on the wall. I glanced up and down the hallway, counting doors. There should have been one here.

"I knew it," Veronica muttered.

Kit drew a rectangular frame on the wall with her finger while chanting a few words. The line she drew glowed green, and the paint rippled, revealing a hidden door. Her movements grew more urgent as she turned the knob and pushed open the door, and we followed her inside.

The room was the same size as the others we searched, large enough to work as a roomy bedroom. Instead of a bed, a long glass box sat on a table.

I thought Octavia had shown her evil side by controlling Kit and forcing her to attack us, but this was something else altogether. Because it wasn't just a box—it was a coffin, and Angela slept peacefully within.

My lungs constricted, but it wasn't only from seeing Angela like this. If Kit, a powerful witch, hadn't stopped Octavia, then I could never keep Veronica safe. I wasn't even close to being strong enough.

As difficult as it would be to say goodbye, I might not have a choice, not if I wanted her safe from harm. I knew she was my soulmate, but that didn't mean she couldn't find love again.

The mere thought of letting her go threatened to consume me with grief and agony until I pushed it away, not wanting Veronica to realize the tumultuous emotions bleeding through our bond was from more than seeing Angela like this. Not until I had time to process my thoughts and what they truly meant.

"How long has she been in there?" Veronica asked, her violet eyes opening wide. Her shock and horror radiated through our soul link.

Kit unlatched the coffin. "Two days. Octavia used her to control me in the beginning until her magic dug its claws in too deep to escape."

The lid clicked open with a hiss, and cold wisps licked

the warmer air of the room before dissipating.

"Was she cryogenically frozen?" I asked.

"Sort of, but with magic," Kit explained. "It's slowly draining her life force."

Angela's eyes remained closed, her white face relaxed in a peaceful sleep.

Panic shot through our soul link, and Veronica gripped my arm. "She's not waking up."

Kit leaned over the coffin's edge and placed a soft kiss on Angela's lips.

CHAPTER 8

Sunday Midday

Letting go of Thane's arm, I crept closer to Kit. I didn't want to spoil the moment, but I also wanted to be within reach if Angela didn't wake up. Kit would go ballistic, and while I wouldn't blame her, I also didn't want to lose my best friend.

Thankfully, I didn't have to worry.

As Kit leaned back, Angela let out a soft sigh. Her long, dark eyelashes fluttered as she opened her brown eyes and focused on Kit. She smiled. "Oh, hello."

A quiet sob tore from my best friend's throat. "Hi." Although not much taller than her pint-sized fiancée, Kit reached into the coffin and lifted her as easily as a baby. She set Angela's feet on the ground but still held her close.

Angela's black leggings and tunic-length shirt showed no signs of long-term wear other than a few wrinkles. She didn't even smell bad.

Jessa closed in to look her over.

"We'll call you Snow White from now on," I said, smiling.

While Angela gave a shaky laugh, Kit brushed her fiancée's curly brown hair away from her face and stroked her cheek. "I didn't have to kiss her to break the spell. I just wanted to."

If that wasn't the sweetest thing ever, nothing was.

After my ex-pseudo guardian angel confirmed Angela would be just fine after a meal and a gallon of water, most of us headed to the kitchen. We were all starving from using so much magic—or being used in Angela's case—but Lena and Ivan refused to eat until they patrolled the area and ensured Octavia acted alone.

The square-shaped kitchen was monstrous, which wasn't surprising considering the overall size of the mansion and the woman who owned it. Surrounded by floor-to-ceiling white cabinets, the kitchen was equipped with top-of-the-line appliances and a two-door, sub-zero fridge that blended seamlessly with the cabinets. Taking up the center of the room was an island big enough to seat four in high-backed chairs.

Kit waved us over to the chairs but refused my offer to help make food. "Girl, don't pretend you know your way around a kitchen. I'll just throw together some sandwiches real quick."

I laughed. "Fine, but I'll grab some water for everyone."

As Kit got to work pulling out deli meat, cheeses, and bread, I rummaged through the cabinets until I found some glasses.

Angela sank onto one of the high-back stools with a heavy sigh. Thanks to the days spent in a glass coffin without food or water, her face was even paler than usual, hiding her smattering of freckles.

Now that I could see how frail she'd become—even if she was rather delicate before—I was sure I wasn't the only one regretting the decision to call for backup. I really wanted to make Octavia pay first—with blood.

Her inhumanity on par with the vampires, and they had the excuse of being dead.

I filled the glasses with water and handed them out, and we all drained ours in one long gulp.

Everyone except Jessa, who didn't need water or food to survive. Perks of the job.

She hugged me, then gave me a knowing, exasperated look that made me grin. "I have to head back, but I'm sure I'll see you before long."

After giving the others quick hugs, the red-headed angel left through the back door. A flash of pearlescent pink shimmered through the windows as she spread her wings and took flight.

At that moment, Shirley and Walter walked in. I couldn't make out what the balding, grey-haired butler said to the vampire maid, but his condescending tone rang loud and clear. So much for thinking he was a nicer guy the first time we met.

The vampire had pulled her blonde hair into a sleek, tight bun at her nape, and she wore a well-pressed black pantsuit just like the last time I saw her. Except today, her uniform included a crisp white apron.

When she noticed us gathered around the island, her brown eyes opened wide. She hurried over to my best friend and tried to take over sandwich making.

Kit shooed her away as she spread out the food on the island. "I can make my own damn sandwich. And my friends'."

Walter sniffed the air like something stank. "While Mrs. Parker is away, you will act as the owner and mistress of Parker House. Shirley's duties include serving you and your guests."

It was anyone's guess how he already knew about Octavia's arrest and where he'd been this whole time. But if he kept talking to my best friend that way, he'd quickly regret his decision.

Kit glanced at the vampire fretting around her and paused as she laid out the bread slices. "In that case, you're free to go. Permanently. No amount of money or magic can return what that monster took from you, but I'll set up a bank account with enough funds to compensate for your service. Thank you."

Walter scoffed and opened his mouth, likely to protest, only to snap it shut when Kit looked his way. Anybody would shut up with *that* look directed at them.

Shirley's eyes rounded even more, and I was almost afraid they would pop right out. Then she would be without eyes or a tongue, all due to Octavia. She glanced nervously around the room as if it were a joke.

Kit took a deep breath and faced the vampire straight on. "What you did wasn't your fault. We all know that, and I don't blame you."

"I don't either," Angela said, placing her hand on top of the vampire's.

The undead woman stilled beneath Angela's touch before nodding, relief loosening her tense shoulders.

I wanted to know what they were referring to, but I knew we'd get the whole story soon. I smiled at Shirley. "Enjoy your freedom."

Me being nice to a vampire? Hell just froze over.

After patting Angela's hand, Shirley removed her apron and set it on the counter. She met Walter's unhappy gaze and flipped him off before turning and leaving.

An undead girl after my own heart.

"Miss Parker, if I may—" Walter began.

"No, you may not. You're dismissed as well," Kit interrupted as she opened the deli meat and cheese containers. "Pack your things and don't come back."

The butler's mouth dropped open comically. I was sure that was the last thing he expected to hear, and I hid a grin behind my hand. I didn't care if he saw, but I was still practicing my etiquette. Baby steps.

Such a shame Shirley didn't get to witness this moment.

"This is outrageous!" he declared.

As Walter continued to splutter and protest, Kit opened a drawer and took out a knife, dipping it into the mayo and spreading it on two slices of bread. Her calm yet firm demeanor showed no signs of cracking.

"If you have any desire for a positive reference letter, I suggest you take your leave," she said when he stopped to take a breath. She pointed the knife toward the door. "*Now.*"

The older man narrowed his eyes at my friend, and I gripped the hilt of one of my knives. He didn't strike me as an especially dangerous threat, but one could never be too careful.

"The covens will hear of this," he warned.

She looked up at him, her gaze emotionless yet electrifying the air with tension. "Yes, they will."

Walter wised up and showed himself out, though not without muttering the entire way.

"Yeesh," I said as I took a seat on a stool. "Talk about a stage one clinger."

Thane grinned at Kit as he took the stool beside me. "You just made someone's day and ruined another in less than five minutes. That a new record?"

Her lip twitched upward as she laid slices of turkey and cheese on the bread. She closed the sandwich and pushed the plate toward Angela, who smiled gratefully. "That's me: maker and breaker of worlds. Must be my new specialty."

Despite her fragile appearance, Angela wasted no time scarfing down the sandwich like a footballer after an intense match.

"So, you going to tell us what the hell happened?" I leaned my elbows on the island counter as Kit set to work on more sandwiches.

"There's not much to tell." She shrugged as she spread mayo across the bread slices. "Octavia welcomed us like we were actual guests. I was cautious at first and ready to leave right after saying the thanks you promised her." She glanced up from her work to give me a pointed look.

I waved a hand dismissively. "Hindsight."

She snorted and pointed the knife at me. No wonder Walter had stopped arguing—she was terrifying while wielding a butter knife. "I warned you before meeting with her. That's not hindsight."

"Honestly, I still can't believe Octavia turned on us like that," Angela said, taking a break from her sandwich to chime in before I could argue again. "I know you told me not to trust her, but she was so… nice."

Her eyes filled with tears and her chin trembled, but she held her head high as she took another bite of her sandwich.

Pressing her lips into a thin line, Kit laid turkey and cheese slices onto the bread.

I would've called Angela naïve, except I'd almost fallen for the woman's charms, too. And then I'd sworn a blood oath.

To be fair, I hadn't agreed to swear a blood oath. Octavia had sprung it on me when we shook hands, jabbing me with something she'd hidden in her palm.

"Anyway, she wanted to show me the greenhouse," Angela continued after swallowing her food. "Kit was taking a shower, and I didn't think much of it." She bit her lip and dropped her gaze, picking at the bread's crust. "Shirley was there. Before I knew what was happening, she was on me, feeding."

She closed her eyes and shuddered.

While a vampire had never bitten me—outside of my nightmares—I imagined the sensation was unpleasant. A vampire as old as Shirley, who was at least a century out of the grave looking as human as she did, would have an arousing bite. A quick jab followed by pure ecstasy, which must be wildly confusing.

I had no intention of ever learning what that felt like, but damn if it didn't pique my curiosity.

"I found them like that. Octavia had forced Shirley to attack Angela, to show me how fragile my human mate is." Kit's upper lip curled in disgust as she plated the finished sandwiches and slid them toward Thane and me. "By that point, I realized she'd been slowly wrapping her magic around me until she had a strong enough hold that I couldn't resist."

Well, now I knew what they weren't blaming Shirley for. I never thought I'd see the day I sympathized with a vampire.

Kit's gaze lifted to meet mine. So much emotion flickered through her eyes—anger, sadness, guilt—it made my breath hitch. "You saw what came next."

"It's not your fault, Kit." I reached over the island to grab her knifeless hand. "Despite what you tell yourself, that woman is your mother. No one blames you for wanting to believe in her again."

Shaking her head, my best friend took her hand back and started on two extra sandwiches. She was a sandwich-making machine. "I never should've faced her without my full powers."

"Now who's got hindsight issues?"

Her cheek twitched again as she finished the last sandwich. Instead of making one more for herself, she tore off pieces of turkey and took small bites. Sandwiches weren't really her thing. *Bread* wasn't her thing.

Since I didn't suffer from the same affliction, I shoved mine into my mouth, nearly groaning at the simple flavors. Magical and physical fighting had left me ravenous.

"What was Octavia preparing for?" Thane asked after

he'd finished half his sandwich.

Kit rolled her eyes. "It's so stupid. There's a rift among some witches, and she planned to seize control of the Elder Flame coven, the oldest still practicing. She's pissed off at the High Priestess for something. I don't even know what, but I'm sure it's petty as fuck."

"Octavia's not a High Priestess?" I asked between bites.

I'd assumed she was since she could control the five elements, an extraordinary ability she'd obviously passed down to her daughter. As far as I knew, they were the only two witches alive with that much power.

Come to think of it, I had no idea who else knew about their abilities.

"No one in their right mind would let her govern anything." Kit snorted. "She might be rich, but that bitch ain't popular."

"Yeah, but she's gotta have enough magic to just, like, take over, right? Do they know about you two controlling all the elements?" I asked around a mouthful of turkey and cheese.

She shot me a disgusted look, but I didn't know if she directed it at my see-food or my question. "No, and alone, neither of us could take on an entire coven. Most coven members support their High Priestess and want nothing to do with Octavia. No surprise there."

I had no doubt that the two of them together could decimate whole cities. I chewed and swallowed. "So now that she's gone and no one cares, we need your help."

Kit folded her arms across her chest. "First, tell me what the hell happened to *you*."

Between Thane and me, the story of our experience

with the dragons went a lot faster than it'd taken our group to tell Adam. Having fewer people adding in their perspectives or corrections saved a fair amount of time.

At some point, Lena and Ivan waltzed in, bickering about something inconsequential until Kit snapped at them to shut up and eat. Amazingly, they listened without complaint, digging into their sandwiches like savages.

By the time we finished our story, ending with the agreement to dissolve the Mirfeniksan monarchy and form a council rather than promise the dragons a daughter, Angela's eyes were as wide as saucers. Even Kit looked impressed.

"Never thought I'd get to meet a dragon," Angela said with a slow, disbelieving head shake.

I grinned. "Did you think they were real before now?"

Angela's cheeks turned pink, which was a good sign because it meant she was regaining some energy. "Well, no."

"Me either." I winked at her.

"I'm glad you didn't have to promise them a kid," Kit said as she stood upright. She opened the fridge and put away the food supplies. "Especially if you had to do it with a dragon. That would've made for some awkward family reunions."

Thane nearly choked on his fresh glass of water. Laughing, I patted him on the back as he cleared his throat. Awkward was the understatement of the century.

After cleaning up the crumbs left behind, Kit rapped her fingers on the counter. "I have something else I need to do before we leave."

I raised an eyebrow. "Burn the place down?"

She smirked, but a wishful glint shone in her eyes. "No, I need to unbind my magic."

CHAPTER 9

Sunday Midday

My eyebrows shot toward my hairline. As much as I'd wanted Kit to unbind her magic ages ago—or, you know, not bind it at all—I also didn't like the devilish look she had going on right now.

I mean, I liked the look in general, but not on her and not at this moment. Kit was known to do some crazy things.

Oh, wait, no.

That was me—*I* was known for doing some batshit crazy things.

Like Thane, Kit was more coolheaded, except for the time she'd gone a bit nuts when she thought Angela had died. But right now, I wouldn't put crazy past her.

"Are you sure?" Angela asked, her voice soft as she reached for Kit.

My best friend moved around the counter until she cupped Angela's face in her hands. "No more hiding from who I am. I can't risk your life, or anyone else's, just because I'm afraid."

"I'm also kind of extra powerful now and could probably kick your ass," I added with a shrug.

Kit's gaze flicked to me. "Don't tempt me to test that theory."

"Yeah, because then I'd be forced to get involved, V, and I do *not* want to fight Kit." Shuddering, Lena pushed her empty plate away, then let out a hearty burp.

"And if Lena jumped in, then I'd have to rescue you both." Ivan ducked beneath Lena's fist and skipped away with a grin.

Angela stood from her stool and nearly collapsed. Kit caught her arms and kept her upright.

Thane's eyebrows furrowed as he rose. "Let's get her to the DEA to rest under angelic supervision."

His concern for her seeped through our bond, and I smiled. It was another reason I loved the man.

"Their magic's pretty amazing," Ivan's voice called out behind a tall cabinet door. He reappeared and held up a few bags and boxes of snacks: chips, pretzels, and protein bars. "But the food there? Not so great. I'll bring some provisions."

Kit grimaced. "I need her for the unbinding spell."

"Then let's unbind your magic after she's gotten some rest." I gathered the empty plates and set them in the sink.

The one thing this fancy kitchen lacked was a

dishwasher, probably because it had always been Shirley's job.

But worrying about dirty dishes was a low priority. I'd pay for a cleaning service—and a psychic cleansing—once Colin was dead.

Angela bit her lip and shook her head, sending her brown curls bouncing. "I'll be okay. We need to do this before anything else happens."

Kit's eyes widened slightly. I would bet she didn't expect Angela to agree with her because I sure hadn't expected it. I liked this dainty human witch more and more each day.

To think, I might not have seen this side of her without this clusterfuck of a situation.

"Wait, why didn't Octavia make you unbind your magic?" I asked.

"She tried once she got Angela out of the way," Kit said. "But when she found out we'd need Angela for the spell, she wanted to wait until she had me totally under her control."

I raised an eyebrow. "You seemed fairly controlled already."

"Not as much as she thought."

That's my girl. I grinned. "Okay, so how do we unbind you?"

"First, we need supplies," she said.

Ivan hugged the bags and boxes to his chest. "I'm still bringing snacks."

Holding her fiancée around the waist, Kit led us back outside and toward the greenhouse. She aimed for the door, despite the shattered glass panes making entry possible from any angle.

After handing Angela over to Thane, Kit moved to the wooden door, which had survived my falcon screech. A testament to its durability.

I blinked as she brushed a few pieces of glass away from the threshold with her foot, then shut the door...

...while she was still outside. She didn't appear to be losing it, but then again, I wasn't an expert on people. Apparently, not even my best friend.

Before I could ask if she was feeling okay, she muttered a few words, licked her thumb, and drew in the air. A looping symbol materialized as she drew, glowing red against the wooden door before slowly fading away.

I should have known better than to doubt her sanity.

When Kit opened the door again, my mouth dropped open. And mine wasn't the only one.

Lena stepped forward, gaping. "What...?"

Beyond the door was a cavernous, rectangular-shaped room with a marble floor. White Grecian columns stood at the corners, holding up the two-story ceiling and adding to the expansive feel.

I leaned sideways to see around the door and stared at the wrecked greenhouse. Everything remained exactly where it had been. The only thing that had changed was what existed beyond the door.

"This is Octavia's storeroom," Kit explained, gesturing inside. "I'd rather use up her shit than mine." She slipped her arm around Angela's waist again and helped her inside.

Lena glanced at me with wide, excited eyes before following.

"I'll keep watch out here," Ivan said, his hand already deep into a bag of chips. His wary gaze tracked Lena as she explored the room hidden within the greenhouse. "Gives me the shivers."

I grinned. I would have felt the same if I hadn't already experienced Kit's hidden locker—more like her very own bat cave. Your eyes and brain just didn't match up.

Thane and I followed the others inside. Like Kit's space, shelves and baskets lined the walls, ingredients and potion supplies covering every inch. One long table with a granite top took up the room's center, and two backless metal stools stood side by side.

Unlike Kit's cave, this place was immaculate; not a speck of dirt in sight. Kit's locker wasn't dirty, but it was still a cave. A witch-made cave folded into the human dimension, but dirt came with the underground ambiance.

On the far side, Octavia had drawn a chalk star inside a circle on the marble floor. The design was roughly five feet in diameter. Because Kit hadn't used much magic in the time I'd known her, I didn't know what the symbol did. Magic, obviously, but no specifics.

I pointed to it. "What's that?"

Her gaze followed the direction of my hand. "An amplification symbol. It strengthens any spell cast within it. Most witches use just the circle, but I'll need the pentagram's five points to remove my binding. The more elements we control, the harder it becomes to amplify."

Letting her get back to collecting ingredients and supplies, I wandered around the room, reading labels and cringing away from certain items that looked especially nasty. Her mother had kept some weird stuff, way more gross and disturbing than anything Kit had. That or Kit just hid those items better.

Eventually, I sat on the steps to wait, and Thane and Lena joined me soon after.

When her arms were full, Kit set the items she'd collected on the table. Angela sat on a stool, grinding up something herb-like in a mortar, then tipped the dusty contents into a glass jar.

The two witches worked in silence, and I wondered whether they'd already practiced this spell for when the time came.

After removing the silicone lid of another glass container, Kit poured in two vials, creating a murky-looking reddish-brown solution. Slowly, she mixed the liquid into the powder Angela made, and the resulting concoction bubbled and fizzed.

When it settled, Kit lifted the glass to her face, peering closely at the contents, and sniffed.

"Okay, we're ready." She lowered the glass, and a slight tremor in her hand sloshed the liquid.

"Are you sure you're prepared for this? Mentally?" I asked as Thane pulled me to my feet. "There's no rush. We can wait."

Kit shook her head and met my gaze. "It needs to be now. Just don't let me…"

She didn't need to complete the sentence for me to understand her fear. The last time she'd surrendered to her magic, she'd nearly lost herself when she thought Angela had died. Angela had brought her back once, and I believed she could do it again.

Mostly sure.

If not, I had a lot more firepower at my disposal—literally. Plus two more phoenixes and a realm walking, scythe-wielding mate.

Licking my suddenly dry lips, I clenched and unclenched my hands, my fingers cold and palms clammy.

Nothing we couldn't handle.

So why was I feeling this nervous?

Kit and Angela stepped into the chalk star and faced each other.

"The rest of you stay outside the circle, no matter what happens," Kit warned.

Well, that wasn't exactly reassuring. I glanced at Thane, debating whether we should stop this while we still could. Sensing my worry, he wrapped his arm around my shoulders and smiled.

If he had faith, then so would I.

She brought the container to her lips and paused, the murky liquid splashing against the sides thanks to her trembling arm. Angela took her free hand and squeezed it. Getting whatever she needed from her fiancée, Kit tipped her head back and downed the brown substance in one gulp.

I scrunched up my nose. Kit's hesitation and fear weren't about the flavor, but if looks had anything to do with it, that had to taste disgusting.

Kit tossed the container to the side in an overly dramatic yet badass move, and it shattered against a wall. She took Angela's other hand, and they chanted the spell, their eyes never leaving each other's. A light breeze swirled around them, fluttering strands of their hair.

As the spell grew in intensity, so did the wind, though it remained calm and peaceful outside the chalk circle. In seconds, a roaring gale tugged at their clothes and whipped their hair into their faces, but they didn't stop chanting.

A spark ignited along the circle and quickly spread, ringing the two witches in fire. Dark storm clouds formed over them, and thunder boomed within the room, echoing off the high ceiling.

Rain poured from the clouds, splashing within the circle and drenching the two women, making their shirts cling to their bodies. Steam rose where the drops met the flames, and Angela's teeth chattered as the wind drove into their wet clothes.

Still, they didn't stop chanting.

I chewed my lip, wanting nothing more than to bust in and help. But I had no desire to disobey Kit's warning this time. I'd learned my lesson.

The floor buckled and heaved, contained within the chalk but nearly throwing the two women to the ground. As if it were trying to separate them. Kit gripped Angela's hands tighter, their knuckles turning white.

Despite the chaos within the pentagram and circle, they didn't stop chanting.

Unease prickled along my skin, and I took a step forward. Yes, she'd warned us to stay back, and I would do my best to obey, but I couldn't stand idly by if things went wrong. Because if such a thing were possible—and it very well could be—the binding spell seemed alive and clung desperately to Kit.

The pentagram lit up with a golden glow, and the chalk lines rose and swirled around the witches' ankles, becoming thin tendrils that slithered up and around their legs. The tendrils thickened as they spiraled, the physical chain-like manifestation of Kit's binding.

When the glowing chains reached both women's

shoulders, the free end around Kit floated through the air toward Angela, transforming into the shape of a lock. The glowing chain's other end, now shaped like a key, extended from Angela's chest toward the lock.

The chain's key dipped inside the lock as the two witches chanted a final resounding word. The air surrounding them crackled with lightning, and a sharp clap had me covering my ears and wincing in pain.

The lock clicked open, and the golden binding fell from Kit and Angela's bodies, falling into a heap, then dissipating.

The tumultuous chaos and noise within the circle stopped so suddenly that it was like it had never existed. Eerie silence stretched through the cavernous room. The floor wasn't even cracked after the buckling and heaving, and both women were dry.

Magic could do some crazy shit.

I peeled my hands away from my ears, catching sight of Lena doing the same.

"Is it done?" Angela asked, panting. Her pale skin had lost the little color she'd gained earlier.

Sucking in deep breaths, Kit's eyes remained closed. She vibrated with power, visible as a rainbow aura, elemental colors churning around her. She dropped Angela's hands and clenched her fists at her sides, grimacing as if in pain.

Angela stepped closer, hesitant with each step. "Babe, are you okay?"

When Kit finally opened her eyes, her already dark irises had turned completely black, blending with her pupils.

My best friend was gone.

CHAPTER 10

Sunday Afternoon

I unfurled my wings and readied for a fight. Although Lena hadn't been there the last time, she drew her sword and stepped in front of me, sensing the danger. I was sure she hadn't forgotten the story about Kit trying to kill me.

A dark, humorless laugh trickled out of my best friend's mouth, sending a shiver up my spine. "Don't worry, Veronica. I don't want to kill you today. Not yet."

Combined with an eerie wink, her words did little to relieve me. Kind of the opposite. Goosebumps rose along my arms.

"Kit…" Thane warned, holding his scythe's device low in his hand. With one click, his deadly weapon would appear.

A deep crease formed between Angela's eyebrows as she drew them together. She reached up to Kit's face, lightly touching her temples. "What's happened?"

Kit's disturbing black gaze focused on her fiancée. "Releasing so much power at once is…addicting. It wants to control me, devour me." Closing her eyes, she inhaled deeply, her nostrils flaring. A vein popped out on her forehead. "I want to give in to release the pressure."

Angela took Kit's face in both hands, drawing her closer. "Don't let it win. Stay with me."

Kit's jaw clenched, and she gripped Angela's arms tight enough to make the human gasp. "You need to get away from me before I hurt you."

"You would never hurt me," Angela said, though she winced from the pain of Kit's hold. She stroked my best friend's cheeks with her thumbs before rolling onto her tiptoes and pressing her lips to Kit's.

With a violent shudder, she returned the kiss and loosened her grip on Angela's arms. She pulled back and opened her eyes—her brown irises had returned.

Breathing a sigh of relief, I let my fiery wings dissipate into ash. Lena sheathed her sword but watched the witches warily with her hand on the hilt. I didn't blame her, but she didn't need to worry anymore.

Angela might have been just a human, but her power over Kit superseded magic.

We should all be so lucky.

A strange emotion from Thane flickered through our soul link but vanished before I could identify it. He gave me a quick smile and tucked his scythe's device back into his pocket.

I frowned, but he'd looked away before seeing my confusion. Now wasn't the time to ask if he didn't want to mention it, but I made a mental note to discuss whatever it was later.

Kit sucked in a raspy breath, her focus solely on Angela. "You're my rock."

Angela smiled and kissed Kit again. "Always and forever."

If they kept it up much longer, their level of sweetness was going to give me diabetes. "As adorable as you two are, let's get the fuck out of here."

Kit nodded and glanced around. "I need to seal this place up. Most of these items are incredibly dangerous and volatile."

Thane helped hold Angela upright since her legs nearly gave out with her first step.

I glanced around as we headed for the door, knowing that the whole place could have blown at any moment during that spell, and only some of us could resurrect. Not only that, but if something had happened to Kit, we might have gotten trapped inside—forever.

It was an eerie feeling that helped me understand the importance of planning even more.

We rejoined Ivan, who stood with an empty chip bag dangling from one hand while staring wide-eyed at Kit. I guess he got to see the whole impressive display from outside.

After Kit closed the door, she sealed hidden storage room with a quick chant. Holding Angela around the waist, she turned away without a backward glance.

Thane and Ivan realm walked us to the DEA, where we found the others in the conference room.

Adam stood when we entered and bowed his head. "My deepest apologies, Ms. Parker. I had not considered your mother to be such a threat."

The corners of Kit's lips tilted up, but her eyes remained cold and hard. "Accepted. Octavia's where she belongs now."

A small gasp came from beside her. Angela stood stock still, her eyes opened wide, and a delicate white hand pressed to her mouth. I followed her gaze to Imos and Tundreg.

Oh right. They were obviously not human with their seven-foot stature, dragon scale skin, and weirdly dilated, matching golden eyes.

As our group filled the empty seats, I introduced the dragonmen to Angela and Kit, who remained standing behind her fiancée. If I felt small next to the two giant men, Angela, who might have topped five feet while wearing shoes, must have felt like an ant.

After the introductions were complete, we brought the witches up to speed on war preparations, should it come to that. Hopefully we could just kill Colin and be done with it, once and for all.

I was also positive it wouldn't be that easy. In my life, nothing ever was.

"We have since learned that Mr. Ó Broin left hidden devices," Adam paused as he considered his words, "magical bombs, if you will, around the building. I do not know for how long, but long enough to render the whole office incapacitated by his nightmare spell."

Ognebog's flames. Did this man's level of deceit know no bounds?

I clenched my fists in my lap, imagining my fingers wrapped around his neck.

Was there *any* good left inside him?

In the chair next to me, Thane reached over and took my hand, giving it a squeeze. His warmth flooded through me and soothed my rising anger. I took a few deep breaths.

Kit leaned against the back of Angela's chair and addressed Ivan. "You mentioned some sort of super weapon?"

He sat up straighter and nodded, an eager gleam flashing through his green eyes. "I tracked it down to the human world but haven't located it thanks to *someone's* impulsive decisions." He gave me a pointed look.

I stared wide-eyed and innocent right back. Sure, I might have a record, but I wasn't the *only* one causing problems. Colin topped the list.

Kit glanced at Adam. "Is this what I think it is?"

A tingling sensation crept across my scalp. Something told me there was more to this thing than I initially thought.

Adam sighed. "Yes. The Daggers of Abaddon."

"The ones William used?" Thane asked with a frown.

I had hoped to never think of those bad boys again. The three daggers were created in the dark ages by powerful necromancers, who used them to kill reapers and angels alike or perform sick acts like removing their wings. We'd almost lost Jessa to one.

Memories of mutilated bodies tried to surface, but I shoved them down and swallowed hard against the rising burn.

"The very same," Adam answered Thane. "If you will recall, however, mages created three daggers, and we have only recovered two."

I knew they could take down an angel, but the way Ivan described it? Able to stop any kind of magic? It didn't seem likely. "The daggers are the super weapon?"

"When combined, the three daggers become Abaddon's Last Hope," Kit explained.

Even though it was a pretty name, I shivered. I wasn't the only one, either. Darkness saturated her words like a bad omen, tainting the air we breathed.

"What kind of weapon is this thing?" Lena leaned forward, and her blue eyes sparkled with interest.

"We do not know. They have never been combined," Adam said.

"How do they combine?" I asked.

Kit shrugged. "Like most things, with magic."

"But I thought this weapon stopped magic." This was too confusing for my tired brain.

"Only once the daggers fuse together." Adam ran a hand over his tired face. "If we do not recover the third dagger, this idea will be for naught."

"Any ideas where the third one is?" Thane asked, his gaze moving between Adam and Kit.

The archangel shook his head. "If I did, I would have it in my possession already."

Kit pushed off Angela's chair. "Time to research. We'll head back to my place so she can rest while I do some digging."

"Ivan, can you get them home and keep an eye on them?" I asked.

Kit raised an eyebrow. "Did you forget who I am?"

"I'm not questioning your ability to protect both of you," I held up my hands in surrender, "but Ivan can jump here if anything goes wrong."

She gave a quick nod and helped Angela stand. The human was teetering and about to collapse. Sleeping for a few days might sound great to most people, but not when combined with no food or water and a spell that slowly stole her life force.

Ivan moved around the table to help Kit with Angela, and a moment later, they winked out of existence.

It was barely afternoon, but I yawned behind a hand. It'd been a long day already, what with the attack on the DEA then fighting Octavia.

Adam caught the yawn. "There is plenty we can discuss without you present, Ms. Neill. Please go rest."

He didn't have to tell me twice.

Thane, Lena, and I realm walked back to my penthouse. Lena wasted no time flopping onto the couch and closing her eyes, while Thane and I decided on a shower and a fresh change of clothes before doing the same.

Despite our mutual states of exhaustion, we took advantage of the calm before the storm and rallied for some much-needed tension relief in the shower.

The warm water had hardly washed over us before our lips crashed together, our kiss greedy and filled with passion. He knotted my hair in his hand, yanking my head back, then licked and kissed his way down my neck.

Every warm, wet flick of his tongue was like fire and ice. Electric shocks burst through my body, igniting my core with insatiable craving. I reached between us and stroked his straining erection, not wanting or needing to wait. My body was more than ready.

Growling low and deep, he pushed me against the marble wall and slipped his hands under my thighs, spreading me wide. His sapphire gaze locked on mine, and with one deep stroke, he plunged inside me, hot and hard, tearing a cry of pleasure from my mouth.

Streams of water cascaded through the divots between his pecs and abs as he drove into me again and again. Each thrust heightened my desire into writhing desperation and amplified my endless need into an all-consuming hunger.

Whimpering, I arched my back, pressing my breasts into the hard planes of his chest, until I exploded into a thousand pieces of pure ecstasy. I clenched around his thick length and dug my nails into his skin, shuddering with aftershocks. The water dripping down our bodies sizzled and popped.

His thrusts grew faster, more frenzied. As my back slid up and down the slick shower wall, his hands gripped my hips hard enough to bruise. He groaned my name and released inside me with a final deep thrust, his shoulder muscles bulging beneath my hands.

He rested his forehead against mine, and we panted together, kissing each other softly until we could move again.

After a quick scrub and another explosive orgasm, I barely made it to the bed before collapsing. Smoke still wafted out of the bathroom.

Beneath the sheets, Thane curled his muscular body around mine, pulling my back against his chest. My body warmed beneath his touch, tingling as he stroked my hair back from my face. He kissed my cheek and shoulder before settling down, one arm cradling me.

Completely content, my eyelids fluttered shut, and I fell into a deep, dreamless sleep.

After sleeping for nearly fifteen hours and feeling like a new woman, I stood facing one of the conference room's glass panels. My gaze tracked the various routes into and out of the Summerlands and the Summer Palace.

The Otherworld's land was more extensive than I'd realized, probably twice the size of Mirognya, if not more. The fae split the four courts into quadrants, with the Summer and Winter regions covering most.

Like Mirdrakona, the Winter Court's territory primarily covered the mountainous region blanketed in snow. Except in the Otherworld, snow constantly fell in that quadrant, controlled by the Winter fae's magic.

I shivered, rubbing my arms as I gazed at that area. It was like the cold drifted from the image and blew across my skin.

Lining the paths into the mountains, scraggly trees reached skeletal arms up and out, trying to snag trespassers unawares. According to Adam, once caught by the forest, you were unlikely to return. The Winter Court fae required permission before visitors could enter their lands.

Although, I didn't know why anyone would even *want* to visit. Winter Court fae were humanoid, exhibiting distinguishing icy features like William's white hair and blue-grey skin, and had chilly personalities. They were well-suited for their quadrant.

But the other fae inhabiting the frigid wasteland, the

true unseelie, were vile creatures that terrified you at best or, at worst, ate you alive.

I dragged my attention back to the Summer quadrant. Colin was a Spring Court fae and had close ties to the Summer Court through Queen Fiadh. That she had allowed Colin a position in her court was surprising until Adam learned Colin was a cousin of hers, making him royalty.

The fae man had certainly failed to share *that* important detail on our dates.

To make Otherworld matters even more complicated, the various fae organized themselves into clans based on an animalistic hierarchy. William had been part of the *Mac Tíre* clan, named after the wolf, and technically, any Court could become a member.

While the Wolves were reasonably high on the political food chain, only the Summer Court Lions or Winter Court Bears had enough force to become a king or queen. Fae had to be born into those clans.

If Colin allied with the Lions—or worse, the Bears— our potential war would become even more challenging.

"Do you have any mages capable of opening a portal on this side?" Pietr's deep voice brought my attention back to the group discussion. "If not, we'll have to open it from the Mirognyan side."

I tore my gaze away from the maps to face the others. Some phoenixes could open portals, though they needed something from the human world to succeed.

The major downside to a portal was that whichever side opened it had complete control. In the unlikely event a coup happened in Mirognya while I was away, they could close the portal to keep me out.

Luckily, the dragons in Mirdrakona still held my primary opponent Adrik, and only our allies knew I had a realm walker as a mate. And after we dealt with the fae, ruling Mirfeniksa would no longer be my concern.

"Once I learned of Ms. Neill's capture, I sent a request out to other agency branches asking for assistance locating one," Adam said. "I am still waiting to hear, but I am confident we will find one soon."

Unless William had recruited them all and gotten them killed, of course. I wouldn't have put it past that power-hungry idiot.

Pietr rubbed his white beard, the colors of his rainbow-hued irises swirling as he contemplated the situation. "Opening a portal on this side as soon as possible is ideal. However, we need to bring over troops, and I don't recommend waiting around for a mage."

Adam nodded. "In the meantime, I have procured a hotel nearby to house your people. The owner is a Community friendly human who will ensure discretion, and a gateway exists between the two buildings."

As he, Imos, and Pietr discussed lodging logistics, a reaper I didn't recognize stepped into the room and cleared his throat.

Adam eyed him. "Yes?"

The reaper pointed to the maps. "Someone's closing the portals to the Otherworld."

CHAPTER 11

Monday Morning

I spun to face the panels again. Sure enough, each yellow dot marking an Otherworld portal disappeared one by one. Dread sank into my stomach like a heavy stone. Fuck.

"Does that mean Colin knows?" I asked, hoping against odds that I was wrong.

Part of our plan relied on getting the upper hand by surprising him. If he knew we were on to him, things would get even trickier.

"I cannot imagine any other reason for the closures," Adam sighed, rubbing a hand over his face.

Dark circles ringed the archangel's eyes, and his wings drooped behind his back. Angels and reapers might not need sleep the way everyone else did, but that didn't mean exhaustion couldn't set in. The poor man needed to take a nap before he collapsed.

"But doesn't Queen Fiadh control the portals?" Thane asked, his brow furrowed. "Do we actually believe she's in on this?"

Steepling his fingers in front of his mouth, Adam's blue eyes flicked back and forth as he considered Thane's question. "I would like to believe she is not, but this appears to prove otherwise."

"She wanted all the fae to return to the Otherworld a few months ago. Maybe this is why." I glanced at the clock. "I can try to catch Joe at the Morning Grind to pick his brain about it. Assuming he's still in this realm."

Getting out of these strategy discussions would also be nice, but no one needed me to say that out loud.

"That would be most helpful," Adam said.

Thane hesitated before rising with me. I placed my hand on his shoulder and pushed him back into his seat. "You stay. I know you'd rather be in this conversation than coffee shop gossip."

He grinned and kissed my hand. "You know me too well."

Lena appeared at my side with a scowl. "Don't even think of asking me to stay."

"I wouldn't dream of it." I patted her cheek. "Let's go stretch our wings."

The flight to the Morning Grind went way too quickly despite taking a few extra loops through the ocean-misted air. Dark storm clouds loomed on the ocean's horizon but brewed far enough away to not cause any problems for flying. Just a few exhilarating gusts that sent us soaring.

When I couldn't stall any longer for fear of missing Joe, I led Lena down to my usual alley a block away from the store, and we shifted back to human form.

Tucked between a restaurant and a clothing store, the narrow coffee shop's front boasted a large window that provided customers excellent views for people watching. The red brick covering the rest of the front had seen better days, but it went well with the overall rustic industrial vibe.

Lena scrutinized the outside of the building as we approached. "You used to work here?"

"Don't judge." I nudged her with my arm. "It was just a cover."

She scoffed. "Oh please. I've seen how much coffee you drink."

I shrugged and opened the door for her. "You haven't tried the good stuff yet."

The morning crush of caffeinated addicts had already come and gone, but the Morning Grind was still bustling, as it would be for most of the day. Along with a handful of four-top tables spread out in the main dining area, a few two-tops stood by the front window, and three metal stools were tucked under the bar top. Most seats were occupied.

I didn't recognize any of the faces behind the counter working, which wasn't a huge surprise considering the high turnover of high school and college kids. Except on this side of the counter, one familiar head perched at his usual stool caught my eye.

"Miss me?" I asked, leaning close to the fae man's ear.

Joe spun around with wide, dark brown eyes and barked out a surprised laugh. His dyed black hair was slicked back, and he wore a light blue shirt under an expensive grey suit. As usual, shiny black Amadeo Testoni loafers adorned his feet.

He was Italian from head to foot—on the outside.

"Ciao bella!" He kissed both my cheeks. "What a surprise. I was starting to think I'd never see you again."

I smiled. He wasn't the only one. I introduced him to Lena, whose hand he kissed like she was royalty.

He grinned at me. "I've heard you received a big promotion in your life, *sì?*"

"The title comes in handy, but I'm looking to rid myself of it soon." I shook my head. "I'm glad I found you here. We've got a situation to deal with involving your people."

His people meaning the fae. Joe might have been born and raised in Italy, but that didn't take away his fae genetics.

He scrunched his eyebrows together. "What's happened?"

I held up a finger. "First, coffee."

Stepping over to the register, I ordered two black coffees. The young barista rang me up and filled two ceramic mugs before handing them to me.

Coffee in hand, I motioned him and Lena to an empty table that was far enough away from curious ears. The grinders, steamers, and overall loudness of the shop would aid in masking our conversation.

Briefly, I went over the details with Joe, sipping the heavenly brew and leaving out as many supernatural words as possible just in case some human heard us over the din.

Lena wrapped her hands around her mug, cradling the

warm coffee like a precious diamond. I swore she purred in contentment the first time she took a sip. *Kofe* in Mirfeniksa had nothing on the Morning Grind brew; not even the fancy beans I kept at home could compete.

The shop had been just a cover job, but it was as comforting as a second home. And they brewed damn good coffee.

When I finished telling him everything, Joe blew out a breath and leaned back in his chair, crossing one leg over the other. "I did not know it'd gotten so bad, but I'll be happy to help in whatever way I can."

"Do you think Fiadh knows about it?" I blew on my coffee, earth-scented steam swirling up and away. "Would she work with Colin on this?"

"I would be shocked if she was." He shook his head. "She and Colin had a falling out years ago. Decades."

A creeping sensation crawled up my back and neck, and I exchanged a look with Lena. "Thirty years ago or so?"

He tilted his hand from side to side as he considered. "Thirty or forty. Years pass so quickly for us."

If their falling out started this whole thing, then maybe she wasn't involved. At least not willingly.

Or maybe she *was* to blame. She hadn't exactly been warm and inviting when we met.

"You know," Joe continued, tapping the table with a finger in time with his bouncing foot, "now that I think about it, I noticed Fiadh was acting strange the last time I met with her, just a few weeks ago. Not quite herself."

Most fae didn't have the pleasure of meeting with their king or queen in their lifetimes, sometimes never even getting a glimpse of one. Joe's unique upbringing in Italy had always intrigued the queen, and he acted as one of her human world advisors.

"She's not normally cold and dismissive?" I asked, recalling my all too brief meeting with the queen. Although maybe she'd intended her coldness for Colin and not the rest of us.

He chuckled. "Not at all. She is as bright as the summer sun in looks *and* personality."

That was definitely not the same Fiadh I'd met. In looks, yes. I almost envied her long golden hair, but she'd basically thrown us out of her castle when we brought William's shenanigans to her attention.

"Well, when we visited, she and Colin seemed to have worked things out," I said.

"Veronica?" a familiar voice gasped out from behind the counter.

I cringed and glanced over, catching Isaac's gaping face before he spun toward the opening that would let him exit the back. Isaac, as in the Morning Grind's manager and my old boss.

I could only imagine how pissed he was that I'd ghosted him. Or had he ghosted me? I couldn't even remember at this point. Too much had happened since then and was way more important than whether I still had a cover job.

Isaac rounded the counter's corner and thundered toward me. He'd lost weight since the last time I saw him, and his clothes looked clean for once under his apron. I didn't spy a single stain.

Instantly, Lena's mug was back on the table, and she gripped a hidden knife hilt.

I placed a hand on her arm as she started to rise and

shook my head. Isaac was a human and far from scary, no matter how much he tried to intimidate his younger employees.

"It *is* you," he huffed out as he closed in on our table. "You're alive!"

My eyes widened as much as his. "What?"

He sniffed, and a legit tear rolled down his cheek. "I was so worried you'd died, and we'd parted on such awful terms."

Ah, crap.

"I'm sorry to drop off the face of the Earth like that." Hey, it wasn't too far from the truth. I stood and faced him, gesturing to his slimmer figure. "Don't tell me you stopped eating because of me."

Isaac barked out a laugh and pulled me in for a hug.

I blinked, caught unawares. The Isaac I knew was about as touchy-feely as Kit. I patted him on the back and extracted myself from his arms.

"I miss your humor," he said, wagging his finger. "No, no, my new, much better half is helping me get back into fighting shape." He pretended to box the air, almost dropping the towel tossed over his shoulder and scrambling to catch it.

That explained a lot. After his wife left him a few years ago, Isaac had gone into a downward spiral and gained a bit of weight and a bad attitude. This whole time, all he needed was a new girlfriend.

Who woulda thought?

Noticing the others at the table, he did a double-take. "Sorry to barge in, Joe. Had to see if I was hallucinating."

Joe grinned. "I almost thought the same."

Isaac gave Lena's glowering face a curious but cautious smile before lifting a hand toward me. "Duty calls, but don't be a stranger, okay?"

"I won't," I said, still feeling a bit mystified by his attitude change toward me. I was sure it wouldn't last long once he remembered he hated me.

Joe checked his watch. "A new man, *sí?*"

"I'll say."

"Duty calls for me as well," he said and stood. "But I'll look into the issue we discussed. Discreetly, of course." He smiled at Lena and took her hand. "It was a pleasure to meet a friend of Veronica's, especially one as fierce as she is beautiful." He kissed the back of her hand.

A light pink tinted her cheeks as she muttered a thank you. Men and women were usually afraid of the warrior woman, and compliments were more often about her fighting skills than her looks. Which was just crazy because the woman was drop-dead gorgeous.

"I can always rely on you, Joe," I said with a smile. "Thank you."

He and I kissed each other's cheeks, and he headed out the door.

I downed the last of my coffee. "Let's check on Kit. Her place isn't far from here."

Lena gazed into her empty mug with sadness. "Do they offer this to go?"

Lena and I strolled down the sidewalk toward Kit's with fresh brews in hand. It wasn't often we got to just hang out, and we both relished the opportunity while it lasted. Time would tell if we ever had this luxury again.

Death would catch up with me eventually. A true death. My new goal was savoring a few centuries with Thane first, but who knew what games the gods played with our lives.

By the time we reached Kit's, I felt more relaxed than I had in weeks, not since before the whole dragons-kidnapping-me fiasco. But I was also ready for some action. As much as I enjoyed a relaxing vacation, I was the type that needed to keep moving, keep getting shit done.

I'd texted Kit before leaving the coffee shop, so the door was unlocked when we arrived. We let ourselves in, and I froze mid-step.

Something was terribly wrong.

CHAPTER 12

Monday Morning

The entire apartment sparkled. Kit wasn't a messy person, but I'd still never seen her place so…shiny.

While my best friend faced her three computer screens in the living room's corner and barely noticed our arrival, Ivan glanced over his shoulder before returning to his game. He sat on the couch facing the TV, playing a fantasy video game featuring elves.

The answer to the mysterious cleanliness scrubbed a pot furiously in the kitchen sink. Angela wore bright yellow rubber gloves up to her elbows, and her cheeks were bright red from the exertion. Strands of her curly brown hair clung to her forehead.

"I don't mean to state the obvious, but that pot can't get any cleaner," I said. Taking Lena's empty cup, I tossed both in the trash can.

Lena drifted over to the couch and sank onto the cushion beside Ivan. Her mouth dropped open as she watched the screen.

Life's little luxuries—in the human world.

Angela blew out her breath and paused her scrubbing. "I know, but I need to keep busy. There's only so much I can do to help you guys. Cleaning is one of them."

I knew how she felt. Yes, I was physically stronger than her and had magic she didn't, but I also knew how useless I felt about not doing *something* when everyone else was busy. That was basically how I got myself into trouble so much.

Thankfully, Angela was channeling her anxiety into something more productive and less destructive than my typical go-to—impulsive decisions.

"My penthouse could always use some love," I teased.

She snorted, which sent one of her stray curls flying. "Your cleaning service would kill me."

I grinned. She wasn't wrong. I paid them way above market price and added hefty bonuses around the holidays. Hoarding cash wasn't my thing, even if I didn't flaunt it like other filthy rich people I knew.

Leaving Angela to her therapeutic cleaning, I sat on the fold-up chair next to Kit. Images and text covered her computer monitors, and she switched between them without pause.

"Adam's reaching out to other agency locations to see

if there's a mage capable of opening a portal to Mirognya," I said.

She nodded. "He emailed me."

Of course he did. I wasn't upset he'd beaten me to the punch—not that it was super exciting news to begin with—but I was already feeling the itch to be productive. Angela's disease must have been contagious.

Ivan shouted Yazyk curse words as Lena fell into a fit of laughter. A quick glance at the TV showed his character lying on the ground, dead, while an innocent-looking fluffy bunny licked the blood off a paw.

Murderous bunnies? So weird.

"Do you know any mages who could open a portal?" I asked Kit.

Frowning at a screen, she shook her head. She clicked away from whatever caused her frown before I could see it. "The two I would've recommended were involved with William's mess."

My upper lip curled with disgust. Even after his death, the fae necromancer had caused way too many problems. Still, it was probably because of his mistakes that we uncovered the entire plan before it was too late.

We needed mages we could trust, which meant not one of William's. They also had to keep a portal open long enough to get an army through, which was no easy feat.

"What about witches or warlocks?" I asked after trying without success to follow along on the screens. The girl moved way too fast for me to keep up. Her brain was like a machine.

Someday she'd figure out how to connect that brain to a computer, and we'd all be doomed.

"Octavia could, but I doubt she would, even if we trusted her."

"You're just as powerful as she is," I said.

Behind me, Ivan let out a whoop of excitement, and musical fanfare drifted from the TV.

"True, but I could only open one at a time, and each would seriously drain my ability to harness magic," she said. "For all their annoying, holier-than-thou, egotistical tendencies, mages are the best suited for opening portals. Their usefulness ends there."

The rift between mages and witches was well known. Witches looked down on mages, who were usually humans who studied and (hopefully) mastered sorcery. It took decades, sometimes longer, to become as strong as William or simply by winning the genetic lottery and born fae.

Mages hated that witches and warlocks were born with magic, tapping into it as easily as breathing. But their superiority complex came from the fact that mages *earned* their magic rather than having it handed to them on silver platters at birth.

Regardless of what they thought about each other—and don't get either started on human witches—they both had their place in our world. Angela was obviously a special case for Kit.

"Any luck with the last dagger?" I asked.

"Not yet." She glanced over at me. "You bored?"

Pots and pans clanked loudly in the kitchen as Angela put the clean dishes away.

"Apparently," I sighed.

"Here's an idea: go apologize to that poor demon whose house you broke into and trashed. Maybe it'll be up for joining the fight."

Did Kit seriously just suggest I apologize to a *demon*?

They weren't even considered Community members, which meant I was well within my rights to kill them outright. Or break into their homes, whatever.

I squinted at her. "Are you high right now?"

"I wish." Kit returned her attention to her screens. "Anyway, I can punch a permanent hole through the Otherworld's veil if necessary."

Whoa. "You can do that?"

"It's easier and less draining than holding a portal open," she explained. "But it comes with some serious cons, obviously."

That was an understatement. A permanent portal would allow the monstrous unseelie fae to come over at will. Even if we took precautions and created the opening somewhere in or near the Summer Palace, the catastrophic idea of unseelie crawling around Miami gave me the heebie-jeebies.

"Let's do it," Lena said at my side, making me jump. I hadn't even heard her approach. "I'd love to kick some fass."

My eyebrows drew together. "Fass?"

"Fae ass. Fass." She shrugged. "Just go with it."

"Don't even think about it!" Angela called from the kitchen.

"Too late!" Lena hollered back. "Fass is a thing now!"

Angela stalked toward us with a murderous look, made even scarier as she dried a large frying pan with a dishtowel. I knew firsthand how much damage a frying pan could inflict in the right hands. Angela might be tiny, but she had some serious steam to vent.

"You know that's not what I meant," she snapped. "If

the unseelie find out, you'll have another war on your hands or an apocalyptic-level crisis."

That was exactly where my imagination went, too, but her level of knowledge about the fae impressed me. She'd been doing some studying since meeting Kit and discovering the Community.

"What are the unseelie?" Lena asked with a raised eyebrow.

Angela shuddered. "Creatures of nightmares."

Lena smirked, resting her hand on a knife's hilt. "Faced nightmares before, and I'll face 'em again. Nothing I can't handle."

No longer rubbing the dish, Angela's eyes glazed over. "There's a reason they're contained in the Otherworld."

"Because humans are weak," Lena said, then grimaced. "No offense. You're special."

"You're absolutely right about us humans." Angela threw the dishtowel over her shoulder and pointed the frying pan at Lena. "But from what I've read, some of the worst unseelie snuck through a century ago, and it took *several* DEA branches banding together to fight them off."

Lena rolled her eyes. "No offense to the DEA either, but they follow moral codes some of us don't have to deal with."

"Are you going to guard the opening day and night?" Kit asked, amusement flickering across her face as she leaned back in her chair.

"Not me specifically." Lena leaned on my shoulder. "I've got duties. But I'm sure we can figure out a guard rotation."

Heading back to the kitchen, Angela shook her head.

"You better discuss this with Adam first. I doubt he'll be up for it."

She was definitely right. Adam wasn't a risk-taker, and the few times he was, it was after persistent heckling. Usually from me.

"If our only option is creating a permanent hole, then we'll figure out how to keep this world safe." I pulled out my phone and dialed Thane on speaker. "For now, let's fill them in on everything and see what they say."

My heart skipped a beat when my mate answered, as it usually did when I heard his voice after any time apart. Lena and I explained what we'd discussed with Joe before bringing up the backup plan.

"Worst-case scenario, Kit can punch a hole through the veil," I said and crossed my fingers, hoping they'd agree.

"I hope I do not need to stress the importance of *not* doing that without every other option considered first." I could practically taste Adam's panic through the phone. "Such an act is irreversible."

Lena snickered.

"Like I said, worst case," I said with a restrained sigh.

"Should we find the queen is implicit in this betrayal, we will consider such an option," he added. "We would want to prepare for an unseelie attack at any moment, with our combined forces in place."

Lena and I gave each other a silent high-five. I understood the risk and danger involved with a permanent portal, but I also really wanted to show Colin he messed with the wrong woman.

He thought he could keep me out by closing portals?
Boom. Think again.

"Good news," Thane said, his deep voice sending delightful shivers down my spine. He had such a hold over me and I loved it. "Or maybe bad news for you. We've located two mages within the US who can open and sustain portals for some time. Reapers will teleport them in later today to verify."

"Why would that be bad news?" I asked.

"Don't tell me you didn't want to punch a hole through the veil."

I let out a surprised laugh. "You caught me."

"Ms. Neill…" Adam's voice warned in the background.

"Just because I want to doesn't mean I'm going to," I said with an exasperated huff.

"You've got a track record saying otherwise," Thane said. Touché. "Once we bring the mages up to speed, we'll open portals to Mirdrakona and Mirfeniksa. Pietr and Imos will ensure their armies are ready to go, then bring them over."

I shivered, remembering the portals I took to the Otherworld and then Mirognya. The cold void between worlds was not a place I wanted to visit via portal *ever again.*

Twice was more than enough, and thankfully, my mate was a realm walker.

We ended the call, and I sighed at the device's background image—a picture of Thane and me at the beach. Back before our peaceful lives had gotten complicated again, as in before the dragons.

I still needed to track down Jackson Reed and kill that motherfucker once and for all—even more after leaving me stranded in another realm—but that task would have to wait. Colin was the mastermind behind my parents leaving

Mirognya and Jackson killing Maddox.

At the moment, the traitorous fae man was my first and only priority.

Kit muttered beside me, pulling my attention back to the present.

I tucked my phone away. "What's up?"

"The last dagger may be in the Otherworld." Her eyes focused on a particular screen.

Fear clenched at my chest, and I leaned in closer. "Colin has it?"

She frowned. "I don't think so, but he may be looking for it. Maybe that's why he closed the portals. He knows we have the other two, and he wouldn't want us getting the third."

"Where is it then?" I asked, my pulse racing. This was the closest lead we'd gotten so far.

"I'm not sure," Kit mumbled as she read through an online forum. "There's chatter about it showing up there just after you and William went to Mirognya. Some of the stronger or older fae can feel potent magical objects, especially when those objects leave or enter the realm."

"But no one saw who brought it in? Or where it went?"

"A rumor's circulating that a legend no one has seen or heard from in centuries has it. A guardian of the fae woods, but it's just gossip at this point. I'm trying to confirm with a reputable source."

Holy shit. I'd met a stag who fit that description. "You mean the Keeper of the Forest?"

Almost in slow motion, Kit turned her stunned gaze on me and blinked. "How the hell do you know that?"

I licked my lips, excitement building. "I saw him in the Otherworld on our way to the Summer Court. He was the one who told me I belonged in Mirognya."

Kit blinked again. "You actually saw and spoke to the Keeper of the forest?"

"Shocking, I know." I grinned, relishing that I knew something my genius best friend didn't.

I might have told her about the encounter earlier if I hadn't followed William through that portal. Instead, I'd kind of forgotten about him.

As if my revelation pained her, she pinched the bridge of her nose. "People have pursued him for centuries, and you just waltz in and find him on your first visit."

"To be fair to everyone else, he found me," I said. "I'm sure it was a onetime experience."

She muttered something under her breath and returned her gaze to the computer screen, resuming her too-fast-to-follow clicking.

I sat back and gnawed on my lip. What if it wasn't a one-time visit?

He had clearly sensed my presence in the Otherworld. Maybe he would again and want to say hi, catch up, and ask if I ever made it to Mirognya. Or maybe I could get his attention somehow, set the forest on fire or something.

It might be wishful thinking, but trying couldn't hurt…

Right?

I looked at Ivan, who'd finished his game and relaxed on the couch with a bowl of pretzels. "Hey, do you think you could realm walk to the Otherworld?"

CHAPTER 13

Monday Morning

"I heard that!" Angela yelled from behind the kitchen counter. She'd progressed from dishes to scrubbing baseboards on her hands and knees. "Don't even think about it!"

"I don't mean right this second," I called back. "Just his ability in general."

Ivan leaned forward and grinned, setting the empty pretzel bowl on the coffee table. "The better option would be Thane. He's been there a few times."

Realm walkers usually needed to visit or see a place before they jumped. Ivan was a unique case, able to realm walk without having to do either first, but crossing dimensions was a whole other risk.

Thane had risked his life with a super dangerous blind jump to Mirognya to find me, a memory that brought a grimace to my face. I wouldn't put him or Ivan at risk again. Not if I could help it, anyway.

"Can we sneak in another way?" Lena asked, undeniable hunger for adventure lighting up her face. That must have been what everyone saw in my eyes all the time. No wonder it terrified them.

"I could open a portal with a few supplies from my locker," Kit said, swiveling her office chair to face us again. "A quick opening to get us through."

"Us?" Angela's voice squeaked. Her head popped up over the counter, sending her ringlets bouncing. "You're thinking about going?"

"Meeting the Keeper of the Forest would be…" Kit's eyes took on a distant, dreamy look. "Unbelievable."

"You thought he was a legend until a few minutes ago." Angela stood and planted her yellow gloved hands on her hips. A deep crease formed between her eyebrows. "And there's no guarantee he'll show himself to you. To any of you."

She had a point there, but I had a gut feeling he would reveal himself to me again. Of course, maybe that was wishful (or egotistical) thinking.

"But now I know he's real." Kit's chair creaked as she rose and headed toward her fiancée. "I believe the dagger's with him. What if Colin finds him first?"

"What's that fae going to do with one dagger?" Angela demanded. "The DEA has the other two."

Another well-thought-out point for Team Angela. She and Thane must get along perfectly.

"One is still enough to kill reapers and angels," Kit said calmly, taking Angela's gloved hands in hers without a hint of disgust. Those gloves weren't totally yellow anymore. "The stag's rumored to grant blessings on certain people, especially those with hearts as pure as yours. Maybe he could extend your life, give us more time together."

As a human witch, Angela wouldn't enjoy the longer than average years that a Community witch did. Not even human mages had figured out how to extend their lives yet, and their ability to harness magic through sorcery far surpassed normal humans tinkering with witchcraft.

With Kit as her tutor, however, Angela might surprise us all.

Her already flushed cheeks deepened to red. "You want me to come with you?"

My best friend smiled. "Of course. There's no way I'm leaving this realm without you by my side."

Indecision was evident in every inch of Angela's expression. After a moment's hesitation, she glanced at me. "You need to tell Thane first, or I'm pulling the plug."

Once again, she was absolutely right, but he would try to talk me out of it. He might even ask Adam to chain me up or something ridiculous like that, even if I had earned that kind of treatment with my impulsive actions.

Decisions, decisions.

"I will," I said. "If he agrees, we can use his realm walking ability. Save us some time."

"What if he says no?" Lena raised an eyebrow suspiciously.

"Then…" I trailed off as I considered her question.

In the past, I would have wasted no time diving headfirst into danger, regardless of who I hurt. After losing Mad, I had little to live for except the adrenaline rush during a heist.

But now?

Now, I had Thane and Kit, Lena and Ivan, and all the others who had become friends and family over the last few months. The only logical option was one I really hated suggesting, but we needed to get that dagger before Colin did, no matter what.

Making up my mind, I gave a slow, one-sided shrug. "Then you guys will go without me and hope the stag wants to chat."

Kit's slack-jawed stare hinted at how much I'd grown. I would have given myself a pat on the back, but I didn't want to spoil the moment.

"But first, let's get everything prepared for Kit's spell so he has less to argue against," I added with a wink.

Baby steps.

Ivan grinned. "I like the way you think."

"I'm surprised you'd let us go on an adventure without you." Kit had narrowed her eyes, most likely thinking I was up to something sneaky.

If only.

For once, I was doing the right thing.

I heaved a sigh. "Trust me, it's not easy. But I can't do that to him again or to any of you."

Speaking of the handsome devil, Thane appeared in Kit's living room as if we'd summoned him. His concerned gaze met my surprised one. "Luka called. The Hollow

Hounds attacked his pack. Something's wrong with the rogues, and the pack needs backup."

I was wondering when the rogue clan would show their faces again. If the Hounds were working with Colin as they had with William, then they were in for a big surprise facing me. I still wasn't over losing my Mercedes-Maybach thanks to those asshole shifters.

Lena sauntered over to Thane with a sly smile, a blade already swinging in her hand. "About time we got some action around here." She gave him a lewd look. "The rest of us, anyway."

I turned to the witches. "We'll take care of it. You guys work on the other plan."

Kit shook her head and folded her arms across her chest. "We're helping."

"What other plan?" Thane raised an eyebrow as he looked at us.

"Nothing that can't wait," I said. "I'll fill you in after we put down the rogues. Let's go."

Our group joined hands, and the colorless void of instant teleportation engulfed us.

A breath later, gravel rolled underfoot as we settled on hard ground, and vicious snarls replaced the silence of the void.

Everywhere I looked, wolves and several shifter species fought around Luka's tiny house on stilts, sending fur and spit flying to the surrounding treeline. Blood splattered across the patches of grass and rocky driveway that wound through the trees toward the main road, but I didn't see any wolves down or critically injured yet.

Instantly, I knew we had a problem. In their wolf forms,

it was impossible to tell which wolf was which—one of Luka's or a rogue.

The good news was the rogue clan consisted of more than just wolves. We could focus on those who didn't howl at the moon and let Luka's pack pick off the wolves.

After telling the others to focus on non-wolf shifters, we spread out, and I immediately lost sight of Ivan and Thane. I drew two of my hidden knives and unfurled my fiery wings. Fire was an excellent deterrent to most of the Community, and these shifters were no exception.

Some sort of big cat—as a bird shifter, I didn't really *do* felines—was getting the upper hand against a smaller wolf. I threw a knife, aiming for the cat's belly. As much as I despised the rogues for siding with necromancers and destroying my car, I didn't want to kill anyone unless necessary.

Other than Colin and Jackson, of course. They were walking dead men.

My thrown knife drove deep into the shifter's side, and the cat let out an anguished yowl. As Lena ran toward it with her sword raised, it backed away from the wolf and ran into the woods.

No one ever accused the rogues of being brave.

The wolf dipped its head to Lena and me before dashing after a fleeing wolf, Lena right behind him with a bloodthirsty grin on her face.

I turned my attention to the next shifter, another big cat. Outside of wolves, feline shifters were among the most common, and just like their domesticated counterparts, they could be such assholes.

This cat had a light tan coat and reminded me of pictures I'd seen of mountain lions. Her icy blue eyes followed my every move, the muscles beneath her skin rippling as she circled me on soft paws.

Too bad for her, I didn't have the time or patience for this cat-stalking-a-bird bullshit.

With my free hand, I tossed out a line of fire, creating a whip of flames. I cracked it overhead like a circus ringleader before bringing it down on the cat right as she lunged for me. The whip snapped across her nose, and I spun away from her reaching claws.

She yowled and landed, rubbing at her singed snout. I cracked the whip again and brought it down on her haunches.

Yeah, that's right. I spanked her like the bad kitty she was.

With a final snarl in my direction, she dashed into the trees and out of sight.

"Julian! No!" Tabitha's panicked voice shouted from the house's front stoop.

I whipped around. Her toddler son Julian ran down the steps and straight toward two giant wolves snarling and snapping at each other with deadly intent. I recognized the grey one as Luka, which meant the brown one had to be Rico.

There was no way Tabitha or I would reach Julian in time, but neither wolf saw the little boy headed their way.

CHAPTER 14

Monday At Noon

As Julian raced toward his stepfather and uncle, everything else seemed to slow down in my vision. Even though I knew I wouldn't make it in time, I had to try. I sprinted toward the little boy with everything I had.

At the last second, the brown wolf snapped his head toward the fast-approaching boy and bared his teeth. Saliva dripped from his mouth, and he lunged for Julian.

Luka intercepted his attack with a pounce of his own and pinned the brown wolf to the ground beneath his massive grey paws. His jaws closed around the other wolf's neck, and with one wrong move from Rico, Luka would crush his throat.

I was almost there, but Julian didn't stop. He ran right up to Luka and pounded on his wolfish head. "Let *tío* Wico go!"

Luka's surprised gaze swiveled to the little boy, and his vise-like grip on the brown wolf lessened.

That was all the diversion Rico needed. He rolled out from beneath Luka with a snarl, kicking the grey wolf in the side, sending him plowing into two shifters. They set on him immediately.

Rico growled and lunged toward Julian again.

"No!" I yelled as I ran, reaching for the boy.

A blur of brown fur swept past me and slammed into Rico. A smaller female wolf clawed and bit him relentlessly, sending tufts of fur flying. Even with the newcomer's fury-filled attack, Rico was much bigger and stronger and slowly gaining on the other wolf.

Before Luka could shake off the last shifter, an enormous bear barreled toward him. It bellowed as its paws thundered against the ground.

I reached Julian and pulled him to me just as Rico flung the other brown wolf away. The smaller wolf slammed into a large rock and collapsed, whimpering as she stood, only to fall again.

"Momma!" Julian cried out, trying to wriggle away from me.

Despite the bear lumbering toward him, Luka's head snapped our way. He searched for the cub, ensuring the boy's safety before his own. The bear smacked him with a massive paw, sending the grey wolf flying into a tree with a resounding crack. The trunk split and half the tree fell with Luka.

Rico's wolfish gaze fell on me as the next potential threat.

I sucked in a breath as we locked eyes and drew my fiery wings around Julian and me. Something was wrong with Rico's eyes. They weren't the usual wolf colors—shades of brown, green, and yellow. His were an icy blue, a color that reminded me way too much of William's.

Goosebumps prickled across my skin. The mountain lion I'd fought had a similar eye color, and a quick glance around proved that many other shifters and wolves did, too.

The bigger brown wolf raced toward me, unafraid or unaware of my fire in his craze to get to Julian. I shoved the kid behind me and raised my knife.

Instead of deflecting the wolf's attack with the blade, I found myself glued in place and unable to move. My wings' fire extinguished, and flecks of ash drifted away.

Panic rose fast. Rico's snarling teeth were only a paw's length away from my face, ready to maim and disfigure, but he was frozen mid-leap.

I glanced around as much as I could. Everyone had stopped in the middle of whatever action they'd been doing. Any attempts at using my magic or shifting resulted in absolutely nothing.

What the fuck was happening?

As luck would have it, I didn't have to wait long to find out.

Chanting, Kit stepped closer toward us, drawing in the air with her finger. The looping and swirling designs glowed red briefly with her magic, and her irises darkened, blackness seeping to the outer edges of her eyes.

Behind her, Angela stared with wide eyes, unmoving. Her mouth parted in a silent cry, her arm outstretched toward Kit.

My heart beat wildly against my ribs. Kit's magic was consuming her right in front of me, and I had no way of stopping it. As much as I hated my next thought, I was terrified she was about to kill us all.

Kit saturated her words with powerful energy in a deep, guttural voice. Red mist rose from the ground everywhere I looked, which wasn't far considering I couldn't move my head. I had a sneaking suspicion the mist covered Luka's property, anywhere shifters and wolves fought.

I didn't think Kit's magic could kill me for real like phoenix fire, but then again, I wasn't entirely sure. Finding out wasn't high on my priority list.

When I realized I couldn't see Thane, my lungs clenched, stealing my breath. Fear and frustration pulsed between our soul link—he was here somewhere and just as worried as I was. Because if Kit killed us all, I wouldn't get the chance to see him one more time. He wasn't a phoenix, and who knew if his scales would activate and protect him.

The red mist grew thicker, moving and condensing around the shifters and wolves. It swirled and thickened around their bodies, devouring them whole.

Surprisingly, it left me alone. In fact, the more I tracked the mist's pattern, the more I realized her magic was only going after the rogues, including Rico.

All across the yard—the parts I could see, anyway— blue and white sparks erupted from the shifters' bodies, bursting and dissipating within the red haze. When the last spark disappeared, the mist sank into the ground and evaporated.

A small whimper brought my attention to Rico, who was still dangerously close to chomping on my face. His irises had changed to a brownish-green, back to a wolf's color.

Out of breath from chanting, Kit raised a hand and snapped.

Rico crashed into me, knocking us both to the ground, but he quickly rolled away. I jumped to my feet as he shifted to his human form, where he knelt, naked and shaking. As brothers, he shared Luka's russet-brown skin, but he'd shaved most of his dark hair into a buzz cut.

With a horrified look on his face, he reached a hand toward Julian, who'd thankfully gotten far enough away that I hadn't squashed him with my fall.

I grabbed the little boy and held him back as he dashed toward Rico again.

"Don't touch my son," Tabitha's voice snarled as she limped closer.

I knew she didn't direct her comment at me—her furious gaze fastened on Rico. She was significantly more fierce naked, dirty, and limping than in her daily mom clothes. A mate worthy of an alpha.

She took Julian from me, holding him on her hip, and glared at Rico.

"Come on, Tabby, you know me," Rico pleaded, still on his knees. His voice sounded familiar, but I couldn't place it. "I don't know what happened or why I'm here."

All around us, shapeshifters had returned to human form, some looking baffled like Rico and others still baring their teeth defensively. But the desire to fight had fled from everyone.

Well, almost everyone.

Naked and ready to murder, Luka stormed toward Rico, his fist raised.

"He's telling the truth," Kit said and stepped in front of Luka, holding her arms out to block him. "They were under a fae spell, and a really fucking strong one."

Rico's face paled.

Although his fist was still in the air and ready to strike, Luka hesitated. His arm shook with the effort to restrain himself.

"Spell or not, I will *never* forgive you," Tabitha spat at Rico. "You're a disgrace to our kind."

Rico's eyes remained wide as his gaze dipped to Julian, who was still struggling to get out of his mother's iron grip. "I'm ashamed. I can't believe I almost attacked my nephew."

"Trust me when I say you had no control," Kit said. Over his head, her soft gaze met mine, and I saw the understanding there. She'd been under Octavia's control the same way.

I felt for the guy, for all of them. Vampiric influences had controlled my actions and thoughts more than once, to the point that I had almost orgasmed in front of an arena full of the bloodsuckers. Their ability to influence wasn't even total mind control like this had been.

Angela rushed up beside Kit, who smiled and pointed to her eyes. "Still me."

The human witch let out a noticeable sigh of relief and took Kit's extended hand.

"How was this possible?" Luka asked, finally lowering

his arm, though his body remained tense and ready to act.

Rico sucked in a deep breath and stood on shaky legs. "A fae mage, William Caomhánach, approached me with a deal I couldn't refuse. He took us to the Otherworld and offered us land. His help and influence would give us something we'll never get here—a place to call our own." His gaze met his brother's. "And respect."

Luka's jaw clenched, but Tabitha let out a loud snort beside me.

"But when I heard he'd died, I thought the deal was off." Rico ran a hand over his buzzed head.

"By taking you to the Otherworld, he was able to weave a spell of control over all of you that followed you back here," Kit explained. "William was strong enough to cast a spell you wouldn't have noticed."

"William or Colin?" I asked, hoping Bill was the only fae that powerful.

Kit hesitated, then gave a slight shake of her head. "Honestly? I don't know. I'm fairly certain that Colin cloaks his magic when he's in this realm. Either way, Colin had to have done this."

Trepidation skittered down my back. We all knew Colin had a great deal of magic, especially for one of the Spring Court fae.

If he was hiding the full extent of his abilities, then just how powerful was he?

Controlling so many people meant pretty damn strong. I couldn't be sure of course, but I didn't think his relation to the queen, as her cousin, had much to do with it, especially since it seemed like she was on his side.

We needed to find out how involved she was, and soon.

"I'm going to start off by saying I really don't like your clan for wrecking my car," I said to Rico, putting my hands on my hips. "But we need to stop Colin and whoever the hell else is involved. Can we count on you and your rogues?"

Rico's gaze traced my body, lingering on my curves as if seeing me for the first time. His entire demeanor changed, and a playful, downright sexy smile tugged at his lips. "As long as I get to watch your fine ass in action, count me in."

Just like that, I recognized his voice. He was the man in the skull mask who had kidnapped Kit and me and threatened to kill her if I didn't play nice. One of several despicable threats.

I pulled my arm back, then slapped him as hard as I could, snapping his head to the side. The sound rang across the yard.

Slowly, he turned his face back to me, narrowing his eyes. A bright red handprint stained his cheek.

I leveled my gaze at him, drawing my ancestral magic forward into my stare. Generations of mothers giving him *the look*. "Would you like to try that again?"

A sudden possessiveness surged through my soul link, and warmth spread across my back as Thane approached our group. Electricity sparked through my body and ignited my core, aching with a sudden need for him. An undeniable sense of belonging pulsed through our bond.

Mine. I could almost hear his mirrored thought.

There was no doubt that I belonged to Thane—mind, body, and soul.

Sure, Rico was a good-looking guy for an asshole; he shared genetics with Luka, for flame's sake. But I wasn't there to mess around and play games with someone like him, someone I really wanted to stab.

No one else spoke, as if sensing the seriousness of our silent showdown. I held Rico's stare until he shifted his weight uncomfortably and flicked his gaze to Thane.

He licked his lips. "Count us in, *señora*."

A low growl came from Tabitha's throat. "You can't trust these outcasts. There's a reason their own families banished them."

Rico met her fierce glare straight on, and his flirtatious act dropped. "And we want to atone for our sins. I'm in."

The entire rogue clan voiced their assent, promising their loyalty in the fight against the fae. A battle for freedom. Because if Colin won, he would control everything, including them.

Luka's narrowed gaze swept over the rogue clan before settling on his brother. "Respect must be earned, but I will honor an alliance between our packs if you prove yourself loyal in this war."

A hushed murmur swept through the wolves and other shifters watching. Such an alliance was unheard of because, like Tabitha said, they were rogues for a reason.

Rico's eyebrows skyrocketed toward his buzzed hairline. He grinned and held out a hand. "We won't let you down, *hermano*."

"Don't make me regret this," Luka growled as he gripped his brother's hand.

Tabitha snorted again and led Julian away by the arm. Or she tried to, except that stubborn little cub wriggled himself free and ran back to the group.

"*Tío* Wico!" he cried as he all but leaped into his uncle's arms.

Rico laughed and swung his nephew around, smothering his cheeks with kisses. Noticing a fuming Tabitha approaching, he put Julian down and ruffled his hair. "Don't give your mom trouble, *mijo*, or she'll put a leash on you."

Julian grinned at his mom, who sighed in exasperation and led him away again. This time her grip was ironclad.

I wasn't sure Tabitha would ever forgive Rico for leaving the pack or almost attacking her son. To a mother, it didn't matter that he'd been under a spell and not in control.

I wasn't sure I could forgive him either, no matter how much I appreciated the extra help against Colin. His pack had wrecked my car, then kidnapped my best friend and me promising to inflict horrors on us in good time.

Forgive? No.

Forget? Also no.

Ignore for now? Sure.

The good news that came from this fiasco was that we had added another group to our growing collection of fighters. Dragons, phoenixes, reapers, angels, wolves, and now shifters galore. We'd involve the vampires if we needed to, though we all had our fingers crossed that wouldn't be necessary.

As the wolves and shifters dispersed, Thane pulled our smaller group to the side. His gaze fell on mine, longing and desire rippling between us. I never wanted this insatiable need to end.

"You ready to tell me what the other plan is?" he asked.

I bit my lip and glanced at Kit. She raised her hands as if saying this was my problem. Rude, but she wasn't wrong, even if she was the one who figured out where we needed to go.

I took a deep breath. "We know where the third dagger is."

CHAPTER 15

Monday Afternoon

Thane

My blood still pounded in my ears from Rico's lecherous reaction to Veronica and the intense feeling of anger and disgust that had seeped through our bond. Yes, she was a beautiful, confident woman who would attract attention for centuries to come.

Still, something in me nearly snapped when I saw how the wolf had looked at her. Like she wasn't a woman or even a person, but a prize to be won.

His reaction brought on my rage so fast it spilled downward like an avalanche that iced over the last of my warmth. I had been ready to murder the man in front of everyone.

Clenching my fists, I refocused on Veronica's face as she bit her lip and glanced at Kit. I might not be the strongest or most magically inclined mate to protect her, but if I needed to give her up, I'd be damned if I let someone like *him* try to take my place.

"We know where the third dagger is," Veronica said, interrupting my tumultuous thoughts.

Only that wasn't what I expected her to say, and the statement jarred me into focus. "Where?"

"The Otherworld," she said with a slight grimace.

I groaned. "Of course it is."

"It gets better—it's most likely with a stag called the Keeper of the Forest."

My jaw slackened as I stared at her. She'd told me about seeing a stag, and I hadn't believed it was anything more than a fae trick, luring her deeper into the forest.

"You know, the one who first told me about Mirognya," she added. Her pointed look made it clear she remembered my panicked reaction in the woods when I thought I'd lost her.

"I remember. I'm just not sure how to process this," I said, rubbing the back of my neck. Glancing at each member of our group, I narrowed my eyes as suspicion grew until I landed on Veronica again. "You were going to leave without telling me."

She opened her mouth to object, but Angela beat her to it. "Actually, she said she'd stay behind if you didn't agree."

I smirked. "How much did she pay you to say that?"

Veronica scoffed, but her purple eyes twinkled with amusement. "How dare you. A lady never reveals her bribes."

"Thank you." I threw an arm around her shoulders and drew her to me.

She tilted her face up toward mine, and I kissed her. Unadulterated love flooded through our bond. Her lips tasted like heaven, like ocean breezes warmed by the midday sun. I could drown in her love until the end of time and never have a single complaint.

"I can open a portal to sneak us through," Kit said, forcing our attention back to the present. "But it'd be faster and less likely to be noticed if you realm walked us in."

"You're a bad influence," I teased Veronica.

A rush of intense desire swept through our soul link, instantly stiffening my cock.

She shrugged casually, though a flush crept up her neck. "I just get things done."

"Okay," I said with a nod. "I'm in."

Because the sooner we got that dagger and took care of Colin, the sooner I could throw her on her back and thrust deep inside her warmth, claiming her once again.

A heavy, dull ache spread through my limbs.

Mine…

…for now.

Veronica

I'm not gonna lie. I definitely thought we would have to bully Thane into going, or I would've ended up staying behind. Excitement fluttered in my stomach. Soon, we would have the dagger, create the super weapon, and kick Colin's ass to the curb.

"If things go sideways, I'll help realm walk back to this side," Ivan added.

"Let's try not to let anything go sideways," Angela said with a slightly panicked expression as she gripped Kit's hand tighter.

The phoenix grinned. "It's always good to have a backup plan."

Ivan was right. Kit and I always planned one or more backup scenarios should things go wrong during one of our heists. But Angela was new to this whole sneaking around business.

Still rockin' his birthday suit, Luka walked over to our group. Dirt smudged across his tanned muscles, which somehow made him even more handsome, like a work of chiseled art. I wasn't the only one who thought so, judging by Lena's open-mouthed stare.

He shook Thane's hand and nodded to the rest of us. "Thank you for rallying help so quickly."

"I'm just glad there were no casualties," my mate said.

Seriously, we got lucky. If Kit hadn't recognized the spell and intervened, we might have been digging graves tonight. To think I'd tried to stop her from coming with us.

As if sensing my thoughts, the alpha wolf turned to Kit and dipped his chin. "I'm in your debt."

"I don't do debt between friends," she said.

Luka smiled, and I swear I would find a puddle of drool at Lena's feet. "I'm lucky to have your friendship, and I look forward to helping you out someday."

Her gaze flicked to me. "Don't get too comfortable, then. Trouble follows this one like night follows the sunset, and somehow I'm always dragged in."

I threw my hands up in the air. "You can't blame me for everything."

"I'm afraid I believe the witch more than you." Luka winked at me. "I don't mean to be impolite after your help, but I need to speak with my pack. Excuse me."

He lifted his hand in a brief wave and turned around, giving us a delightful view of his shapely backside. I caught Lena's crestfallen expression as he walked away and nearly laughed.

I rubbed my hands together. "No time to waste. Let's head to my penthouse and load up."

Luka already forgotten, Lena whooped, earning a few curious glances from the wolves lingering nearby.

"I need to grab a few supplies from my place first," Kit said. "Ivan, can you be our chauffeur?"

The phoenix bowed low, swooping his arm across his middle. "At your service, ladies."

"Don't be too long," Thane said. "I'd rather not be in the Otherworld when the sun goes down."

Ivan raised an eyebrow. "You won't get lost. Some of us have avian night vision."

"He means because of the other fairy creatures," Angela said quietly. "The ones you pray to never meet and *never* at night."

A shiver crept up my spine. That was exactly what Thane had meant. Banished from walking during the day, some unseelie fae prowled the night, preying on anything they could sink their claws into. Some would kill you outright, while others would make you wish they had.

The newly-turned human world vampires that resembled rotting corpse monsters didn't even come close.

Thirty minutes later, we were ready to roll. Ivan had jumped Kit and Angela over to my penthouse only a few minutes after leaving Luka's place. We had stocked up on weapons, and I'd helped Angela find a few suitable potions to bring along in a messenger bag.

Lena had donned her leather armor from Mirfeniksa, her excitement radiating like an aura, while I changed into cargo pants, a tank top, and a light jacket.

We didn't know what dangers we might face in the Otherworld, but we wanted to be prepared for almost any scenario, especially if we stayed after the sun went down. I sent a quick prayer to Dazhbog that we made it back long before then.

As we gathered in the open space between my kitchen and living room, Kit scribbled a note with charcoal onto a piece of paper. She lit a small flame in her hand and set the paper on fire, chanting a quick incantation.

"What's that?" I asked, watching the fire consume the paper.

When the ashes dissipated, she closed her hand, snuffing out the flame. "A message to Adam."

Since when did she become a snitch? "Ugh, you told him?"

"Only in the event of my death."

"But you're the least likely to die," I pointed out.

"Exactly." She hefted a backpack over her shoulder and took her place in our circle.

A twinge of fear nipped at my lungs. If she was leaving a message in case she died, then that meant the rest of us were already dead. The archangel would have to write our obituaries. Scary thought.

"Ready?" Thane looked at each of us as we joined hands. "Here we go."

The void swallowed the light, sound, and even gravity, eating me up and threatening to devour me whole. No one in our group was visible in this absolute nothingness, not even to my avian vision. No heat existed to generate a signature.

While realm walking through dimensions was far faster than a portal, it still unnerved me that it took longer than a heartbeat like any other human world jump. The idea of getting stuck in between realms was beyond terrifying, and I hated that I'd made Thane experience such an uncertain, awful feeling when he followed me to Mirognya.

Never again.

Solid ground reformed beneath my feet, and I took a steadying breath before opening my eyes.

We stood on a dirt path that sliced across a grassy clearing and wove its way between tall, leafy trees. They resembled pine or oak, except their branches twisted and turned in ways human world trees never did.

As the sun shone above in a cloudless, bluish-lilac sky, every color splashed across this world appeared heightened and brightened. Every flutter of leaves caught my eye with their brilliance. It was like seeing the world through my falcon eyes while in human form. Disorienting and mesmerizing.

Glancing around, I recognized where we were—the path from the last time I'd visited, as in the exact location of the portal that used to exist here.

"Is this a safe place to arrive?" I asked, flicking my gaze around for anything creeping up on us.

"I'm thinking it's the safest," Thane said. "Colin will think we'd open a portal closer to the Summer Court."

I hoped he was right, but doubt still plagued my thoughts. Colin was anything but predictable, and he'd had plenty of time to snoop on us and study our behaviors before we caught on to him.

"As Veronica found out before, it's easy to get distracted here," Thane said to the group, winking at my scowl. "But whatever you see or hear, do not stray from the path. This realm is designed to trap visitors, especially those without a fae guide."

Lena adjusted one of her vambraces. "Not everyone is as impulsive as V."

I threw my hands up. Arguing with this crowd was pointless—they knew me too well.

Thane pointed down the path, which disappeared between the trees. "It wasn't far in that direction that you said you met the stag. Let's go."

After giving Ivan a moment to memorize his surroundings so he could realm walk here safely in the future, the six of us headed deeper into the forest. Like my last visit, birds sang among the branches, their calls as unique as their colors.

Something new and exciting drew my attention and urged me to explore everywhere I looked. Only this time, I expected the allure, and I grinned when I caught Lena and Ivan holding hands, keeping each other on the trail.

As much as she boasted about her superior fighting skills, this wasn't the kind of battle she was used to having.

We crossed the bridge spanning a bubbling brook, whose water tempted me to follow it to the ocean. Once back on the dirt path, I nudged Lena as she took a step into the grass.

She blinked at me and looked down, her mouth falling open. "I didn't even realize…"

"Just my impulsiveness, huh?" I teased.

She gave me a sheepish look and let Ivan drag her back to the middle of the trail.

We continued a few more yards before Thane stopped us. He pointed into the trees. "This is where you disappeared."

Kit stepped toward the edge of the dirt, her eyes narrowed as she scanned the woods. "What happened last time?"

"I looked over, and he was just…there," I said with a weak shrug.

Now that we'd arrived and no stag was in sight, my confidence in him showing up again waned.

"You're sure it was here?" Lena gripped her sword's hilt, though it remained sheathed.

Thane and I nodded. It wasn't easy to forget such a

pivotal moment in our lives—for me, meeting the stag, and for Thane, thinking he'd lost my crazy ass to the fae woods.

"Maybe we need to find him this time, out there," I suggested, pointing to the trees. "All of us. Safety in numbers, right?"

Thane and Kit exchanged glances, but Kit tightened her lips and nodded. "We've come this far. We need that dagger."

"Everyone needs to buddy up, take someone's hand." Thane pointed at Ivan. "You're with V again."

The phoenix nodded and threw his arm around my shoulders with a grin. As much as I hated not having Thane by my side through this entire adventure, I knew he would dig in his heels on this issue.

But afterward, he needed to get over this insecurity and stop hoisting me off onto other people. Besides Kit, I was the strongest one here, even if Lena claimed she could kick my ass.

When we had someone's grip in one hand and a weapon in the other, we stepped off the path. I wasn't sure what I was expecting to happen, but I breathed a sigh of relief when nothing did. Being so nervous about a forest felt silly, yet I knew how tempting the magical call was.

Thane and Lena led the way, his scythe slicing a narrow trail through the tangled undergrowth. It probably wasn't a wise idea to harm anything growing here, but the foliage was too thick and spiky to pass through otherwise.

I wasn't sure how I'd gotten through the first time, but I was willing to bet the stag had something to do with it. If my memories were correct, I'd basically waltzed through to him, which was what Kit had accused me of.

As the forest closed around us the deeper we went, I glanced back. A shiver ran up my spine, and I gulped.

The path had disappeared, and I prayed to any deities listening that we hadn't made a huge mistake.

Continuing on in silence, we moved as quickly as possible through the dense plants. We didn't know where we were going, but with luck, the stag would reveal himself soon.

Goosebumps crawled across my skin, and a chill seeped into my bones. The temperature hadn't changed, but something around us sure had.

We were being watched.

CHAPTER 16

Monday Afternoon

My heart thundered against my ribs, and I glanced around the trees as discreetly as possible.

"Do you feel that?" I whispered to Ivan.

Beneath nearly translucent eyelashes, his eyes were narrowed like mine. He gave a clipped nod without taking his gaze off the trees. "I can't figure out where it's coming from."

Ahead of us, Thane stopped, and his shoulders stiffened. Lena growled beside him and took a defensive stance.

Oh shit.

"What's going on?" asked Angela's high-pitched voice behind me.

Brushing off Ivan's attempt to keep me back, I pushed through the snagging branches to stand by Thane. My eyes widened, not sure what I was seeing. Ahead of us, the trees were moving. Like, on their own.

Rumbling and cracking sounds spread through the air as the trees tugged their roots from the ground, upheaving dirt clumps and the distinct scent of wet earth. Bark crumbled from their trunks, and eyes blinked open, staring straight at us.

Their intense gazes didn't appear pleased, and a menacing presence pressed in around our group. More noises erupted behind me, and I whirled to find more trees uprooting themselves and closing in.

Surrounding us.

I raised my empty, though slightly shaky, hand. We trespassed on their turf. "We're here to see the Keeper of the Forest and mean you no harm."

I didn't think it was possible, but a few trees growled. Then again, I never thought trees could grow eyes, and look how wrong I'd been about that.

"Only the worthy shall pass," a ghostly voice whispered through the leaves.

No tree had formed a mouth, so I had no idea who had spoken.

It was also the only warning we got.

The trees charged forward, moving much faster than I would have expected for something having roots for legs, and snapped their branches toward us like whips.

Instinct kicked in, and flames whooshed across my body and limbs as I drew a knife. The branches closest to me jerked back, and Ivan and Lena also called forth their fires. The three of us formed a protective triangle around the others.

"What do we do?" I asked no one in particular as I deflected a daring branch with my blade. We were all out of our elements in this situation.

"Leave this to me," Kit answered, her eyes taking on a green glow as she raised her palms to the sky. The moss-covered ground rumbled and burst as vines shot out beneath the attacking trees and wrapped around their branches.

The trees groaned and heaved, trying to break the vines' hold. A few snapped, but Kit called more from the ground, overwhelming the trees.

When she'd contained the last, Kit closed her fists, her eyes darkening as she focused on our attackers. The vines tightened as she closed her hands, and an inhuman squealing emitted from the trees.

I rotated in a slow circle, prepared for another surprise attack.

Her face stricken, Angela grabbed Kit's arm. "Stop! You're hurting them!"

Kit blinked and shook her head as if waking from a trance. She flattened her palms toward the ground, and the vines loosened enough to stop the squeal while still containing the trees.

You've returned, said an ethereal, tinkling voice in my mind.

A stag as black as midnight stepped into view. He moved soundlessly across fallen leaves and twigs as if he wasn't actually present but a mere shadow. A ghost. Starlight reflected from his eyes, and his antlers rustled the branches above, proving he was truly there.

Sharp intakes came from the others as they noticed the stag approaching. Not just any old stag, either.

This was the Keeper of the Forest.

You can release the Guardians, he said, and I swear he sounded amused. *They will attack no more.*

Without hesitation, I doused my flames and tucked my knife away. The others did the same with their weapons, and Kit released the vines. Lena remained leery of the trees, even though they had dug their roots back into the earth and returned to their unmoving state.

"Thank you for coming," I said, bowing my head. "We're hoping you can help us."

The stag regarded me with his starlit eyes. *I see you've found your rightful place in life. Do you plan to rid this world of the growing pestilence?*

"If you mean Colin, then yes," I said.

The stag chuffed and pawed at the ground. *The fae risk the very balance of nature with their actions.*

"It's not just Colin, then?" Thane asked, confirming my suspicions that the others could hear the stag.

I wish it were, the stag said. *Too many have forgotten the old ways.*

"We believe one of the Daggers of Abaddon found its way here," I said. "It's the last of the three, and we need it to create Abaddon's Last Hope, a weapon capable of stopping them."

You are correct that it is here. Shortly after running through a portal from his realm, a foolish human mage dropped it. We were lucky to find it before anyone else. He tossed his head, knocking leaves loose with his antlers. *It is a dangerous weapon that never should have existed. Its power is too great.*

My shoulders drooped, defeated. Our entire plan had relied on getting that damn dagger.

I will take you to the dagger, the stag continued, *but be forewarned: the Last Hope is a misleading name. As with its namesake, the weapon desires death above all else and will attempt to corrupt any who wields it. Few are strong enough to withstand its unquenchable thirst.*

Nothing like a dire warning to accompany a weapon that could save us all.

"Kit, you're the strongest here. Looks like you'll be using it," I said.

She shook her head. "Not the way he means. It's hard enough not giving into my magic."

Come. The stag turned back to the forest's depths.

Casting quick glances at the unnerving trees, we followed the Keeper.

Despite the Guardians' return to normal, the uneasy feeling of being watched lingered. Hairs rose along my neck as I walked, and I looked back every few feet.

"I still feel like we're being watched," I said as my apprehension thickened.

You are safe here. The Guardians will ensure we come to no harm. The stag's voice remained calm and peaceful.

Despite his reassurance, I couldn't shake the eerie sense of foreboding creeping through my senses. Every rustle and chirp had my head whipping around, expecting another attack.

The others were also on edge. Lena's gaze shifted constantly, and she muttered under her breath more than usual.

Just when my imagination was getting the best of me, we broke through the trees into a clearing, and I breathed a sigh of relief. White and yellow flowers dotted the area, filling the air with a light floral scent, while butterflies fluttered among the petals.

A rough rock wall barred the way forward at the clearing's far end, and a rumbling waterfall cascaded into a pool with soothing splashes. The water was so blue it was disorienting, like you would fall into the sky instead.

Lush vegetation and boulders bordered a sandy beach leading to the water's edge. Birds swooped down for a drink or a bath, calling out to each other with curious tilts of their heads.

The dagger lies within. The stag tilted its antlers toward the waterfall. *You may only retrieve it at dusk.*

"Why dusk?" I asked, glancing up at the cloudless sky. We'd arrived in the Otherworld late afternoon, which meant evening wasn't too far off.

"It's the magic hour," Kit answered. "Sometimes called the witching hour. It marks the separation between light and dark and provides some of the most powerful harnessing magic."

"How long until dusk?" Angela asked, rubbing her arms as she glanced back the way we'd come.

A trio of butterflies left the flowers and flitted around her legs, dancing up to her face. Smiling, she released her arms and held a finger out. One brave bug settled on it and proceeded to wash its face.

Or whatever bugs did.

Kit checked her watch, an analog that still functioned in this world. She was smart to bring it. "An hour at most. Enough time to decide."

Lena raised an eyebrow. "Decide what?"

"Who will use the weapon," Thane said, eyeing the base of the splashing waterfall.

"Not it." I raised my hands and backed away.

"No offense, V, but you weren't in consideration," Kit drawled.

I glared at her, but I wasn't mad and she knew it. Impulsive decisions wouldn't go well with this weapon's kind of magic. I'd go evil in a snap for a fresh slice of mushroom and truffle oil pizza.

"That leaves Thane, Lena, and Ivan," I said, counting them off on my fingers.

"And Angela." Thane nodded at the human.

I cast an apologetic grimace in her direction. "No offense, but your magic isn't as strong as theirs."

"No offense taken," she said with a smile, still watching the butterfly groom itself on her finger.

I smiled back. We could use more of her humility in the world.

Once the daggers unite, the Last Hope will form a bond with whoever wields it. The stag bent his legs and settled onto the grass. Butterflies flitted closer, swirling between the tines of his antlers.

My smile drooped. "What does that mean, exactly?"

It means the weapon and its wielder will find it challenging to be apart, he replied with a note of caution.

I eyed my friends, trying to decide who was best suited for this job. "Does it come apart again? Or can we destroy the whole thing?"

That is unknown. Abaddon's Last Hope has never been created.

Lena cocked her head and frowned. "Then how do you know this much?"

The stag turned its starry-eyed gaze on her, making her fidget. Even while sitting, his gaze was almost level with hers. *When necromancers forged the daggers, the Last Hope was their ultimate purpose. But no necromancer could harness enough magic to create such an object.*

Lena's frown deepened. "I don't get it. Why does anyone expect the daggers to turn into this super weapon if they couldn't do it? Sounds like a myth."

My thoughts drifted back to the little I knew of the daggers, but my memories were murky. A lot had happened since then. Necromancers had created the daggers in the dark ages, but they were stolen and disappeared for centuries, lost to the world until William brought them back into play.

They made a pact with a demon and imbued the daggers with its demonic magic. When combined with an angel's holy magic, the weapon will form. It contradicts nature's two most basic essences. An abomination.

I shuddered. I had definitely forgotten about that detail involving the demon.

"I'm surprised William didn't try to combine them," Thane said.

Very few know the original intent of the daggers, the stag explained. *That knowledge was lost to time.*

Except to the stag, angels, and Kit of course. William had gone after angels, but we assumed it was for creating Risen en masse. Maybe we were wrong. "Unless that's what he was trying to do by kidnapping and torturing angels."

"Thank God he didn't succeed," Thane murmured, his gaze distant.

Our group fell silent as we waited for the sun to disappear behind the trees' leaves, aiming for the horizon.

We still had time to kill, so Ivan and Lena took turns skipping rocks across the pond, competing for the farthest skip. Everything turned into a competition with them, and Thane joined in the fun before long.

Sitting on a large, flat rock near the sand, I leaned back onto my palms and soaked up the last of the sun's warmth. I still hadn't recovered my tan after my resurrection dealing with William. Once this was over, I'd make that a priority, no matter how silly the goal seemed right now.

It made me feel normal and in control, something I hadn't had much of lately.

My anticipation grew as the golden rays faded and the sky's edges darkened. I chalked it up to nerves about what was to come, but I couldn't shake the sense of impending doom. Like something terrible was about to happen.

Was getting this dagger and creating the super weapon worth the risk of it falling into the wrong hands?

Were any hands the right hands?

Or would we all end up succumbing to our dark sides?

CHAPTER 17

Monday At Dusk

By the time dusk arrived, my nerves were shot from the sensation of being watched. Also because we hadn't settled on who should wield the Last Hope. At least we had more time to decide before creating the damn thing.

No sense rushing into such a monumental decision, right?

Not like it would cause chaos if we chose the wrong person…

Oh, wait.

The last traces of sunlight filtered through the surrounding leaves and sparkled like gold amid the specks of dust. Fresh noises joined the forest chorus as nocturnal animals began their shifts.

The witching hour was calm and peaceful and truly magical.

So why the hell did I feel so uneasy?

The stag tilted its massive antlers toward the waterfall and huffed. *It is time. The dagger is at the bottom of the pool beneath the falls.*

"I can go get it." Ivan reached for his shirt's hem to pull over his head.

With a flick of Kit's wrist and a single chanted word, the pool's water separated down the middle, forming a path over smooth stones straight to the waterfall's base. A cave burrowed into the rock, its opening barely large enough for an adult to crawl into.

Ivan grinned sheepishly as he pushed his shirt back down and stepped toward the pool.

A twang rang from the trees a breath before an arrow pierced the sand an inch from his boot, pulling him up sharp.

I spun to face the attacker, knives in hand.

A sound I hoped to never hear again echoed all around us—the skittering noises of newly-turned vampires. Except these weren't any kind of vampire that I'd ever seen, and my mouth ran drier than a desert.

Malformed faces materialized in the shadows between trees like they had formed from the darkness. As the unknown creatures climbed down tree trunks and slunk forward beneath bushes, saliva dripped down their nonexistent chins. Horrors that belonged to someone's worst nightmares crept closer, leaving the forest's gloom in their wake.

Razor-sharp, splintering claws extended from their gnarled hands and legs. A dark, greenish-black skin clung to their somewhat humanoid bodies, but ooze leaked from their pores. Steam and the nose-burning stench of sulfur rose anywhere the tar-like goop dripped.

Their empty eye sockets regarded us without emotion, and I knew deep within my soul that they would kill us and eat our innards without an ounce of remorse. I swallowed hard.

These were most definitely not human world vampires.

No, it was so much worse than that.

The unseelie fae had arrived.

"Oh my goddess," Angela breathed, her face draining of color, "those are the *neamh-mairbh*."

I wasn't an expert on fae by any means, but I knew the name meant something like "walking dead." They were a fae version of the vampire but with no desire to join society except to feed. As far as I was concerned, a vampire was a vampire.

Unfortunately, they weren't alone.

Other figures glided from behind trees like wraiths, revealing dusky skin and shades of blond and white hair—Winter Court fae. They were also considered unseelie but weren't forbidden to walk the day like the others.

My stomach curled in on itself. No wonder the nightmarish creatures had approached without the guardians stopping them. The trees must not see them as a threat while accompanied by the Winter fae. Talk about a loophole that needed a firm plug.

As we formed a defensive line to guard the pool, one of the Winter Court fae stepped forward ahead of the others.

His icy blue gaze appraised us, a condescending sneer on their lips.

"Step aside." The fae man's lovely tenor voice belied his true nature. "The Otherworld and anything within belong to the fae."

The weapon is under my protection, the stag's voice tinkled in my head. He pawed at the ground and snuffed, lowering his head in a distinct challenge. *You are not welcome here.*

"So be it," the fae said, devoid of emotion.

Grotesque and inhumanly beautiful fae streamed out of the forest, snarling or hissing as they flowed toward us. Fae of any kind were graceful, even when getting ready to tear you limb from limb.

As I raised my arm to throw a knife at the closest vampire-fae, a gust of wind whipped past me, tugging at my jacket and hair. The closest attackers ran into an invisible barrier and stumbled backward with high-pitched squeals and cries. Some creatures bounced off and back into the forest.

On the other side of Thane, Kit held her palms out toward the barrier, grimacing as she held the wind shield that kept them at bay. Blasts of ice magic crashed against it as the Winter Court fae retaliated.

I tapped into my inner flame and blended the magic with Kit's shield, creating fiery tendrils that whipped out toward the creatures approaching. Their oozing skin caught fire quickly, sending them squealing and fleeing into the forest.

The stag let out a harsh bray. Outside the shield, a group of vampire-fae surrounded him, but he was holding his own, using his antlers and hooves to keep them from getting too close. He must have been too far from Kit's protective reach.

Ivan and Thane blinked out of existence and appeared outside the wind barrier. Setting himself on fire, Ivan reached for a Winter Court fae casting spells at the stag. The fae shrieked in pain as searing flames licked his skin, and the next spell missed the stag and embedded in a nearby tree.

Thane's black scales rippled across his skin right as a vampire-fae bit down on his arm. The creature's shark-like rows of teeth scraped across the scales but never found purchase. Thane's scythe swept through its neck with ease, and its body crumbled to the ground.

Tsarina, the stag's urgent voice echoed through my mind, and I met his gaze through the haze of smoke and wind. *Dusk is nearly finished. You must get the dagger.*

I fed the shield more of my magic. "Lena, go get the dagger!"

"Like hell I'm leaving you for a second," she growled back, adding her fire to mine until the windy blaze reached high above our heads and lashed out hungrily.

"If we don't get it at dusk, we won't get it at all," I argued, then winced as I held our magic against a wave of ice shards. The cold seeped deep into my bones despite the shield, and my teeth clattered together.

"I'll go," Angela said behind us, staring wide-eyed as she took in the fight. She spun around and ran down the path between the walls of water, disappearing into the tiny cave with little trouble.

I'd almost forgotten she was with us, which I immediately felt bad about. She was the right one to go after the dagger since there wasn't much she could do against the fae, and she was far more vulnerable.

Plus, she'd fit into the cave a hell of a lot easier than the rest of us.

"My magic's not as strong here." Kit grunted as another spell battered into our shield. "I can't hold both the air shield and the water back much longer. I'll have to drop the shield first if she's not back soon."

I opened my mouth to agree as a fresh wave of unseelie fae swarmed out of the forest. My blood chilled to glacier level as I tried to count their numbers. They had outnumbered us already; now, they would overwhelm us.

Releasing a frustrated cry, Kit dropped her hold on the wind and moved behind Lena and me to protect the pool.

Our fire barrier still held, but the fae's ice magic battered against and froze pieces of the flames, which broke off and shattered against the rocks and ground.

"No!" Ivan's anguished voice traveled through the inferno.

The stag let out a horrible whinny as it sank to its knees. Vampire-fae scrambled over every inch of the magnificent beast like a horde of ants, tearing into his hide with teeth and claws.

He met my gaze once again. *Go. Save this forest.*

Then he was gone, the life in his beautiful star-filled eyes snuffed out forever.

The Keeper of the Forest had died.

A shocked gasp tore from my lungs. The ground trembled and shook, and a high-pitched keening wailed through the forest. Trees groaned as they tugged their roots from the earth and swung their branches at the fae.

Behind me, Kit let out a strangled yell, then took up chanting again. I chanced a glance over my shoulder with blurry eyes—vampire-fae scaled the waterfall's rocky walls from above, heading straight for the cave.

The rocks trembled and crumbled beneath the creatures' grasps as Kit's earth magic shook them loose, dropping them into the water.

Angela tumbled out of the narrow entrance. Raising the jeweled dagger above her head, she ran forward. "I got it!"

As soon as she cleared the water's edge, her gaze fell on the stag, and she slowed to a stop. She shook her head, a disbelieving look on her pale face.

Kit released her hold on the pool. The two walls of water crashed together, drowning the creatures who'd made it to the bottom.

"How could you?" Angela screamed at the *neamh-mairbh* consuming the stag, devastation ringing in her accusation. Gripping the dagger tight, she pointed it at them as they twisted their necks to stare at her, blood staining their teeth and mouths.

A burst of dark energy rocketed out from Angela and the dagger, slicing through the creatures like a sharp blade. With gaping mouths, their bodies separated wherever the magic touched, and they collapsed to the ground. The desiccated bodies shriveled away, dissolving into the moss.

Thane appeared beside Angela and grabbed her free hand, earning a surprised yelp from the witch. Her eyes rolled up, and she collapsed into his arms. Without hesitating, Thane jumped them away. A twinge in our soul link meant he'd left the Otherworld.

"You're mine, Veronica…" a phantom yet familiar voice whispered, the words carrying through the trees and flames on wings of magic.

I whipped my head toward the sound, squinting to identify individual shapes behind the thick smoke. Then I saw him.

No…

The natural red highlights in Colin's auburn hair sparkled in the firelight as he stepped forward. His blue-green gaze met mine, set within a face I once considered handsome. Now, his smug smile promised nothing but cruelty and immeasurable horrors.

He thought I was his?

I narrowed my eyes, fueling my gaze with every ounce of hatred I possessed.

No fucking thanks.

Roaring flames burst outward from Ivan's body, creating an inferno and incinerating the remaining nightmares in his radius. He disappeared and reappeared beside me, grabbing Kit and my hands. I reached for Lena, gripping her hand tight as the world fell away.

When we reappeared in my penthouse living room, we stumbled forward and nearly collapsed. The city's twinkling lights sparkled through the giant windows, mocking me with their cheeriness.

A quick glance around the penthouse showed Thane and Angela weren't here, but my soul link pulsed with his presence in this realm. They were safe.

Holy fuck, that had been way too close.

And now Colin knew we had the third dagger.

Fucking fuck!

Before my legs gave out completely, I sank onto my L-shaped couch and dropped my head back onto the cushions. I stared at the vaulted ceiling. My emotions were all over the place, but grief seized my heart in a vise above all others.

The world had just lost a legend, a powerful being that humans knew nothing about and whose presence Community members only mentioned in whispers. If they even knew enough to whisper.

I might not have known the Keeper long, but no one in their right mind could deny the stag's ethereal beauty or his otherworldly presence. He had protected the fae realm for millennia, and thanks to one fae man's creepy infatuation with his cousin and subsequent thirst for power, the stag was gone.

What did his death mean?

Who would protect the Otherworld now?

Despite my sorrow, I was also relieved we retrieved the dagger before Colin arrived. Seeing him again had reignited all the anger and hurt I'd experienced over the last few months. Make that the last few years.

Hell, my entire godsdamn *life*.

My nostrils flared with my quickening breaths. Colin was the reason my parents fled the Mirognyan realm and kept my brother and me in the dark about our true identities. He was the reason they were all dead.

Since that wasn't enough emotion to deal with, anticipation also churned through my stomach, knowing what was coming, that the actual war was beginning.

We'd lost so many lives already—how many more would he claim in his ridiculous quest?

And for what? Why the fuck was he doing this?

Any of it?

The couch sagged as Ivan and Lena dropped to either side of me.

"*Chyort!* What just happened?" Lena asked, her voice quiet despite the harshness of her words.

I didn't know how to answer her, and judging by the ongoing silence, no one else did either. Winter Court fae weren't totally unexpected, but the *neamh-mairbh*'s arrival had thrown me off, way off. There were so many of them, and it hadn't even been dark yet.

Then *he* showed up. Thinking back, he didn't seem overly upset that we beat him to the punch. Because I was mentally, emotionally, and physically exhausted, I didn't have the brainpower to think through what his lack of reaction meant or if I should even worry about it.

"I can't believe he showed up," Ivan murmured as if reading my thoughts. "Thank sweet Mokosh Thane had already gotten Angela and the dagger out of there."

Glass clinked together as Kit rummaged through my kitchen cabinets. She pulled out four shot glasses and a bottle of tequila and filled each glass to the brim. We definitely deserved—and needed—a few drinks after that shitshow.

My phone vibrated in my pocket. I took it out and answered Thane's call.

"Oh, thank God you made it back," he said, relieved. "Is everyone else with you?"

"Yes," I said, too tired to say more.

Kit deposited the drinks before us, and we wasted no time tossing them back.

The alcohol burned its way down my throat, and I

wished it would burn away the sorrow burrowing deep within my heart. A few more shots might numb the pain, for tonight anyway.

"Let Kit know Angela's fine," Thane said. "She was only out for a moment, but whatever spell she channeled through the dagger took most of her energy. The angels are monitoring her vitals just to be safe."

I relayed the message to Kit, who immediately looked at Ivan. "I need to hitch a ride."

He pushed himself to his feet and reached for her hand. They disappeared a breath later, and I heard Kit's voice on the other end of the phone. I smiled as she fussed over Angela.

The phone went dead, and a warm, tingling sensation spread across the back of my neck. I knew without looking that Thane stood behind the couch.

Realm walking was amazing.

He sat beside me and wrapped me in his arms, where I all but melted into his warmth and entwined our fingers. Lena leaned into my side, and I lifted my arm to let her snuggle closer. We all needed comfort right now.

"That was insane," I murmured against Thane's chest. "Colin showed his face right after you and Angela left."

His body stilled, and his heart thudded against my ear. "What did he do?"

"Nothing." I tightened my hold on his hand and gave it a reassuring squeeze. "Ivan got us out of there real fast."

He released a deep breath, and his heartbeat slowly returned to normal. "I'm surprised you didn't try to fight him."

I chuckled. "That makes two of us."

"Three," Lena muttered against my stomach. "What kind of spell was that? The one Angela did."

"Shadow magic. It came from the dagger," Thane said.

"Is that kind of thing normal here?" she asked as her eyelids drifted shut.

"Not at all. I'm not sure how she cast it, but shadow and death magic are closely intertwined," he explained. "That's why the daggers are so effective against reapers."

Even with Thane's warmth blanketed around me, chills crept across my skin. Three insanely powerful weapons had been in William's hands, and I hadn't even known what they could do. I still didn't know the full extent, and I couldn't help but wonder if we were doing the wrong thing by using them.

Were we dooming the world to chaos and ruin?

CHAPTER 18

Tuesday Morning

Thane had convinced Adam to give us a night to grieve and recover before providing him with a full debrief. I needed that time to process everything that had happened. We all did.

The following day, Thane realm walked Lena and me to the DEA to fill everyone in on what had occurred in the Otherworld. As if the Earth herself was mourning the stag's loss, the clouds were heavy and grey and wept in a slow drizzle.

The welcome scents of warm, buttery bread and freshly brewed coffee drifted out of the conference room door as we approached, making my mouth water. As my stomach grumbled its agreement, I didn't know which I wanted more of—food or coffee.

Before the three of us had finished filing inside, Kit, Angela, and Ivan appeared, and Angela eyed the dagger on the table warily as she took her seat. None of us knew how she'd accessed its magic, but I was eager to find out if she could do it again.

Shooing everyone away from the kitchenette, Ivan and Lena loaded up plates with fresh pastries and fruit, filled cups to the brim with coffee, and placed both in front of those of us who ate. They'd turned into saints overnight.

When we finished telling the others what had happened, and Angela had explained the surge of power she'd experienced followed by a total drain, the conference room was silent.

Well, silent of voices. As the last to take their seats, Lena and Ivan were still munching and crunching on their breakfast while the rest of us sipped on our second or third cups of brew.

Adam sat with his eyes closed, his fingers steepled at his lips. Imos, Tundreg, and Pietr might not have known the Keeper of the Forest, but their expressions were solemn. More so than usual, anyway.

After a lengthy silence, Adam opened his eyes and lowered his hands. "Losing the Keeper at such a time is unfathomable. Once word of his death gets out, which Colin will ensure happens sooner rather than later, the unseelie will infringe upon the other fae courts. The Otherworld will be in chaos, if it isn't already."

"Maybe that was the plan all along," Kit said as she ripped off pieces from a napkin. Probably because she couldn't rip Colin's head off just yet. "For all we know, Colin engineered this whole thing as a diversion or to cripple any fae enemies he has while hoping to get the dagger before we did."

Adam dipped his chin. "It is possible. Unfortunately, this new knowledge makes opening a portal more challenging. Providing the unseelie an easy way through would be catastrophic."

"He didn't seem super concerned about losing the dagger. Maybe he doesn't know about the Last Hope. We need to speed this up." I pointed at the blade. "How do we make the super weapon?"

Adam nodded at Nathan, who sat beside him. The beefy, blue-winged angel extracted the other two daggers from thin air. Literally, just reached up and plucked them out of nothing.

Gods, I loved magic.

He set the daggers next to the one already lying on the table, creating a triangle. All three had expensive jewels embedded in the hilt and swirly designs etched down the blade. Pretty, yet deadly.

"Demonic magic forged the Daggers of Abaddon, but it is holy magic that assembles Abaddon's Last Hope," Adam explained. "Nathan, please proceed."

The other angel held his palms above the triangle and closed his eyes.

Talk about ironic. Only angels could create a super weapon named after an angel of death, yet capable of extinguishing their souls. Had William known, things would have ended very differently…

…for *us*.

A soft white glow emanated from Nathan's hands and illuminated the daggers beneath. Tendrils of white light wrapped around the three blades, which started to spin in place. The tendrils drew them closer together, still spinning, and the light brightened until it exploded in a flash that had me throwing my arm in front of my eyes.

When I lowered my arm, the light had faded. So had the three daggers, and in their place was one beautiful sword.

My lips parted with awe as I examined the new weapon pulsing with holy light. The double-edged blade wasn't super long, only slightly longer than Lisa, my trusty short sword named for a she-fox. Like the daggers had been, flowery sigils were etched along the steel and jewels embedded in the hilt.

Veronica…

I licked my lips and sat up straighter. No offense to anyone else, but this divine weapon wasn't meant for them. It was meant for me. I leaned forward, eyeing the sword as it sang to me, enticing me with visions of grandeur.

We could do amazing things together, bring Colin to his knees or topple whole civilizations. Wielding this weapon was what I was *born* to do.

Nothing else in this world mattered but the sword.

It was *mine*.

"There is only one here strong enough to withstand the blade's seduction." Adam's words filtered through the outer edges of my thoughts, but I barely registered them.

My fingers itched, ready to seize the hilt and claim what was mine. This was it, my moment. With this sword, I would rule not just Mirfeniksa but the entire world. With Thane at my side, we would be unstoppable, and no one would hurt our loved ones or us ever again.

"Angela."

I reached out and—

Wait, what?

I blinked, suddenly aware of what I was doing and how close my fingers were to brushing against the sword. My face burned, and I snapped my hand back.

I glanced at Thane beside me. He hadn't moved like I had, but sweat glistened across his forehead. The others around the table leaned back with sheepish looks and pink-tinged cheeks that likely matched mine.

Everyone except Angela, whose face had drained of color as she stared at the archangel. "Me?" her voice squeaked out.

Adam nodded. "The sword is an anomaly, a mixture of all that is good in this world, as well as the evil. Of everyone here, you are the least likely to submit to its seductive song. As you just witnessed, several almost gave in to its allure without the slightest touch."

I blushed again, but I knew I was in good company.

"But what about you? You're an *angel*," Angela argued, recoiling farther into her chair as her wide-eyed gaze flicked to the sword. She gestured wildly at it. "I don't know how to use that."

"As unlikely as it may seem, that weapon's dark magic can sway even angels." His blue-eyed gaze shifted to it for only a fraction of a second. "The weapon will form to whatever shape you wish it to be. I hear you have gotten quite talented with the staff?"

Kit took her fiancée's trembling hand, a proud look on her face. "He's right. Your heart is pure, especially compared to the rest of us."

"Speak for yourself," Lena grumbled, rubbing the hilt of her sword. Her hungry gaze remained on the Last Hope.

I rolled my eyes. "Just because you served us breakfast doesn't make you a saint."

"Is that your way of saying thank you?" she asked.

"Only if you clean up, too." I grinned when she finally tore her gaze away from the sword to glare at me.

Her chair scraped against the linoleum floor as she stood and grabbed my empty plate. "I'm holding you to it."

She reached for my coffee cup, but I clutched it to my chest like a precious jewel. I needed every delicious drop.

As Lena made her way around the table collecting trash, Angela gulped and suddenly found the floor fascinating. "What if you're wrong? What if I'm not strong enough?"

"I mean no offense by what I'm about to say," Kit said, turning Angela's chin to look at her, "but as a human, you're the least powerful. Should you succumb to the blade's darkness, it would be far easier to stop you than someone like V."

Oh hey, I was top of the list. I would have almost felt a sense of pride if it wasn't such a bleak conversation.

"Or you," Angela said quietly, biting her lip.

"There's no way I could resist," Kit agreed. "It's hard enough to ignore my own magic's temptation."

Lena dumped the plates into the dish bin and returned to her seat. She looked at me expectantly.

"Thank you, Saint Lena," I said with as much fake reverence as I could muster.

She shook her head and grumbled, and her gaze wandered back to the sword again.

Taking a deep breath, Angela nodded. "Okay. What do I need to do?"

Adam opened his hand toward the sword. "Pick up the Last Hope, and it will form into the weapon you desire."

Pushing back her chair, Angela stood and reached for the weapon with a shaky hand. She paused just before touching it.

"You've got this, babe," Kit said reassuringly. "I'm right here."

Angela took another deep breath and gripped the hilt. The slightest twinge of jealousy pinched my heart, but I brushed it aside. That reaction was exactly why I wasn't the right person for the job, no matter how much the damned tempting sword tried to convince me otherwise.

As Angela lifted the blade off the table, a slight shudder passed through her body. The blade and hilt extended, lengthening and changing shape until she held a steel staff.

She rolled it in her hands, examining the new weapon with awe shining in her eyes. "This thing's capable of doing what you said? Resisting all magic?"

"It is indeed," Adam said. "Much like yourself, great power lies in unexpected places."

Angela blushed. "I don't have great power, not without this thing."

The archangel smiled. "Do not underestimate yourself."

"One weapon to rule them all," I said, trying to hide the wistfulness in my voice.

Thane chuckled, but Kit stared at me across the table like I'd grown a second head. "How do you do that?"

I raised an eyebrow. "Do what?"

"Make references to pop culture things you should know but definitely don't." She pinched the bridge of her nose. "One ring to rule them all? Ring a bell?"

"So you're calling your fiancée a hobbit?"

I mean, no one could resist that, right?

If looks could kill, I'd be dead so many times over from Kit alone.

"I know how to use a staff," Angela cut in before any deaths occurred and peered at the sigils engraved in the steel, "but how does this magic work?"

"Mr. Munro, would you be up for the challenge of teaching Ms. Smith to wield her new weapon?" Adam asked.

Thane raised his eyebrows. "I'd be honored, but surely Kit would like to train her?"

Kit hesitated before shaking her head. "Want, yes. But I won't be able to push her as hard as you can."

Angela glanced between them with a gulp.

"I can push her, but I'm still just a human," Thane said with an unusual tightness in his voice. "An angel like Nathan is a better choice to handle that kind of magic."

His frustration leaked through our soul link. My mate was far from *just* a human, but I understood what he meant. He didn't think he was strong enough to help her. I knew otherwise, and I'd spend as long as it took to prove it to him, too.

"The weapon should work similar to your scythe," the archangel explained, his calm expression showing no concern over the decision. "Nathan and I are busy focusing our efforts on finding a mage capable of opening portals."

"Weren't you bringing in two mages earlier?" Kit asked.

Adam sighed. "They overestimated their skill."

"This would be a good time to teach you control over your scales," Tundreg said. The skin around the blind dragonman's pale yellow eyes crinkled as he smiled in Thane's direction.

"Plus, you can test out your dragon scales against the Last Hope's magic," I added, urging my confidence in him through our bond.

"Let's not waste any time then." Thane stood and leaned down to brush his lips across mine. "We'll be in the training room."

I smiled, feeling immense pride that my mate was selected to help Angela. It was the next best thing after wielding the weapon, and he'd finally get the training he needed to manage his scales.

Angela gave Kit a shaky wave and followed Thane and Tundreg to the door, trying not to knock anyone in the head with the staff. Ivan ducked playfully even though she wasn't even close to hitting him, then grinned at her scowl.

Having Angela wield the weapon might have been a terrible idea.

"Mages are best suited for it, but I can open portals one at a time," Kit said to Imos and Pietr once the others had left. "They won't be permanent, but long enough to get your people through."

Both men tilted their heads down in respect.

"We welcome your assistance," Imos said.

"Thank you for the generous offer, Ms. Parker. What supplies will you need?" Adam asked.

"None. I gathered them all yesterday for our trip to the Otherworld, just in case." She patted the backpack slung over her seat. "I'm ready to roll if you have an area prepared."

Adam's white wings fluttered behind him as he stood. "Your foresight is a boon to us all. We will open the portals in the hotel we acquired. Come."

The rest of us pushed our chairs back to follow him out of the conference room.

In the hallway, a reaper pushing a mail cart waited for me. "Ms. Neill, a letter arrived for you."

I accepted the envelope, eyeing it with a slight frown. "Thanks."

As the others disappeared down the hallway, Lena and Ivan hung back with me, and the reaper resumed his mail delivery route.

I tore open the seal and took out the paper. My lungs constricted, making it hard to breathe as I read the letter:

My beautiful little bird,

The time for our reunion has finally arrived. I request the pleasure of your company—and yours alone—at the Brickell City Centre's parking garage. Meet me at noon.

Forgive the inhospitable ambiance, but I'm sure you'll understand my need for discretion. Trust me when I say you won't want to miss this meeting. I have something you desperately *desire.*

Your loyal friend,

X

Only one person signed letters like that—Xavier. The godsdamned Master Vampire who'd tried to enslave me was alive. I *knew* it.

The paper shook in my hands as my vision blurred. He had to think I was stupid to agree to meet with him alone. And by meet, I meant kill. I had no intention of hearing him out. Whatever he had to say, he could take it to oblivion along with his ashes.

"What's it say?" Lena asked, leaning over my shoulder to scan the paper. A low growl rose in her throat. "Not happening."

Ivan raised an eyebrow.

I took a deep breath. "It's Xavier. I'm not meeting him alone, but I'm definitely going to face him. And this time, I *will* kill him."

CHAPTER 19

Tuesday Morning

Thane

I countered Angela's swing with my scythe and stepped back. Sweat dripped down both our faces and soaked into our clothes. "Again."

After leaving the conference room, she and I had changed into DEA-issued training gear and met Tundreg in the training facility. For the last hour, I'd tested Angela's ability with the staff while the dragonman explained how to control my scales.

The latter was simple. Where I had been trying to force the dragon scales *out* of my skin through sheer will, Tundreg had me focusing on sinking *into* them, surrendering to the change.

According to the dragonman, the process was the same for shifters and done subconsciously once mastered. It explained why I hadn't thought of it and why Veronica hadn't mentioned trying it.

Unfortunately, none of us had figured out how the staff's magic worked. Abaddon's Last Hope was holding its cards close.

Once I had mastered accessing my scales at will, Tundreg left us to train while he assisted Imos with the incoming dragons. His parting words to Angela were to listen to the staff's magic, but neither of us knew exactly what that meant.

It was all I could do *not* to listen to its seductive call.

Panting, Angela wiped her sweaty forehead with her arm. "I think this is a sign I'm not the one meant to use this thing."

Instead of replying, I rushed toward her, swinging the scythe at her unprotected arm.

She yelped and raised the staff just in time to stop the curved blade from connecting with her skin. Grimacing, she shoved the scythe back, then dropped to a crouch and swiped at my feet.

I evaded her swing and spun, tapping her lightly on the back with the scythe's blunt end. "Good. Again."

She flopped back onto her butt and held up her hand. "I need water."

To her credit, she hadn't complained or asked for a break once over the last hour. I stepped back and deactivated my scythe before grabbing the two bottles of water we'd left near our mat. I handed her one, and she gulped it down greedily.

"It may not feel this way, but you're picking it up quickly for how little training you've had. Your reflexes are fast," I said and sipped my water.

"Not fast enough." She pressed the cold bottle to her cheeks, flushed from the workout. "And there's still no magic. I don't think it likes me."

"What does it feel like?" I asked.

"Like a stick. A long, thick rod."

I grinned at the innuendo she probably didn't even hear. "No, when you try to connect with the magic."

She squinted at me. "It doesn't just do its thing on its own?"

Okay, back to the basics. "What did you sense about the weapon when it was first created?"

She glanced at the staff. "Nothing. Was I supposed to sense something?"

Adam had been right in choosing Angela. Anyone else in that conference room would have drawn on the magic as soon as they picked up the sword. I'd felt its energy pulsating without touching it, calling me to take what was mine.

Even now, the dark magic whispered enticing fantasies in my ear.

I finally understood Tundreg's message.

"Try it now. Close your eyes and reach out to it with your mind," I said, hauling Angela to her feet and taking the empty bottle. "Try to connect with the staff and listen."

Her dubious expression spoke volumes, but she did as I asked. Holding the staff in both hands, she closed her eyes and concentrated. Black wisps drifted up from the metal, wrapping around her hands.

She yelped and opened her eyes, panic taking over her expression. "I can't let go!"

"Don't be afraid of it." I gripped her shoulders. "*You* are in control, not the staff. Assert your dominance."

She grimaced as the black wisps traveled up her arms. "You know I'm not the dominant one."

My cheek twitched as I held back a laugh. I didn't think she meant I knew from the time I'd teleported in on Kit and her in a compromising naked situation on the couch. She probably meant their personalities.

"You're stronger than you give yourself credit for," I said, squeezing her shoulders.

Her knowing gaze met mine. "So are you."

I knew I had a fantastic poker face, so I'll admit her intuitiveness surprised me. Unlike Veronica, who sensed my unease and frustration through our soul link. Reading people wasn't one of her strong suits, though she'd gotten better.

Perhaps it was time I listened to my own advice. After all, if the gods saw fit to throw an ex-grim reaper and a phoenix queen together, who was I to say no?

Concentrating once again, Angela's eyebrows drew together, forming a deep crease. The black wisps snapped off her arms as if slapped before withdrawing and dissipating back into the staff.

She gasped. "I did it!"

I smiled at her innocence. She was like a new grim reaper in training, excited by the slightest hint of magic.

"I can feel it now without having to try." She cocked her head as if listening to something. "I can *hear* it."

"Good, that's what we want." Glancing at a group of reapers in training, I found Brandon's familiar face and called him over. He'd helped in the fight against the dragons and quickly gained favor with Adam.

"Agent Munro," the reaper said when he joined us, nodding his head in respect.

Brandon had been young when his human life ended, and he'd kept his dark brown beard and hair well-groomed while alive, both of which stayed with him in death. He was a few inches shorter than me but built like a tank.

If he didn't have such a friendly face, he would intimidate most Community members, even without his reaper abilities.

"Still ex-agent," I corrected. "I'd like your help with something."

He stood at ease, hands clasped behind his back. "Sure. What can I do for you?"

I pointed at Angela. "Attack this woman with everything you've got."

Kudos were owed to the newer reaper—he didn't hesitate for a second. With a click of the device in his hand, his scythe snapped into view.

Angela's eyes widened, and she squeaked as he attacked. To her credit, she deflected each of his blows, protecting herself well, but it was clear she was losing ground.

I circled around them as they sparred. "Don't resist its help."

"I'm trying not to," she argued between clenched teeth, ducking beneath a swing.

"Exactly. Stop trying. Give in."

"I'm afraid of giving in! What if I can't resist it, either?" She winced as a hard blow against her back nearly knocked her off her feet, but she twirled away before falling.

I understood her fear, but this was the perfect place to test it, to see how strong its hold would be. "Brandon, I said *everything* you've got."

The reaper hesitated for only a moment before blackness bled outward from his pupils, covering the whites of his eyes. He threw his arm forward, and dark shadows hurtled toward Angela. They wrapped around the staff and spiraled around her hands, slithering up her arms toward her chest.

Panic flashed in her eyes as she tried to shake the shadows off, but the shadow magic held tight.

"Give in, Angela," I said. "Or was Adam wrong about you? Are you really just a weak human?"

Brandon met my gaze, questioning whether he was pushing too hard. I shook my head, and he held. If he pushed too hard for too long, he would not only kill Angela, he would shatter her soul.

We were riding a fine line, but I had to trust she could do it. She had to. If not, we could never face Colin and win.

All of our lives depended on her ability to resist.

As the reaper's magic crept closer to her heart, Angela backed up as if that would help, but the shadows crept closer.

"Give in," I urged, my pulse racing as I readied my scythe. If she didn't, I would sever the connection between them and pray that I did it in time. "If you don't master this, Kit will die."

Angela tightened her grip on the staff and screamed—not from pain but sheer frustration. The steel warped and hummed beneath her palms before a midnight-hued wave exploded from Angela's chest, knocking Brandon and me off our feet.

We flew backward several yards before sliding and tumbling head over heel for a few more feet. Thank God I'd mastered my dragon scales. Immediately, I jumped up with scythe in hand, ready for another attack. Brandon was right beside me, though he was nursing a sprained ankle.

Wide-eyed, Angela fixed her gaze on the staff, her chest heaving as she panted. "I did it."

Grinning, I lowered my scythe and approached her. "All it took was thinking about Kit dying, huh?"

She blew out a shaky breath and tucked a strand of curly brown hair behind her ear. "That's a powerful motivator."

I knew that feeling profoundly. It seemed most days were like that with Veronica, moving from one crisis to the next with hardly any time to catch my breath. I loved that woman with every fiber of my body and soul, but if she didn't rein in her impulsive behavior, then she and I would need to have a serious come to Jesus meeting.

However, I would have to worry about our future together after we defeated Colin. Bringing it up before then would be a moot point if none of us survived.

Uncertainty flickered through my thoughts. My death was a very real possibility in this war. If Veronica worried or became distracted because of something happening to me, she might get herself captured or even killed.

She might not be the last phoenix, but there was no denying that she was special. This world needed her as much as I did.

Taking a deep breath, I forced my runaway thoughts back on track and nodded at Angela. "You've proven you can harness its magic, but now you need to learn to do it without relying on fear."

Brandon handed us new bottles of water, which she wasted no time chugging. Fighting was draining physically, and using magic added an extra layer of exhaustion.

After finishing her water, Angela tossed the empty bottle in a nearby trash can, then gripped the staff. She rubbed her thumbs along the steel. "I can feel it trying to seduce me, teasing me. If this is only a fraction of what the rest of you feel, I can see why it'd be hard to resist."

As she examined the staff, what looked like a sliver of inky shadows twisted through her brown irises. When she blinked, it was gone, most likely an optical illusion born from my paranoia. But…

What if it wasn't?

Abaddon's Last Hope had never existed before now. We only knew the legend passed down through generations of mages and angels. Necromancers had chosen the name Abaddon for a reason: the word was a place of destruction and an angel of the abyss, a chasm with no light and no end.

A shudder of apprehension rolled across my shoulders.

Were any of us truly able to resist its dark call?

CHAPTER 20

Tuesday Midmorning

The doors to the DEA's training facility were closed, and a prominent Do Not Enter sign warned visitors away. Not heeding the warning last time, I'd interrupted a dangerous training session and found myself enshrouded in the Reapers' Shadow about to lose my life and soul.

Thankfully, I'd learned my lesson. Enough not to hurl the doors open this time, anyway.

I cracked the door open, ignoring Lena's grumpy muttering behind me. She'd argued that if anyone should do the peeking, it should be her or Ivan, with her preference given to Ivan.

Not that I disagreed, even though I did, but I kind of knew what I was doing this time.

As I peeked through the door, my eyebrows shot toward my hairline. Shadows and black tendrils flew back and forth between Angela and a reaper I knew—Brandon. While Angela had a look of fierce determination on her flushed face, sweat soaked the reaper's clothes as he attempted to hold his ground. A stance he was slowly losing.

Everyone in the facility had gathered around to watch, so I tilted my head for Lena and Ivan to follow. We made our way around the crowd and joined Thane on the opposite side.

Although my mate remained focused on the fight, he wrapped his arm around my shoulders. A wave of warmth and security swept through my limbs.

Angela deflected a blow from Brandon before the staff's dark magic shot out toward him like a wide rope. It wrapped around his middle and squeezed. As he struggled for breath, she caught sight of us watching. Her sweaty face lit up, and she waved.

That moment of distraction was all the reaper needed. His scythe sliced through the magic, breaking the hold, and he swept Angela's legs out from beneath her. She landed on the training mat with a loud thump and a whoosh of breath. Before she could recover, Brandon had his curved blade at her neck.

"Checkmate. *Finally*," he said with a grin, his broad chest heaving.

Laughing, Angela accepted his offered hand and let him pull her to her feet. She probably weighed next to nothing for the big reaper.

The other trainees clapped Brandon on the back and praised Angela for doing so well. She blushed and brushed aside the compliments as she gulped down a bottle of water.

"Sorry to distract you," I said after the reapers had returned to their training.

She rubbed a towel over her face and neck. "It's all good. I need to learn to keep my focus, no matter what."

"What's the score?" Ivan asked, an eager gleam in his eyes.

Lena scowled at him. "No betting."

Holding up his hands, Ivan managed a perfectly innocent look, complete with puppy dog eyes. "Who? Me?"

They could bicker for days if no one stopped them. As luck would have it, Brandon interrupted with a groan and rubbed an already fading bruise on his arm. "Five to one, in her favor."

As Lena and Ivan congratulated Angela and teased Brandon, Thane turned toward me with a curious look. "I thought you'd be with Kit while she opens the portals."

"I thought so too until I got this." I handed him the letter. "It's from Xavier."

Shock widened his eyes, and his expression darkened as he read it. "Are you sure it's him?"

"I can feel it in my gut."

"Feel what? Gas bubbles?" Lena asked by my side.

I nearly jumped out of my shoes. That was the second time she'd snuck on me. Maybe my nerves were permanently frayed.

Catching my reaction, Ivan snickered.

"That Xavier's alive," I said, glaring at Lena for the scare.

Thane sighed. "There's no talking you out of this, is there?"

I wrapped my arms around his middle, hugging him tight. "Nope."

His chuckle rumbled through me pleasantly. "Then let's meet with a Master Vampire who's escaped death for too long. To the armory we go."

This man *got* me.

"Brandon, can you keep working with Angela while I'm gone?" he asked as the rest of us joined hands.

The reaper grimaced and nodded. "I might regret it tomorrow, but I'll stay on my feet as long as possible."

We left them to it, and Thane jumped us into the DEA's armory. The check-in foyer was a closet-sized room with just enough space for our small group to squeeze inside.

Behind a bullet-proof window, a grim reaper stood from his chair and logged our names and identities, requiring us to place our hands in a biometric hand reader. Once finished, he pushed a button on his computer, and the massive steel door—missing any kind of handle, keyhole, or keypad, I noted—on our left slid open, revealing an even tinier room barely the size of a standard elevator car.

"Head on in," he said, gesturing us through the opening. "Mr. Munro, you know the drill."

Intrigued at the level of security required and imagining what sorts of goodies we'd find in the armory, I followed Thane with a bounce in my step. To make room for our group, I wrapped my arms around his middle and cuddled in close.

Ivan's grin proved he was as excited as I was, but Lena's scowling face scoured the steel walls as she pressed in. Her grip on her sword's hilt tightened.

With the four of us squished inside the second room, the opening we'd entered slid shut and clicked with a somewhat ominous sound. Add in the lack of other doors or exits, and I was glad I wasn't claustrophobic.

"I don't like this," Lena muttered, a sheen of sweat covering her forehead.

Thane grinned. "Not a fan of small spaces?"

Her gaze flicked toward me. "With this woman in here, too? Not a chance."

A loud clanking sound came from the handleless wall before the entire thing swung open, and Thane ushered us into the armory. Only one step in, Ivan, Lena, and I stopped and stood with our mouths hanging open.

If Lena thought my penthouse's hidden cabinet full of weaponry was impressive, it had nothing on this place.

The armory was beyond enormous, much larger than I'd expected for such a peace-loving organization. An expansive warehouse sprawled out before us, complete with an upper level running around the perimeter, much like the DEA's training facility.

Two levels of guns, blades, and weapons I didn't even have a word for, along with every type of armor imaginable. There were even cannons and rocket launchers behind a thick steel gate locked with a top-of-the-line keypad, and I was sure it was encrypted with magic, too.

My fingers itched to break that lock, but I wasn't a thief anymore.

Besides, Adam would likely give me the code if I asked, which kinda took the fun out of the breaking-in fantasy.

"You've been holding out on me," I accused Thane.

His smirk sent shivers down my spine, though the sheer sexiness of all those deadly blades and bullets might have added to the effect. "I need to keep some secrets to impress you."

Lena stepped farther inside, turning around and craning her neck like Belle in the castle library, taking it all in. "I've died and gone to Dazhbog's hearth, haven't I?" She held up a hand before anyone answered. "No need to agree. Just leave me in my happy place."

Laughing, I browsed my way over to some racks of wooden supplies I'd noticed as soon as we walked in, Thane close behind me. I stopped at the row of custom wrist bows that would launch tiny stakes at their targets. I'd worn a similar one during a previous encounter with vampires.

"Did Kit make all those?" I asked, pointing.

Thane grinned. "She sold the design to the DEA after word got out about the one you used."

"That girl was doing charity work helping me out with my jobs." I shook my head, slipped one off the rack, and held it to my wrist. "I always knew she could make plenty of money from her ideas."

"It's not the first design Adam's purchased from her," he said as he helped me secure the straps. His mere touch spread warmth through my limbs, relaxing my nervous energy, always grounding me.

Along with the bow, I added a few sharpened stakes and a gun that had been custom retrofitted to shoot wooden bullets. Perusing the bottom shelf, which mainly contained shoes and boots, I gasped. I pulled out a pair of ankle-high, black leather boots with two chunky metal buckles and held them up.

Flicking a button on the heels, small wooden points jutted out from the toes. A simple heel tap on the buckles would activate these bad boys.

"A Kit original," Thane said, seeing the awe on my face.

I scowled at him. "You've both been holding out on me."

Besides the weaponry and my shiny new pair of boots, we added metal cuffs around our necks and major arteries. Except for Thane, who could now activate his dragon scales at will.

There was no way to protect our entire phoenix bodies against a vampire's bite, not without a chain mail bodysuit, which I was *not* wearing. Talk about uncomfortable. Still, not immediately bleeding out would be a bonus, even if we could resurrect.

Coming back to life sounded cool, but it could be such a hassle, mainly because we resurrected as Mother Mokosh made us—buck naked.

When we finished adding everything we could think of (plus a few extras for fun), we left the armory. Lena cast a forlorn look behind her shoulder before the steel wall slammed shut, trapping us inside the tiny room again. The lock engaged with a resounding click.

I laughed. "I'm sure we can come back and play another day."

Her face lit up. "Promise?"

Xavier had requested a meeting at noon, so Thane and I realm walked to Brickell City Centre's underground parking garage at precisely 12:00. That was a huge benefit to realm walking—no more late arrivals.

Although, it also meant no more fashionably late arrivals unless I did it on purpose, which I definitely enjoyed doing when wearing couture.

Ivan and Lena had shifted into falcon form a few minutes before we arrived and hid among the piping lining the ceiling. They stayed far enough away not to attract attention, yet close enough to provide backup.

They would inch closer once the bloodsucker showed up, but I'd made it very clear I wanted the kill.

Pouty Veronica was not a pretty sight.

Because we were in downtown Miami on a weekday, cars filled just about every parking spot. We had no way of knowing how Xavier would arrive, so we stood in a corner with our backs to the windowless walls. Usually, that would sound like a recipe for disaster—cornered with a Master Vampire—but not with Thane's instant teleportation ability.

If only I'd gained his ability through our soul link.

I wasn't sure if realm walking was a genetic trait, but I would keep my fingers crossed our kids would inherit it. Butterflies danced in my stomach—our kids.

Since vampires always had to ruin a good moment, footsteps echoed across the garage.

It was midday, but being underground meant the garage had no windows, so dark shadows spread throughout our level. Flickering light bulbs provided a little extra light to see the man approaching.

As memories of my ongoing nightmares flooded my mind, fear rooted me in place. Ice seeped through my skin and coated my bones.

The Master Vampire I loathed with a passion stepped into the light.

CHAPTER 21

Tuesday At Noon

If I was being honest with myself—which we all knew I hated to do—I wasn't sure how I would feel seeing Xavier again. Yes, he had planned to cage me and apparently breed me—for what purpose, no one knew—which stoked my anger into an all-out rage.

And yes, his face filled my nightmares, not just the ones from Colin's spell, but ongoing nighttime visions that made my stomach plummet to my feet and my legs turn to jelly.

The problem was that he had also warned me not once but *twice* about a greater threat. Once on the streets of Miami after he'd escaped from the DEA's holding cell, when he tried to kidnap, slash asked me to run away with him. Then a second time when he sent a letter warning me to dig deeper just before I went to the Blood Trials to save Thane's life.

This mother fucking vampire had helped me twice, maybe even saved my life, and now I was super conflicted about my feelings toward killing him as soon as he showed his face. Only a handful of months ago, I wouldn't have hesitated. Curbing my impulsive side came with some serious cons.

Especially now as he strode forward. I'd forgotten how fucking good-looking he was, which shifted my emotional spectrum back to the angry-as-fuck side. Because it wasn't his *influence* talking—just plain old vampire genetics (if it was called that).

The man had thick, wavy hair that curled around his ears, each strand showcasing the rich hues of autumn. His dark brown eyes were laser-focused on me, set within the latte-colored painting that made up the rest of his beautiful facial features.

His light blue suit jacket hung open, revealing a simple white shirt beneath, and the sleeves rolled up to his mid forearms to display the floral pattern on the inside. He tucked his hands casually into the pockets of his matching linen pants. Not a care in the world as he approached two incredibly powerful Community members, if I say so myself.

Sharp canines hid behind his full lips, the corners of which were currently twisted upward into a conceited smile. His gaze drank me in from head to foot, his subsequent arousal pressing against the fabric of his pants.

"Ah, Veronica Neill," he purred in a sultry voice that likely made most women's panties drop, "what an absolute pleasure to see you again."

I put my hand on Thane's arm as he stepped forward, anger emanating from him like a heatwave. "I can't say the same."

"My apologies for the late arrival. I had a minor issue to attend to first." Xavier's gaze flicked to my mate for the briefest of moments. "And I believe I asked you to come alone."

Thane crossed his arms.

"If you actually expected me to follow through with that, you're dumber than I thought," I said.

Xavier's eyes flashed dangerously. "How I missed your…ladylike sass."

Like before, the man hadn't come to grips with women being his equal and often his better. He was stuck in his millennia-old ways, and I was happy to take advantage of that mindset again.

"Let's get this over with so I can move on to killing you," I said with a hurry-up gesture. Just because I was emotionally conflicted didn't mean I wouldn't kill him. "And I'm only giving you one minute before I do because you technically helped me with Emilia."

Xavier's smile deepened. But coming from the vampire, it was like a cat teasing its prey. "How kind of you."

"Her generosity won't last long," Thane said, narrowing his eyes. "You're stalling."

"What do you have that I want?" I eyed him up and down with contempt. "Because I can't think of anything except your ashes in the trash."

The vampire's pupils burned red as he telepathically communicated to his creations. I wasn't stupid enough to think he hadn't produced more vampires, which was part of the reason we'd armed up as much as we had.

Like nails on a chalkboard, the skittering sound of claws on cement surrounded us. Newly-turned vampires crept out of the surrounding shadows and from beneath cars. As their hungry eyes fixated on us as if we were their lunch, I counted five with varying degrees of desiccated skin and stringy, patchy hair.

Although we kept our weapons sheathed, Thane and I shifted our weight into more defensive stances. Five wasn't a lot, but who knew how many more waited. If things got dicey, our plan was to inflict as much damage as possible, then high-tail it out of there.

I let out an exasperated sigh. "An ambush? Really?"

"Of course not. I've no intention of harming you," the Master Vampire said. "However, I knew you would not come alone, and you brought more than just one ex-reaper."

Before I had a chance to feign innocence, he removed a key fob from his pocket and pushed a button. A nearby black sedan's trunk popped open, and two vampires scrambled over. From the trunk, one vamp lifted a birdcage, just large enough to hold two birds.

Correction, two *falcons* with red and orange under plumage.

Fuck.

My pulse thumped against my eardrums. Lena and Ivan screeched angrily and flapped their wings in protest. That they hadn't shifted and burst through the cage meant it was iron or magic-resistant material.

How the fuck had bloodsuckers snuck up on and captured them?

"My insurance policy during our meeting," Xavier said with a flourish of his hand. "Play nice, and I'll hand them over unharmed."

The second vampire by the car heaved a limp figure out of the trunk and laid him on the concrete. Iron chains secured cuffs attached to his wrists and ankles, and a bag covered his head.

"You may consider this one a gift." Xavier sauntered over and removed the bag.

My breath left my body in a whoosh.

Jackson Reed.

The Master Vampire had captured the realm walker responsible for killing my brother. The man who had actually done the deed and one of the last dangling threads I needed to cut to get complete vengeance for Maddox's death.

He laid there, unconscious, ready to die.

Talk about a gift.

I blinked at Xavier. "How? Why?"

"A motley crew of shifters owed me a favor," he said with a sinister smile. "As for why, it pleases me to know you like my gift."

Puzzle pieces snapped into place when I remembered that Rico's rogue pack had met with a vampire. It couldn't be a coincidence.

If Rico's gang had helped capture Jackson Reed and proved loyal in the fight against Colin, then I would totally forgive them for ruining my Benz.

I took a step toward Jackson, but Xavier shook his head, sliding over with a graceful step to block my path. "Not so fast, little bird. I'd like something in return for my generosity."

A falcon squawked its displeasure, startling the newer vampire holding the cage. Fangs extended as it hissed at the bird.

I should have known a gift would come with strings attached. "You said this was a gift."

"Seeing that the man who killed your brother is a captive on his way to my torture chamber is the gift," he explained. "Getting to touch him will require a bargain."

Thane growled beside me, and his rising anger fused with mine.

Of course a gift would require something in return. How silly of me to think otherwise. I ground my teeth together. "What do you want?"

His brown eyes gleamed. "Immunity."

That single word slammed into my gut like a hard punch. I hadn't been the Master Vampire's only target for his collection of rare Community members. Before me, he'd caged several others, torturing them until the DEA freed them or, more often, they died.

How could I even consider this kind of deal?

Because this was for my baby brother, to finally bring justice to Maddox's murderer. It wasn't enough to know he'd be in Xavier's custody and tortured for the rest of his life. I clenched my hands into tight fists. Jackson needed to die for what he'd done.

Thane stepped closer to me, his warm presence and familiar bergamot scent wrapping around me. He probably sensed my indecision through our bond. That or my horrible poker face gave it away. "Veronica, no. You cannot make this deal."

I met his deep blue gaze, sinking all my emotions into our soul link. The years of pain and grief, the fear and shame, even the bloodthirsty rage and desire for blood. All of it. For once, I didn't hold back.

He winced at the onslaught of emotions but didn't stop me. Instead, he cupped my face in his palms. "Maddox wouldn't want you to do this."

My heart shattered with the truth of his words, and I closed my eyes against the crushing regret and sorrow that threatened to consume my soul.

He was right. I couldn't make this trade just for a few moments of satisfaction.

If I did, I wouldn't be any better than Jackson.

I turned my head to kiss Thane's palm before opening my eyes and facing Xavier. "I'll accept on one condition."

The falcons flapped their wings and chirped, and a sound of intense frustration came from Thane's throat. He dropped his hands, disappointment streaming through our link.

Trust me, I urged through our bond. We couldn't communicate telepathically, but he would know through the emotion.

Xavier's eyes flashed with excitement, and he gestured for me to continue.

"You can have your immunity from the inside of a DEA prison cell and not just a holding cell." I examined the vampire's face for any reaction, but he locked down his emotions. "We'll spare you from the death you earned and so obviously deserve, but you'll live out your years in a maximum-security prison."

He tilted his head as if considering my words. "That doesn't seem like a fair exchange. You get satisfaction from killing Jackson, and I'm left to rot?"

"Jackson will be in the cell next to yours, available as your private meal whenever hunger strikes."

It was the next best alternative to not killing the fucking asshole. Either of them.

Pride and humor seeped through our soul link, and I looked up to catch Thane's smirk. He might not condone murder, but he had also never experienced what I had.

At least this way, he could look me in the face every day.

If Xavier accepted my offer, that is, and judging by his expression, that option wasn't looking good.

Patience had never been one of my strong suits, and it certainly wasn't one of them today. Waiting for this sadistic vampire to agree with my only offer was like waiting in line at the DMV. I wanted to punch someone, preferably Xavier or Jackson.

After what felt like an eternity, Xavier heaved a dramatic sigh. "It pains me to say I cannot accept your deal."

The bloodsuckers surrounding us inched closer, their gazes lusting after Thane and me hungrily. Lena and Ivan flapped their wings again, rocking the cage until the vampire shook it, forcing them to settle with avian scowls.

My fingers twitched, ready to draw my weapons and fling their ashes to the wind.

Or, you know, the cement floor.

"But," Xavier held up a finger to keep anyone from doing something drastic, "I'd like to up the ante. In exchange for full immunity to live life as I please, I'll help you bring Colin Ó Broin to his knees."

I raised an eyebrow. "Why?"

His upper lip curled in a look of distaste, flashing a hint of fang. "I've been trying to stop that overly entitled fae since before you ever knew a problem existed. Despite my proclivity to collect rare objects," his eyes flashed with desire as his gaze traced my curves, "I'm quite content with how this world works. I have no interest in answering to a fairy."

Putting aside my disgust for the word *object* when referring to people such as myself, I had to admit I was shocked. I never would have guessed Xavier was on our side against Colin. As in one of the good guys.

Seeing Xavier—make that *any* vampire—as a semi-heroic figure was an oxymoron that I wasn't ready to process just yet.

"I find that hard to believe," Thane said through clenched teeth.

Xavier lifted a shoulder in a casual shrug. "Your beliefs, or lack thereof, aren't important. Facts are facts. Not to mention, the archangel knows everything."

Wait, what?

"You're seriously claiming that Adam knows what you were doing?" Thane asked, his tone incredulous and mocking.

"Oh, yes." The Master Vampire grinned, displaying both of his elongated canines. "Catching me with Sophia was an unfortunate turn of events for him *and* me. But don't you find it interesting that the archangel kept me in a simple holding cell the weekend before my beheading?"

Shock ran through me like a bucket of ice water

dumped over my head. This crazy, bloodsucking motherfucker was insinuating that Adam, of all people, knew about his supposed attempts to stop Colin and kept him in the DEA's small prison for an easier escape.

Thane barked out a laugh. "Nice try."

Xavier shrugged. "Like I said, your beliefs are inconsequential."

"If what you're saying is true, why don't you just ask Adam for immunity?" I asked.

"He must *appear* to do the honorable thing, doesn't he?" Xavier winked. "I understand if you need time to make this decision. Shall we reconvene this evening?"

There was no way in hell I'd let this fucker out of my sight again.

"No need to wait," I said, gripping a stake as I prepared to kill him. "We don't need your help with Colin."

One of the falcons chirped and tilted its head to the side. I really wished I could tell them apart in falcon form.

Xavier's next smile was as sinister as they get. "Ah, but you do. You see, I know something you don't."

I rolled my eyes. "Of course you do. You're old. Like, ancient. You have centuries of knowledge on me."

His dark eyes narrowed at my jab. Gods, he was so easy to rile up. "Something that will ensure your win against the fae."

"And how do you intend to prove that?" Thane asked.

"You'll understand once you agree to the terms."

This sonofabitch knew exactly what lures to dangle in front of me, which was infuriating because of course I was hooked.

I held up a finger. "One moment. And don't even think about running."

Xavier put his hand to his chest, feigning a hurt look. "I wouldn't dream of running from you, my pet."

"And yet it's a common occurrence with you." I drew Thane away, glancing back every few steps to ensure the vamps stayed put. Keeping my voice low, I asked, "Could he be telling the truth about Adam?"

"As much as I hate to admit it, it's unlikely but possible." The lines of his jaw moved as he ground his teeth together. "I'd wondered why Adam hadn't transferred Xavier to the maximum-security prison, even for the short time between his sentencing and execution."

I'd wondered the same thing, but I'd let it go with everything that had occurred after. I had believed Xavier's skull graced the foyer of the Miami vampires' hive.

Well, I had until I received that first letter, but I'd been living life in the fast lane since then.

"There's no way I'm giving him a chance to escape," I said. "How do you feel about me lying to him? We can agree to the deal, get the info, then I'll kill him."

"As much as I'd love that, it's a no."

"But no one would know," I argued.

His soulful, blue-eyed gaze met mine. "We would know."

Him and his godsdamned morals. Sure, he was absolutely correct. I would feel great watching Xavier's ashes pile up on the oil-stained cement floor, but I would regret the betrayal over time. Too much regret hung over my head already.

Besides, I wasn't Xavier, and I had no intention of becoming the bad guy, even if I thought I was once upon a time.

"So, do we agree to his terms? With no crossing our fingers behind our backs?" I asked.

Thane glanced back at the Master Vampire, who smiled and fluttered his fingers at us in a little wave. "Yes. We need any information we can get to stop Colin, no matter the source. If he doesn't hold up his end of the deal, he goes to prison."

"Or maybe the vamp'll have an unfortunate 'accident' on the battlefield," I said with a wink.

Thane chuckled, and we returned to the vampires.

"We've made a decision," I announced, my voice echoing across the garage.

"I can hardly contain my excitement." Xavier's tone was thick with sarcasm.

The newly-turned crouching around us shifted from side to side, the scrabbling sounds of their claws against cement sending tingles up my spine.

Sun above, I hated vampires.

"We agree to your terms," I said. "Full immunity in exchange for information that leads to our win. Failure means life in prison."

Xavier's gaze flicked to Thane. "I have your word as well?"

Thane's eyes narrowed. "You have my word."

"Now, tell us what you know," I said.

Xavier grinned and took a few steps backward. "I'll do better than tell you. Meet me tonight at N-V, ten o'clock sharp, and you'll see for yourselves. Oh, and be sure to change your clothes to fit in. Can't have you standing out in the crowd any more than you already do."

A flush rose along my neck. In a flash, two stakes were in my hands, and the newbies swarmed around their master. "You backstabbing bloodsucker."

Xavier's malicious chuckle echoed off the cement walls. "Is that any way to speak to a new ally? As a show of good faith, I'll leave your friends and the murderer with you."

With speed only a Master Vampire possessed, he was gone. Chasing him down would be a lost cause. His minions crept back into the shadows and disappeared, leaving the birdcage and Jackson Reed, who remained unconscious and chained up on the ground.

As promised.

I whirled toward Thane. "Did we just get played?"

A deep crease formed between his eyebrows as he stared in the direction Xavier had gone. "Surprisingly, I don't think so."

Xavier wasn't the type of undead guy to string us along. He was way too fucking cocky. So while I was still angry as fuck, I felt the same as Thane.

What was the world coming to?

CHAPTER 22

Tuesday Evening

After we released Ivan and Lena, they shifted back to human form. Immediately, they squabbled over who was to blame for their capture, then with us about why there was no bloodshed, much to their mutual disappointment.

Once they calmed down and progressed to sulking, Thane jumped to the DEA with Jackson Reed, and Lena, Ivan, and I headed back to my penthouse.

Kit was too busy opening portals to help me, but I needed to do some digging. I wanted whatever dirt Xavier had, and I couldn't wait until the evening.

Unfortunately, hours of research proved fruitless without Kit's expertise. I had no idea what Xavier knew that might turn the tide of war, so we would have to go in blind and hope it wasn't a colossal mistake.

Night had fallen by the time Thane returned to our place to jump us to the club. Although, the lights illuminating downtown Miami outside the two-story penthouse windows never made it feel that way. The city was awake no matter the time.

While I hadn't gone for my standard club gear, I would still fit in wearing tight black leather pants, a sparkly silver top, and my new boots from the armory. I pinned my hair up with a small wooden stake that wouldn't draw attention and tucked a few extra stakes attached to an elastic waistband beneath my loose top.

Ivan returned to the DEA in case anyone there needed his realm walking ability, and Thane changed into a casual linen suit. Lena had refused to change. She wanted comfort over fashion, and I finally gave up arguing.

Her combat boots and oversized vest might earn a few curious looks, but there was always one odd bird in every group. We wouldn't stick out more than anyone else.

The club's music boomed through the open front doors as our group approached. It had been a while since I'd last visited N-V, but the bouncers still recognized me as I headed straight for the doors, skipping the line despite the angry protests from those waiting. Special perks came along with the obnoxious amount of time and money I used to spend at places like this.

As soon as we entered the club, perfumes, cologne, and body odor assaulted my senses, while the deep bass vibrated down to my soul. I used to thrive on all of it, dancing and drinking the night away, and I kind of missed it.

Not necessarily the grabby hands and drunken blackouts, but I missed feeling unburdened by anything other than my guilt. Glancing around the packed club for Xavier, I promised myself a night out soon.

One more thing for my ever-expanding future Veronica list. Although, I might be putting off too much until after this was all over.

Was that time ever going to come?

Against a wall, the club's main bar stretched from the front of the massive room to the back. The rest of the first floor enclosed a square-shaped area in the middle for dancing, sunken a few steps below ground. Guests at the tables and VIP booths lining the walls had a perfect view of the dancers.

Four columns at each corner held up a second VIP-only level, opened up like a theatre so those lounging like gods above could see just about everything.

An unfamiliar beefy bouncer with a shaved head and a trimmed goatee pushed his way toward us. He looked us up and down. "Follow me."

Thane and I exchanged a glance, and Lena muttered something about sketchy people behind me. But if we wanted answers, we had to follow.

We trailed after the bouncer's broad shoulders through the sea of gyrating, sweaty bodies to a door at the club's back. Another giant of a man I didn't recognize pulled a door open and waved us inside the stairwell. We descended a level and exited into a long hallway.

My pulse picked up speed the farther we went. If this

was an ambush, then we hadn't brought nearly enough weapons to fight our way out of here. Using phoenix abilities on humans would likely cause more deaths because outing the Community was a big no-no—we'd have to kill anyone who witnessed our magic.

Or we'd have to involve the DEA for clean-up, which was a nightmare unto itself. So much paperwork, it almost made killing the preferred choice.

The bouncer led us to another door and stopped. He knocked three times before opening it, then stepped to the side with his hands over his broad chest.

I followed Thane into the room, Lena close on my heels and growling softly. She hadn't gotten past the cage incident yet, and she much preferred open battlefields to backdoor brawls.

The room contained several empty poker tables, dimly lit by a few wall lamps. A uniformed bartender stood behind a wet bar stocked with high-end liquors and hand dried glasses with a towel.

Next to the bar was a comfortable sitting area. Xavier and another man relaxed on a couch, drinking whiskey and smoking cigars.

I wasn't sure what I was expecting tonight, but this easygoing scene wasn't it.

My eyes widened as I recognized the other man—Edric, the fae prince. I had never actually met the guy, but there was no mistaking his likeness to his mother, Queen Fiadh. His blond hair was the same rich gold as hers, his eyes the same hue of sky blue, and his skin shimmered with a golden undertone.

The last I'd heard of him was from when we attacked

William. Colin had mentioned the prince escaped the Winter Court fae's clutches—allegedly. Knowing what I knew now, I questioned that story.

Had we just walked into a trap?

"My little bird has arrived at last," Xavier said, raising his glass in my direction. "Drinks?"

My gaze darted around the room for a setup. As far as I could tell, we were alone besides the bartender, but vampires were sneaky little fucks. "No."

When my gaze settled on Edric, he inclined his head. "I hear rumors you're my equal now."

"I wasn't aware you were king of the fae," I said, even though soon, I would no longer be a queen or his royal equal.

He chuckled and tapped his cigar over an ashtray set between them on the couch. "Royalty is royalty."

Lena snorted beside me, and I definitely agreed with her opinion.

"Have a seat. Relax." Xavier motioned to the two cushioned chairs across from them. "Despite what Colin might've told you, Edric is not his man."

The fae man's lip curled with a sneer. "Far from it."

Considering the fae couldn't lie, that was a fact. However, fudging the truth was their specialty. His vague response to Xavier's equally vague description could mean several things, like maybe Colin was Edric's man. Doubtful, but possible.

"I'm not following how Edric plays into this." I stepped closer but didn't sit. "You said you'd show us something that would ensure our victory. Are you saying he can stop the war?"

Holding his glass and cigar in one hand, Xavier leaned

back, draping his free arm along the couch's back. "Nothing so simple, I'm afraid, but I guarantee you'll want to hear what he has to say."

Frustration built within me, and I didn't hide it from my expression or tone. "This isn't showing me something that will help us win against Colin. You could've just told us when we met earlier."

"Patience, my pet," Xavier teased with a wink.

It was just like a vampire to throw my weaknesses back into my face. Everyone knew I was too impatient for my own good.

"Sit." Edric took a drag of his cigar and slowly blew out the smoke. "You are aware Colin and my mother are cousins, yes?"

"Yes." For now, I wasn't his equal. I was above him, which meant to hell with his commands. I would sit when I wanted.

Annoyance flickered across his face, but he didn't address my snub. Maybe he was more intelligent than he looked. "Despite their close genetics, Colin decided at a young age that he would marry my mother and become King of the Otherworld while the Summer Court was in power."

I blinked. That was some hefty news.

"Only that's not how it works in your world or mine," Edric said. "As they grew older, Colin's obsession with my mother deepened until he demanded she change the fae law and allow him as her consort. She refused and asked him to leave the Summerlands.

"When he resisted, she told him she'd never loved him more than as a brother and that a Spring Court fae would never rule the Otherworld. Especially not at her side."

Ouch. I slid onto a chair, totally engrossed in the story.

"If only more people knew their places in this world," Xavier sighed.

I raised an eyebrow. If the vampire followed his own advice, he would be dead. Because his place in this world was six feet under and rotting a millennium ago.

"I'm sure you can imagine how well Colin took that news," Edric continued. He swirled the ice in his glass before taking a sip. "To punish his subsequent egregious behavior, my mother stripped him of his wings and banished him from the Summerlands. Forever."

My jaw dropped open, and Lena sucked in her breath behind me. That explained why he hadn't shown his wings in the Otherworld. He didn't have any.

But taking a fae's wings was absolute blasphemy, even for a queen. I shuddered to think what he'd done to deserve such a fate, how far he must have pushed her.

"What did he do to her?" I asked.

Edric's grip on his glass tightened. "We do not speak of it, but he deserved her punishment and much more. She should have killed him."

"This doesn't make sense," Thane said, frowning. During the story, he sat in the chair beside me, and I hadn't even noticed. "When we last visited, he escorted us into the Summer Palace and gained an audience with Queen Fiadh. They're still close, or at the very least, he's no longer banished."

Edric's jaw clenched. "The woman you saw is *not* my mother."

"Well, that's not completely true." Xavier puffed on his cigar.

"She's spellbound, and he controls her like a puppet," Edric argued. "That may be my mother's body, but nothing she says or does is her own. She's trapped in her own mind."

"How was he able to bind the queen?" Thane asked. His eyebrows were drawn together tight.

"Everyone has a weakness, and Colin knew my mother's from their early years as friends. And no, I won't tell you what that weakness is, but it worked." Edric gulped down his remaining whiskey. "She knew he was planning something, for years. She even ordered our people home for the inevitable war, but it was too late."

Ah. So it wasn't because she had a thing against half-bloods like rumors suggested. Too bad her plan hadn't worked.

The prince set his empty glass on the side table harder than necessary "Regardless, Colin has an extraordinary amount of magic for a member of the Spring Court and an inflated ego to match."

The bartender slipped out from behind the bar to retrieve the glass. As he bent forward, his eyes stared ahead with a glossy look. He wiped the table with a crisp white towel and returned to his station behind the counter.

"I still don't get how this helps us," I said, eyeing the human bartender. I wasn't sure who controlled him, but it seemed hypocritical considering the prince's outrage at Colin doing the same to his mother. "Except now we know the Queen isn't in control, which doesn't ensure a victory."

A smile played across the prince's lips. "It does when I can get close enough to her to break the spell."

"What's stopping you?" I asked, annoyed. We wouldn't be in this mess if he had broken the spell.

"Despite his lesser court status, Colin's magic outstrips mine. I simply don't have enough to break it," he explained with a shrug.

"So you left her there to rot while you ran like a coward?" Thane asked, condescension dripping from each word of his accusation.

Edric narrowed his eyes at my mate. "When I realized what he'd done, I had to hide or face the same punishment as my mother. I can't help her if he binds me as well."

Thane made a sound of disapproval and pressed his lips together. Knowing him, there wasn't a chance in hell he would leave his mother behind, tortured by a madman.

Glass clinked together behind the wet bar as the bartender cleaned the surface.

"Wait, were you ever held captive by the Winter Court?" I asked, remembering Colin's reason for his late arrival in the fight against William.

Edric scoffed. "If you can call it that. Those fae can hardly form complete sentences, let alone keep someone like me behind bars."

I wasn't an expert on fae politics, but having dealt with William and the fae in the woods, I knew the prince's perception wasn't totally accurate. I had to assume there was some beef between the Summer and Winter Courts.

As they say, perception is reality, which might explain how the fae skirted around the truth so well.

"Can I break the spell?" I asked.

Xavier took a sip of his whiskey, his gaze never leaving mine. "No, but your little group has recently acquired a weapon that can."

CHAPTER 23

Tuesday Evening

With the Master Vampire's revelation that he knew about us having the Last Hope, Lena tensed behind me, followed by the sound of steel sliding from leather.

Goosebumps rose along my arms. Surely Adam hadn't told him about that. "How do you know about that?"

"I make it my business to know everything," he said with a predatory smile.

"We're not giving you the weapon." Thane leaned back in his chair. His pose seemed relaxed, but his body was as tense to fight as Lena's.

"I don't expect you to," Edric said, waving aside the idea. "I can get the wielder inside the palace."

Thane and I exchanged an uneasy glance. If Angela broke the spell binding the queen, then the entire fae army would be on our side. We would decimate Colin.

But the danger involved was extraordinary, especially since she was a human.

I rubbed my temples as a dull throb crept in. "This is a lot to process."

"I'd say take your time to think it over, but we know that's not possible," Xavier said.

Thane's phone rang. He showed me it was Adam calling and answered it. His expression darkened as he listened. After a few tense moments, he agreed to something and hung up.

"What is it?" I asked, my scalp prickling.

"Xavier's more right than we realized," he said. "Colin has amassed an unseelie army at the Summer Court palace, preparing for war."

Dread sank deep in my stomach like a boulder, and Lena muttered some colorful Yazyk curses.

He knew we were coming for him.

As much as I loathed letting Xavier out of sight again, we had work to do. Thane, Lena, and I left the club to join the others at the DEA. There was no way we could show up with Xavier without giving everyone a heads up, and doing it over the phone wasn't ideal after the news Adam had just shared.

Leaving the Master Vampire was a tremendous risk, but my priority had to be Colin. If Xavier betrayed me, I'd stake the traitorous bloodsucker *after* I killed Colin.

Yeesh. My to-kill list was getting long. If it got any longer, they'd have to take a number.

To say things were chaotic when we arrived at the DEA was a massive understatement. Reapers scurried down hallways or winked in and out of view via teleportation circles. Conversations outside our usual conference room were much louder than normal as everyone tried to be heard on phone calls or in groups.

Already in the conference room and at the table were the leaders or VIPs of each major Community group involved: Imos and Tundreg, Pietr and Ivan, Adam and Nathan, and Angela and Kit, who'd reluctantly agreed to represent the covens after they insisted.

Word of Octavia's imprisonment had spread, and witches from various covens had sent their heartfelt thanks. Kit would have to deal with a newfound celebrity status.

Not present were Luka and Rico, who were busy preparing their packs.

My best friend had dark circles under her heavily lidded eyes. Keeping the portals to Mirognya open for so long was taking its toll, and taking on her new role as coven representative hadn't helped.

"What's the status?" Thane asked Adam as he pulled out an empty seat for me.

Even in times of war, he was the perfect gentleman.

"We will enter the Otherworld at first light," the archangel said, his voice grim. "We have brought over the dragons and phoenixes thanks to Ms. Parker's skill with portals." He nodded in her direction, receiving only a tired blink in return. His gaze fell on Thane. "I would like to ask you and Ivan to realm walk a small contingent to the

Otherworld before we open the portal tomorrow morning."

Thane gave a brisk nod. "Of course. We'll ensure the location is secure."

My heart thudded wildly. He must have felt my anxiety through our link because he reached over and took my hand, giving it a squeeze. I knew Adam's plan made sense and was a shrewd tactical move, but I hated knowing my mate might be among the first casualties.

I swallowed down rising bile, grimacing at the burn.

"Any questions?" Adam asked, readying to stand.

Here we go.

I cleared my throat. "We, uh, have some news. Colin has spellbound Queen Fiadh and controls her every movement. The Last Hope can break the spell and free the queen, ensuring our victory."

Kit narrowed her eyes and leaned forward onto the table. "How'd you find that out?"

"What, I can't be good at digging up dirt like you?" I asked with a huff.

She just stared at me.

I sighed. "Fine. We have a new source—Prince Edric. He can get us close enough to the queen to unbind her."

"But he's on Colin's side, isn't he?" Angela asked, her gaze flicking around the ground for confirmation.

Thane shook his head and explained what the prince had told us about Colin and Fiadh's history, leaving out one important undead detail for now. "We have no real reason to believe the prince isn't telling the truth."

Angela frowned. "Fae can't lie, right?"

"Not outright," I said, "but they can fudge the truth fairly well."

"How did he know about the weapon?" Kit asked, her narrowed eyes glinting dangerously.

"He didn't," I said.

"So you told him?" Her tone was incredulous, instantly setting off my defensiveness.

I glared at her. "No, he's got his own sources."

"How did you come to meet with Prince Edric?" Adam asked before she badgered me more.

I turned my glare on him, struggling to control my anger as I remembered his involvement with Xavier's escape. "We know the same vermin."

Adam looked between me and Thane, realization lifting his eyebrows. "I see. I presume you would like an explanation."

The others adjusted their positions and shared puzzled looks.

"You presume correctly," I said, trying hard to keep the bite out of my tone.

Adam steepled his fingers together in front of his lips. "What the rest of you do not know is that Xavier Garcia is alive and has worked with the DEA for the past several years."

He let that sink in, and I swear we could have heard a pin drop.

"Until the situation with Sophia Clark, I was unaware of his illegal extracurricular activities," he continued with a sigh. "I was as shocked as you were. Unfortunately, we had not finished our work at the time of his arrest, and I needed his unique skills and contacts to collect information."

Kit slammed her palms down on the table. "Are you fucking kidding me right now?"

"This was long before you agreed to work with us, Ms. Parker."

"Had I known you would ask that bloodsucking shitstain for help, I would've agreed earlier," she fumed.

While I understood her anger and felt it as keenly as she did, it wasn't like Kit to get riled up so quickly. That was my job. Even though her colorful and accurate description of Xavier impressed me, she was in dire need of a nap.

"It is in the past, Katherine," Adam said gently but firmly. "My pride does not stop me from accepting all help dealing with matters of utmost importance to the Community." His attention returned to Thane and me. "What did you promise him?"

"Full immunity," Thane said.

If I thought Kit was angry before, it was nothing compared to outrage contorting her face now. As she clenched her fists on the table, the lights flickered and the building shook, knocking things off the walls.

Outside the conference room's glass wall—which hadn't shattered yet, much to my amazement—a reaper carrying a giant stack of paperwork lost his balance and fell over, sending papers flying everywhere.

It would've been comical if it weren't because my best friend was losing her shit.

Angela laid her hand on Kit's arm. "That's not helpful."

Instantly, the lights stopped flickering, and the building ceased its shaking. Kit rubbed her face with her hands and groaned. "I'm sorry."

"Go get some sleep," I said.

"Don't tell me what to do," she snapped back with a withering glare. As the silence stretched on after her outburst, she sighed. "Sorry. You're right. I'm exhausted."

I glanced at Ivan, who caught my look and nodded.

"I'll take you both home," he said. He got to his feet and stood behind their chairs, placing his hands on each woman's shoulder.

Kit gave me a half-hearted smile just before they winked out of sight.

She didn't need to apologize—this was a shitty situation and grim news to digest.

"How does Edric plan to get Angela close enough to Queen Fiadh?" Adam asked.

"He didn't say, but whatever it is, I think it'd be best for me to go with them," Thane said.

I blinked at him, my pulse immediately racing. "What? Why? Not that we trust Edric completely, but why *you*?"

"My dragon scales will keep her protected if we're attacked, and I can jump us away," he explained.

"If you go, I go," I said.

He shook his head with a look that said he wouldn't budge. "Colin's turned his obsession on you, for whatever reason. Maybe he has a thing for gorgeous blondes. Whatever it is, you need to keep him distracted, away from the queen."

Ugh. This was why I hated living my life by logic. His plan made perfect sense, and I hated every part of it. I also hated knowing he thought the queen was gorgeous, even though it was completely accurate.

Jealousy was never a good look on anyone, but we all had flaws. Some more than others, and I never claimed to be flawless.

"Fine, but I still get to kill Colin first," I sighed.

Thane grinned. "I'm not sure we'll need more than one kill, but sure."

I shot him an exasperated look. "Never underestimate a determined necromancer."

A warning signal lifted the hairs on the back of my neck. Was I right without realizing it?

Had Colin figured out a way to escape death?

CHAPTER 24

Wednesday Morning

The day had finally arrived. Today, we would bring Colin to his knees, and I would have the glorious experience of seeing the life snuff from his eyes. By my hand if everything went according to plan.

I didn't care how immoral or evil that sounded—this man had destroyed my family, and plenty of others. His time in this world was up.

While Thane had chosen all black for his castle excursion, Lena and I had dressed in leather armor. We'd returned to the DEA's armory and suited up with every weapon imaginable long before the sun rose. That might have been a record for me.

I even strapped on the sheath holding Lisa, my short sword named after the phoenix word for she-fox. She'd come a long way from her days dealing solely with demons.

Instead of cramming everyone willing to fight into the DEA's lobby, we agreed that the hotel where the Mirognyan visitors stayed made far more sense. Not that anyone was there for a vacation, but it provided far more space to maneuver an army.

It was a good thing the humans running the hotel were familiar with the Community because otherwise, our gathering was sure to cause more than one heart attack. Their wide eyes threatened to pop right out of their human heads as we gathered.

Reapers, angels, dragons, phoenixes, werewolves, shifters, mages, and a handful of witches and warlocks milled about the convention center. We took up most of the hotel's first floor, decked out in all kinds of armor and weapons, waiting.

Some of the more ferocious dragons and phoenixes couldn't hide the excited gleam in their eyes. That was what happened when you spent your whole life training for war.

Hundreds, maybe even thousands, of magical fighters were ready to destroy one fae man who threatened our world, all because the dude couldn't take no for an answer.

Apprehension and excitement swirled around me, almost electrifying the air. The hotel staff had removed the partitions between their three convention rooms, allowing our army enough space to move and stretch or lay down against a wall and rest as we waited for Adam to give the go-ahead.

Scanning the crowd, I sighed. If only all humans knew

about our existence because this scene would make for an epic viral video. I could be such a sucker for social media praise, but my latte art skills would have to suffice.

The steady drum of beating wings drew all of our attention to Adam. His glittering white wings spanned ten feet or more and raised him high enough above our heads for everyone to see.

"Brothers and sisters of the Community," he began, opening his arms, "the time has come to unite against a force of evil threatening our way of life. Perhaps our very existence."

After the booming echoes of his words faded, a heavy silence settled over the crowd as we took in the full ramifications of his statement.

"Over the last thirty years, Colin Ó Broin has taken too much from our three realms. But his betrayal of our trust will end today," he continued defiantly. "We must stand together and show him the might of the Community."

Shouts of encouragement rang out, but Adam raised his hands to quiet the crowd. His bright blue gaze swept across the faces looking up at him. "I will not lie to you. He has power most have not faced before, harnessing his fae magic, as well as shadow and death.

"Whether or not we are victorious, some will not return home. No one will fault or judge your decision should you choose not to fight today."

People adjusted their stances and looked around, but no one stepped away. Pride blossomed in my middle, warming me to my core.

This was why Miami would always be my home and this group my people.

This was my Community.

A familiar voice spoke up, "What a delightfully empowering speech."

I closed my eyes and groaned.

Xavier slunk through the open doors and clapped softly, his smile mocking. He wore an expertly tailored black suit and tie like he was simply attending a formal event rather than war. At his side, Edric held his chin high with a haughty look that clearly said he expected everyone to bow.

Growls and snarls erupted around the massive room, and some shifters morphed into their beast forms. Okay, make that most shifters.

Shit was going to get real ugly, *real* fast.

"Silence!" Adam's single word boomed across the room, laced with angelic power. It worked. "The vampire holds the key to our success and is under *my* protection. He is not to be touched."

Despite his call for silence, the mob flew into another uproar.

"You must be joking," Luka shouted above the din. From his place among the wolves, he glared at Xavier, and his eyes glinted dangerously. "He's been tried and sentenced to death for torturing and killing Community members. Or have you forgotten?"

"What you say is true," Adam said, somehow rising above Luka's insult. Nothing like a little angelic patience when defending a murderous bloodsucker. "However, he has played an integral part in this endeavor's success and has received full immunity from the DEA. My decision is final."

Gasps and grumbles filled the air, but no one argued against the archangel—a true testament to how much the

Community honored his word. As much as Colin wanted to topple our way of life and allow the realms to form whatever governing bodies we wished, most of us respected the angels and their judgment.

Of course, respect didn't mean we had to agree with, or even like, every decision.

"I've brought some hungry new friends to play with the fae today," Xavier drawled, his pupils blazing red.

Dozens of newer vampires clambered into view through the door behind their creator or scaled the walls like ants. Ill-fitting clothing covered their half-decayed skeletal remains, but at least we didn't have to see them fully naked in the light. Or *ever* would be great.

Thank the gods for silver linings.

More angry mutters rumbled through the vast room, and the assembly squeezed farther away from the foul-smelling creatures. Technically, vamps were as much a part of the Community as anyone else. Xavier was our main issue.

"With *that* situation out of the way, let me introduce Prince Edric of the Summer Court," Adam said, and the prince in question dipped his head regally.

The archangel relayed the information we'd learned from him about the queen.

"Our mission is to hold Colin's attention on our armies for as long as possible," Adam said. "A small group will infiltrate the palace and free the queen. With her freedom, Colin's reign of terror will finally end."

Cheers and shouts for getting this show on the road rang out, near-deafening in volume and intensity. Beside me, Lena raised her sword in the air and joined their cheers, and I couldn't help my grin.

Many here were warriors like Lena, born and bred for battle. This was what they lived for, and their excitement was contagious.

"Before we open the portal, a team will secure the location in the Otherworld. Please complete your preparations." Adam lowered himself back to the ground, disappearing among the throng of people.

Thane's warm presence grew closer, and I spun around to face him, clutching his arms. I hated this part, any time I had to leave his side, but even more when it involved so much danger.

If I lost him…

No, I couldn't go there. I needed to focus only on the present.

My gaze traveled across his handsome features, beginning with his thick midnight waves, lingering on the sharp angles and planes of his face and very kissable lips, and settling on his deep ocean-hued eyes. I drowned in them each and every time, and today was no exception.

His palms cupped my face, and he brushed my cheeks with his thumbs before leaning down to kiss me. Sparks ignited within every nerve with that simple touch, striking down to my core. Our soul link blazed with heat and love, with adoration, respect, and desire.

Whatever happened, he was my flame's chosen mate. I would do *everything* in my power—and more—to protect him. Whatever it took, I would be with him.

In life or in death.

He pulled his head back much too soon and smirked, directing even more heat straight between my legs. Memories of tangled sheets and laughter, his lips and tongue between my thighs, and his rock-hard length thrusting deep inside me swirled through my mind, dizzying and intoxicating.

My cheeks flushed, and I clenched my thighs together as an intense throb ached for release.

I would never get enough of this man.

"Don't worry, I'll ravage you again soon." Grinning mischievously, he kissed the backs of my hands and released me, making his way through the crowd toward Adam.

Grumbling at his absence even though I knew it was coming, I fanned my face. Good thing I didn't have to hide a hard-on in my pants.

"Think I'll find my flame's mate someday?" Lena asked, sighing as she watched Thane disappear into the crowd.

I looked at the longing on her face with surprise. She'd never hinted at that desire before. "I hope so. Maybe you should take a trip to Italy after this."

Expecting an elbow to the ribs or a glare, I laughed when she just nodded with a wistful smile. I couldn't say whether Holly, Kit's witchy friend in Rome, was Lena's mate. Still, she'd turned the warrior woman soft in a way I'd never seen before.

Speaking of witches, I nudged my way through the mob until I spied Kit with her eyes closed, breathing deeply. Close to Adam, she stood in the middle of a chalk circle, which I'd learned would amplify her magic and make holding the portal open easier and less draining.

Angela stood nearby, and I aimed in her direction, Lena right behind me.

"She ready?" I asked when I reached her.

The human witch had pulled her thick curly hair up into

a black beanie and donned all black clothes like Thane. She nodded and tightened her grip on the staff. "But I wish she could come with us."

I rested my hand on her shoulder. "You'll be in excellent hands. Thane will protect you and jump you guys away if things don't go as planned."

"If only that made me feel better, but I appreciate you for trying." Angela gave me a rueful smile.

Considering how little time she'd spent in the supernatural world, I had to give the girl some credit. Few humans would acclimate as fast as she had. Maybe practicing Wicca beforehand made it easier.

Whatever the reason, I was glad to have her on our side and about to marry my best friend.

The tingling sensation of my soul link winked out. The bond was there, just barely, which meant Thane had jumped his group to the Otherworld.

This show was officially on the road.

As the minutes ticked by, my nerves crumbled. I chewed my bottom lip raw as I gazed around at the room, not really seeing faces but constantly searching for the one that held my heart.

I wouldn't feel anything through our link unless the worst happened, and then all hell would break loose because I would lose my ever-loving mind. Nothing and no one would stop me from ripping Colin apart, even if it meant losing my life.

I couldn't live without Thane.

When I was convinced that the link was about to fade, Ivan popped back into view bedside Adam. He was breathless but smiling, and I released a huge sigh of relief.

"We surprised a small unseelie patrol, but the way is clear," he announced, earning a resounding cheer that vibrated down to my bones.

Adam met Kit's gaze and nodded.

About fucking time.

Exhilaration and anticipation zinged through my limbs and veins in equal parts, mixing with the vibrant energy spreading through the convention center rooms.

Everyone fell silent as Kit raised her arms, palms facing up, and chanted. Inside the circle, wind gusts tugged at her clothes and hair, and lightning pierced the linoleum floor, sending chunks flying. Several Community members backed up with startled looks on their faces.

It was hard not to feel nervous with the vast amount of magic Kit was harnessing, even though she'd told us nothing would leave the circle. Proving her point, the pieces of linoleum struck an invisible barrier and bounced back toward her.

A spiraling oval built from nothing but air, light, and magic materialized outside the chalk in front of Kit. It expanded until it stood several feet taller and much wider than she was. Mist and shadows were all that billowed within, but Kit lowered her arms and took a deep breath.

"It's ready," she said, her eyes somewhat glazed as she held the spell steady.

Without delay, Adam ordered various groups through the portal.

Ivan appeared at my side, his eyes glowing yellow from his recent realm walk. "Need a lift?"

I grinned and took his hand. "Absolutely. I hate portal travel."

Seriously, portals were awful. They were cold, desolate wastelands that I never wanted to experience again. It was a damn shame that realm walkers didn't exist in larger numbers or that they couldn't jump more than a handful of people at a time.

After Angela took a moment to kiss Kit goodbye, she gripped Ivan's free hand, and I grabbed Lena's. I met my best friend's worried gaze within the chalk circle and nodded, understanding her silent plea to keep Angela safe. Then the world disappeared.

A moment later, soft grass formed beneath my feet. I'd only been in the fae realm twice, but I recognized where we were. The only difference was the strange lack of sunlight.

We stood atop a hill facing a wall of thick, towering trees with branches that bent and curled in odd formations. A worn dirt path stretched through them, leading away from the capital city.

"Oh my goddess," Angela whispered. Her face was paler than usual, her eyes open wide as she stared at something behind me.

I turned to look and gasped.

Holy fuck.

Below us, nestled within a valley and bordered by a lake and mountain range, was the Summerlands. Except the colorful crystal city with its sparkling palace that thrust spires into the sky like unicorn horns was gone.

Darkness had leaked into and overtaken the glass and crystal castle, and they had walled off the city from the surrounding area. Fae soldiers patrolled atop the walls and positioned cannons at various strategic points.

Everywhere I looked, angry storm clouds rolled overhead, and gusts of frigid wind battered against us.

A shimmering grey dome streaked with black lightning covered the whole city. Its looming menace emanated like an approaching hurricane, threatening anyone who dared to approach or failed to flee.

An intense sense of foreboding weighed me down like a bag of bricks thrown into the ocean's darkest depths.

How the fuck would we get through *that*?

CHAPTER 25

Wednesday Morning

If it were me watching the approaching army from a palace window, I would have been terrified. In fact, I might have even shit myself. I hoped that Colin experienced the same level of fear, no matter how strong his defensive magic might be.

We would be stronger.

We *were* stronger—we had to be.

As I stood atop the hill overlooking the gloom-filled city, Adam directed our people to prepare for the assault. Even though we hoped to avoid significant bloodshed by sending in a team to infiltrate the castle and free the queen, we had to keep up appearances out here until they succeeded.

Gnawing on my bottom lip, which was already raw and cracked from my constant worrying, I wished yet again that I could go with Thane and Angela. Colin was unlike any threat we'd faced before. He was the mastermind behind it all, which scared me to my core.

"Such a shame, isn't it?" Xavier's voice slithered down my back.

I shivered and rubbed my arm against the rising goosebumps. He better not plan on fighting beside me, or he might get an up-close and personal introduction to Lisa. "You being alive? Yeah, that's a shame."

Angela snort-laughed beside me and adjusted her grip on the staff.

He chuckled. "I love your sense of humor. Tell me, what will you do with your life after this?"

What a strange question coming from him. I had no idea what he was getting at, but it couldn't be good. I glanced at him out of my periphery, but he fixed his gaze on the city, his face expressionless. "As if I would tell *you*."

He angled his face toward me, and his dark brown eyes searched mine. "We may have gotten off on the wrong foot, but I mean you no actual harm. I never did."

Angela glared daggers at him. She knew as well as I did what a crock of shit his comment was, but for a human, this chick had balls of steel. The Master Vampire could rip her to shreds before I blinked.

It was my turn to chuckle, though mine was a darker sound than his. "You don't think using someone as a broodmare is harmful?"

"I may have exaggerated my intentions a bit," he said with a shrug, returning his piercing gaze to the palace. "I wanted to set you free."

Before I could ask what the hell he meant by that, Thane and Edric joined us. My mate's gaze shifted between Xavier and me, and his eyes narrowed.

Edric inspected Angela from head to foot before eyeing the staff. "It's too bad your girlfriend isn't the one wielding that. Her skin color would blend into the shadows easier. Unfortunately, glamours and camouflaging magics don't work on other fae."

She rolled her eyes. "I'll be sure to remember the face paint next time."

"Or a ski mask." I winked at her, then gestured to the dome. "Glamour or not, it won't make much difference if we can't bring down the bubble thingy."

Edric shook his head. "The shield only keeps out non-fae. They'll have no trouble walking through it with me. The plan is to get to the queen as fast as possible. We can sneak inside the palace through a hidden entrance, but it won't be easy getting there without being seen."

"That won't be a problem," Thane said. "I'm a realm walker."

The prince raised his eyebrows. "Well, that certainly makes it easier, doesn't it? I'd suggest realm walking right into my mother's room, but the gods only know what state she'll be in or who she might be entertaining."

This plan nagged at a memory I couldn't place. Furrowing my eyebrows, I put my hands on my hips. "I feel like I've been here, done this before."

"You have, with Galina," Thane reminded me.

The memories returned in a flood, and I cringed as the onslaught of accompanying emotions swept through me. I almost wished I could forget that day.

"Imitation *is* the highest form of flattery." Xavier's white fangs glinted as he grinned. "Plus, it worked the last time, didn't it?"

It did, and I hoped and prayed that it would work again. It had to.

Dwelling on the fact that we lost Pavel, among too many other lives, in the last battle against William and Galina would lead nowhere good.

After Xavier wandered away to round up his minions, Edric and Thane agreed they didn't want to waste any more time. The sooner they freed the queen, the better for everyone.

I understood, but I tugged Thane to me for a quick goodbye. Rising onto my tiptoes, I wrapped my arms around his neck and pressed my body against his, relishing in the heat I felt only with him—my mate.

His hands gripped my hips as he leaned down to kiss me. As soon as our lips touched, an inferno of desire swept through me, intensified through our bond. I never wanted to let him go; just stay here and melt into him forever.

We separated much too soon, and I gazed up at him through damp eyelashes. "Don't do anything stupid."

"I think that warning is better directed at one stubborn phoenix," he said with a grin.

We'd said these exact words only a few months ago before facing William and my subsequent discovery of Mirognya.

"Hell hath no fury like *this* stubborn phoenix. I've kept

myself alive and free despite repeated attempts to fix that problem."

"Seriously, Veronica." My heart skipped a beat when he said my name, as it always did. His soulful gaze danced between my eyes. "I love you, and I need you. No heroics."

I was so tired of not getting to enjoy a normal life with this man, but after today, I would get my happily ever after or die trying. "I love you, too. If anyone's the hero here, it's you."

I let him go and watched as he, Edric, and Angela clasped hands and disappeared.

Heaving a sigh, I turned my attention to the palace as shouts of alarm rang out.

My eyes widened a second before a sphere of writhing black shadows slammed into me. I flew backward, my breath whooshing out as my body jackknifed until I slammed into a group of Community members with the force of a well-thrown bowling ball.

The shadows wrapped around our arms and legs as we tumbled and tangled together, utter darkness and frigid air engulfing us. I winced as an elbow or knee jabbed into my side, and a shrill scream came from somewhere within our pileup. It was quickly drowned out by the sounds of rising snarls and shouts.

If this fae spell was anything like the Reaper's Shadow, then we didn't have long before it destroyed our lives—and possibly our souls. My pulse quickened as I called up my fire and latched onto the closest shadowy tendril binding my arms. The dark thread crackled and shriveled into ash, releasing one arm.

Hoping I didn't burn anyone, I set more of the shadows

on fire. The black magic writhed as my flames raced through it, devouring the shadows. Hands reached into the pileup and pulled us to our feet.

Panting, I gripped the arms of the person who helped me up, coming face to face with Xavier.

I yanked my hands from his and glared at the vampire. "Don't expect thanks."

His grin was lecherous. "I always knew you'd end up in my arms."

Ugh. My upper lip curled into a snarl, but there was no time to come up with a good retort.

All across the hill, Community members were on the move as Adam's booming voice called for the attack, and other Community leaders echoed the command. Shifters, wolves, and vampires sped down the slope toward the city while witches and warlocks set up ranged offensive spells from the hilltop.

Glittering white and blue-tinged feathers mixed with black, red, blue, and gold scales as a squadron of angels and the dragon horde spread their wings and launched into the grey sky. Reapers teleported to and from different spots against the dome's base, slicing at the shield with their scythes and magic.

Spells, bullets, and even arrows flew back and forth, but everything we sent at them bounced harmlessly off the dome shield protecting those within. There had to be a way to bring it down.

An earthshaking boom roared across the field as the fae within the city detonated a magical bomb. The spell shot through the dome as if it didn't exist and landed on a group of shifters, exploding with icy shrapnel. Debris and crystalized body parts flew in all directions.

The first casualties had arrived, along with the first wave of grief. It wasn't a big surprise that the Winter Court fae had sided with Colin, but they would soon regret that decision.

I drew Lisa from her sheath and unfurled my fiery wings. Beside me, Lena shifted into falcon form and loosed a defiant screech. We left the ground and followed the swooping falcons, bellowing dragons, and soaring angels as we all raced for the dome.

The battle had begun.

Black lightning snapped out from the shield, electrocuting a falcon who'd reached the upper exterior. The steaming bird dropped like a stone to the ground, where it disappeared beneath dozens of unseelie fae streaming out of the city gate. The creatures had left the safety of the magical bubble and scrambled toward the approaching army, hunger all too obvious in their focused expressions.

Sorrow blended with fear squeezed my lungs. The shifters caught by the earlier bomb and the trampled phoenix were among many who would die today, and even more who would wish for death if caught by an unseelie. There was nothing I could do now except fight.

And win.

I swooped down toward the nightmarish fae and rained liquid fire upon them. My magic poured from my hand like lava, an inferno washing over their grotesque bodies. It drowned and melted anything that moved.

As I shot back up to join the dragons, Imos's serpentine tail smacked against the wavering dome, generating sparks but failing to make a dent. He dropped his giant maw open and spewed deadly fire onto the shield.

Spanning out beside their alpha, the other dragons added their billowing flames to his, attempting to burn a hole through the dome.

I drew on my inner flame and threw my arm out, aiming for the same location. A fiery spear whistled through the air and slammed into the bubble, but the lance splintered into sparks and ash.

Deep rumbles shook the earth below me, and I spun to search for the source. A wide swath of trees and leaves trembled behind our army as something moved through the forest at a breakneck pace. Some *things*, and there were a lot of whatever it was.

I wanted to scream a warning, but my heart had leaped into my throat, rendering me speechless. My pulse thrashed in my ears as I gasped for air.

Oh my gods…

We had walked right into a trap.

I dove toward the hill, toward my friends and Community, beating my fiery wings with all my might and praying I would reach them in time.

Except the sight that came next stopped me short and nearly shocked me right out of the sky. I stared with my mouth hanging open, not sure I believed what I saw.

Moving trees with branches for arms and roots for legs charged out of the forest—the Guardians. They surged from the treeline like a tsunami, surpassing the gaping witches and warlocks and using their branches to thwack the unseelie who'd made it past our infantry.

Squeals of agony blended with the cacophony of battle as the trees' branches launched the fae into the air or splattered their shattered remains over the others. The unseelie tried to stop the enormous trees with their claws and teeth, only to find themselves barreled into and right over, leaving behind unrecognizable blobs and bloody smears.

Unable to resist, I let out a whoop and raised my sword. No victory yet, but our unexpected ally had to surprise Colin, too.

Spying two of the *neamh-mairbh,* the vampire-like fae we'd faced in the forest, about to surprise a distracted witch, I landed just behind the fae and swung Lisa at their exposed necks. She sliced through the first in a clean cut, its body and head toppling to the side, but she stuck partway through the next one's bones.

Screeching, the creature tried to spin around despite the blade in its neck and lashed out at me with razor-sharp claws. Black ooze that dripped from its pores splashed across the exposed part of my arm near my elbow, and a fierce sting dug into my skin.

I hissed through my teeth as I blocked its claws with my vambrace. I tapped my boot buckles together, activating the stakes. With a well-aimed roundhouse kick, the wooden points tore through the vampire-fae's throat.

Gurgling from its own black goop, the creature struggled to recover enough to retaliate. I tugged Lisa free and thrust her through the greenish-black skin covering its heart. Or what I hoped would be a heart, if it had one.

The vampire-fae's empty eye sockets locked on my face as the life drained from its body, and a chill swept over me. Even though the creature didn't have eyes, I knew it watched me, somehow, craving my flesh until it died.

I kicked the body off my blade and inspected my arm. My skin sizzled and charred wherever the liquid had landed, emitting a sulphuric scent that stung my eyes. Rubbing the remaining ooze against my pants and flushing it with my fire did little to stop the spreading burn.

A cry of fear from a warlock nearby drew me back into the battle. I would have to worry about the mysterious toxin later and hope for the best.

Because that kind of thinking always worked well, right?

CHAPTER 26

Wednesday Morning

Thane

Beneath the wavering magical dome, a sinister atmosphere encapsulated the city and palace, trapping whatever inhabitants remained in unnatural darkness. I'd realm walked us to a bushy area along the palace's foundation, where Edric assured us there would be a secret entrance.

He hadn't been wrong, and we snuck up a staircase and inside the palace halls without being caught. As we slunk farther into the castle's depths, my pulse sped up until it droned in my ears. I prayed we would reach the queen without incident.

Unlikely, but miracles did, in fact, happen.

Glued to my side, Angela trembled with each step. She adjusted her grip on the staff she carried, her wide-eyed gaze darting around like a cornered rabbit. As adjusted as she was to the supernatural world's existence, but instinct rode deep within our genetics.

It impressed me she'd made it this far without having a panic attack or trying to back out. Kit had found a worthy partner to share her life with, and I would do everything within my power to get her home safely.

A thunderous boom resounded through the palace. As the walls shook and the overhead light fixtures swung precariously from the aftermath, I met Edric's knowing gaze over Angela's head, and my mouth went dry.

The fight had started.

Edric slowed and peered around a corner before waving us forward. We snuck after him, our footsteps silent against the marble floor as we crossed a wide hallway.

Voices echoed down an adjoining corridor. Judging by the increasing volume and rushed footsteps, they would round the corner and discover us at any moment.

The prince cursed under his breath and ushered Angela and me toward an open door. "Do not make a sound," he warned as we darted inside.

The room was cozy, boasting floor-to-ceiling bookshelves on both sidewalls and several cushioned chairs. An unlit fireplace that was six feet tall from floor to mantel embellished the back wall.

Edric ruffled his hair and unbuttoned his pants,

untucking his shirt haphazardly. As he stepped back into the hallway and shut the door, the footsteps halted. I withdrew the teleportation device that held my scythe and gripped it tight, ready to activate it.

"Ah, you there," Edric addressed whoever had stopped. "My lady guest and I would like some refreshments."

"Prince Edric," said a surprised male voice, accompanied by creaking armor, "why are you entertaining on this level? We're at war."

"A guard dares to question my comings and goings in my own home?" Edric's voice rose in volume, and he slurred his words convincingly. "I can *entertain* on any damn level I want, whenever I please!"

"Yes, Your Majesty, forgive me," murmured the voice. "We will have food sent immediately to the, uh, medicinal library. Although, I would advise you and your guest against wandering the halls until the threat has passed."

I understood the guard's hesitation. Reading about medicinal herbs and remedies—or, based on my few interactions with the man, reading in general—didn't seem like something Edric often enjoyed.

As the footsteps departed, the prince called out, "And drinks! Desserts, too! I want a variety of choices. Do not return without a buffet fit for a king!"

If we weren't in hiding and killed if discovered, I would have chuckled. For all his royal haughtiness, he was sharp. His last request would keep them distracted for a few extra minutes.

We wouldn't need more than that once we reached the queen, but we had to get to her first.

The door swung open again, and Edric waved us out.

"The next patrol will be along shortly. Let's go."

Angela and I hurried after him. I'd congratulate his acting abilities later.

A few doors down, he slowed in front of a giant grandfather clock and glanced up and down the empty hallway before reaching behind it. Something clicked, and a small section of the once-seamless wall slid sideways.

I raised my eyebrows, impressed, but unexpected voices pierced the hallway's silence, including one I recognized—Colin. Judging by Angela's gasp, she recognized his voice, too. I took her hand as a precaution and hovered my thumb over the button that would trigger my scythe.

Fuck. Was this whole attempt for nothing?

Would we fail so soon?

Edric shoved us inside the dark tunnel just as Colin raised his voice to be heard from the distance, "Edric, where have you been hiding?"

"Follow this to its end, and you'll find my mother," the prince whispered, then the opening slid back into place and sealed itself shut.

Without the light from the hallway, Angela and I found ourselves in total darkness, the only sounds our ragged breathing and thumping hearts. No voices drifted through the wall, and I hoped the sound dampening effect worked both ways.

The massive clock had hidden our hasty departure, but I had to pray that Edric hadn't just forfeited his life for ours.

After waiting in the pitch black for a full minute, I determined it was safe to continue.

"Can you conjure a light?" I whispered.

Angela squeaked, followed by a shuffle, thud, and whoosh of air.

"Did you forget I was here?" I tried not to laugh as I reached toward the sound she'd made. I found her arm and pulled her to her feet.

"I'm *not* cut out for this breaking and entering crap," she muttered.

A moment later, a flickering orb illuminated the path forward.

Looking back at the wall we'd come through, it was completely smooth, with no seam marking where it had opened and no visible button or switch to activate it again. I ran a hand over the wall, admiring the work, then turned to face the awaiting darkness. "Let's go."

The orb traveled a foot ahead of us, lighting enough of our way to keep from tripping on loose rubble or tangling in cobwebs. Like rats looking for a meal, we moved within the innards of the castle with no one the wiser save Edric.

I wondered if anyone else knew of this tunnel or if the queen had created it to escape if her life was in danger. When she wasn't under Colin's magical control, that is. Perhaps the passage had always been here.

Whatever the case, I looked forward to having the time to ask those kinds of questions again soon. We would succeed, no matter the cost.

After several more twists and turns, the corridor ended at a knee-high grate close to the floor. Angela extinguished the light, and we crouched beside the slats.

Peeking through the thin angled gaps was difficult, but the room beyond appeared to be the queen's private quarters, just as Edric had said. To the left, a four-poster bed rested against the wall shared with the grate, and a small sitting area and vanity sat opposite.

One wall was glass, which would have provided an impressive view before Colin's corrupted magic spread over the city. Because it was so dark outside, fae lights flickered in wall sconces around the room.

Queen Fiadh sat on a cushioned purple and gold stool at the vanity, brushing her long golden hair and staring vacantly into the mirror. A silk robe nearly the same color as her hair covered her body and flowed to her ankles.

Edric had warned us that Colin controlled the queen like a puppet, trapped her in her own mind. But if he sent us here, I had to assume it was safe to enter.

If not, well…

I had every faith in Veronica finishing the job.

I took a deep breath and pushed the grate forward out of the wall. The queen's blue-eyed gaze flicked to meet mine in the mirror, not a trace of fear on her face. It was almost as if she expected us. My muscles tensed, but there was no going back.

The queen swiveled to face us as we climbed out of the tunnel and dusted ourselves off. Her expression was cold and impassive as she inspected us, but her gaze was sharp and focused. No sign of mind control.

"I hadn't realized I'd be entertaining guests this morning," she said as she rose, the silk robe's hem falling to brush the tops of her bare feet. "Especially with such an interesting entrance."

Okay, not expecting us, but not entirely surprised, either.

"Forgive our intrusion, Your Majesty," I said, bowing

my head. "Prince Edric sent us."

"He's alive," she breathed and clasped her hands in front of her mouth, her eyes lighting up like a summer sky. "He wouldn't tell me what he'd done with my son."

I assumed she meant Colin. "Yes, but we need to get you out of here before Colin realizes we've arrived."

Her upper lip curled in disgust. "I knew I shouldn't have simply banished him. Our long history as friends clouded my judgment. I should have killed him."

"Why did you take his wings?" Angela asked, her voice quiet. "What did he do to you?"

Despite an outer appearance of calm, the skin around the queen's eyes tightened, her gaze hardening like ice. "On the night I became queen, Colin stole my innocence and virtue against my will. His warped mind has conveniently forgotten that part, claiming it was consensual, but I will *never* forget that night and what he took from me."

Mixed emotions vied for space inside my heart and set my pulse racing. What he did was unforgivable, and I understood her regret for not killing him. Adding to my rage was how close he'd been to dating and possibly doing the same to Veronica.

Thank God she saw through some of his façade.

Angela pressed her hand over her heart, her wide brown eyes sparkling with moisture. "I'm so sorry."

"Now's your chance to remind him of the truth and execute the proper punishment." I gestured to the staff Angela held. "We have something that will break the spell binding you."

Understanding filled her eyes, and her demeanor morphed from strength and confidence into raw, vulnerable fear. "That cannot be here. He will—"

The rest of her sentence was cut off as the double doors flew open and slammed against the walls. Queen Fiadh's mouth snapped shut, and she closed her eyes. A tear rolled down her bronzed cheek.

Colin strolled into the room, smiling widely as his guards entered behind him. Beneath reddish-brown hair, his hazel gaze met mine. Despite the smile, there was nothing friendly in his expression.

"Wonderful. I was hoping you'd accompany the human," he said.

Angela gasped, gripping the staff until her knuckles turned translucent, but she didn't make a move to stop him. She simply hadn't had enough training to act from instinct yet.

Fuck!

I grabbed Angela's arm and realm walked us out of there.

Except our feet slammed back onto the same ornate floor, and we pitched forward, catching ourselves just before we fell. I glared at the fae traitor. "What did you do?"

Colin gestured to the walls and ceiling as he stepped toward the queen, stopping at her side. "The smallest amount of iron goes a long way. This room desperately needed a new paint job, and it was such an efficient way of keeping Fee from doing anything she'd regret." He stroked her cheek with the back of his hand.

Undisguised anger lashed out with his question, and the queen flinched away from his touch in a telling way. He'd hurt her before, recently.

My nostrils flared as I tried to control my outrage.

However long it took, he would pay dearly for his poor choices.

"We've put the past behind us. Isn't that right, my dear?" Sliding his arm around Fiadh's waist, he drew her to him and kissed her tear-streaked cheek.

Her chin jerked up and down, but humiliation and fury blazed from her eyes. He was controlling her movements.

Edric stumbled through the door flailing his arms, pushed from behind by a fae guard. The prince's mouth was swollen and bleeding, but he wasn't restrained.

I narrowed my eyes at him. "You betrayed us?"

"I had to," he snapped, kicking at the guard as he righted himself. He missed and almost went sprawling again. "It was the only way he'd let her go."

White-hot fury sliced through me, and I clenched my jaw tight. I knew it had been wrong to trust Xavier and a fae, and they'd used our desperation against us.

Terror clawed at my heart, every muscle in my body tensing. Xavier fought beside Veronica now, and she might not know of their betrayal yet. I glanced at the glass wall but saw only dark clouds outside. We were too high to see the battle below.

I slid my thumb over the scythe's activation switch. I had to get to her, to warn her before it was too late.

Edric glared at Colin, looking every bit the spoiled child not getting his way. "You promised."

"So I did." Colin removed his arm from Fiadh's waist and lifted her hand to his lips. "Goodbye, my love."

As he let her hand drop, her eyes flicked from Edric to Colin, widening with surprise and hope. Then her face contorted with pain. Dark shadows spread beneath the skin and veins of her hand, expanding up her arms.

"What are you doing?" Edric shouted.

Two guards grabbed his arms before he could run to her aid.

"What I promised. I'm letting her go," Colin said, watching as she backed away, shaking her head with horror.

The queen dug her nails into her skin, scratching until she bled, ripping at the ink-like magic overtaking her limbs. As the tainted spell worked its way up her neck and face, trickling into and replacing the whites of her eyes, she grabbed at her throat, gasping as if she were choking.

With a final raspy breath, she fell to her knees and collapsed sideways, dead. An oily black substance dripped onto the floor from her mouth, open forever in a silent scream.

Angela covered her mouth with a hand, her shoulders shaking as she sobbed. Edric's anguished cries and yells echoed through the room, and a deadly chill seeped deep into my bones.

I'd seen a great deal of evil in my day, both before I died and during my years as a grim reaper. I thought I'd seen the worst with Octavia and William.

I was wrong.

CHAPTER 27

Wednesday Morning

Veronica

Fucking hell. My arm hurt like a sonofabitch, and looking at it made my stomach churn. The venomous ooze—or whatever the fuck the *neamh-mairbh* secreted—had resisted my attempts to burn it away. It had eaten down to my bone, cutting through blackened skin that stunk something fierce.

I dragged my good arm across my forehead, wiping away sweat and other liquids I didn't want to think about.

The temperature had risen fast, although I was pretty sure that it was my internal heat.

What was with me and contracting crippling Community infections?

A blurred shape charged forward and slammed into me like a freight train. Then I was airborne. My butt hit the ground hard, my teeth smashing together painfully as I skidded back several feet, too stunned to move.

What the…

I blinked at the figure standing where I'd been only a moment before.

Xavier grimaced, his hands held to his chest where a thick, splintering wooden point protruded from his suit jacket. Several other spears were embedded in the ground around him, still quivering from the force of their landing.

Seriously, though, who wore a fucking suit to a war?

I mean, come on, it was—

As flecks of ash peeled off his skin and floated away, my mouth dropped open with realization. I scrambled to my feet and stared at him. "Did you just sacrifice your life for mine?"

He chuckled, then immediately winced and coughed, sending flurries of black ash fluttering from his mouth. "I'd hoped the spear would miss my second most valuable organ."

This bloodsucking shitstain (thank you, Kit, for that lovely description) had the audacity to wink. He was decaying—literally dying, the official no-coming-back kind—and cracked a dick joke, then fucking *winked*.

What in the actual fuck was wrong with men?

"But why try to save me?" I asked between clenched teeth, pissed beyond reason.

I had wanted to kill him, not some random, well-aimed fae spear.

His light brown skin color faded to an ashy grey, cracks spreading over every visible inch like fractured glass. "Because you're the only one who can do it."

One of his ears crumbled to dust and spilled down his jacket.

Gross. "Do what, Xavier? You're running out of time."

His eyes, once a rich shade of brown, dimmed. "The only one who can stop Colin if—"

More of his body disintegrated, blowing away in the wind or piling on top of his expensive dress shoes.

Was he seriously going to fall apart before telling me what the fuck he meant? "If *what?*"

"…if they fail."

His dying words caught in the wind and blew away, along with the rest of him.

The cool breeze swept across my sticky skin, bringing a hair-raising sense of foreboding. My injured arm throbbed harder as my pulse quickened.

I glanced up at the palace's spires stretching high into the sky. There was no way they would fail. They couldn't. Because that would mean the worst had happened to Angela and Thane.

And if they failed, then I would have nothing left to lose.

No one could stop me from demolishing this realm and decimating everything within it.

That was a promise.

Thane

Colin turned his icy gaze on Edric, who had slumped in the guards' hold, tears streaming down his cheeks. "Thank you for bringing them to me. You've outlived your usefulness."

He nodded to a guard, who stepped behind the wailing prince and seized his head in two gigantic hands. The guard broke Edric's neck with a quick jerk to the side, and the other two dropped his body to the floor with a thud.

Beside me, Angela went silent and stiffened, dropping her hand from her mouth back to the staff. Her knuckles whitened as she gripped it in both hands, and her wide eyes moved from Edric to Fiadh to Colin. "How could you? You said you *loved* her."

"I did, yes. Before she betrayed me." Nodding, Colin pressed his lips together as he approached us.

I stepped in front of Angela, and black scales erupted across my skin. My scythe flicked to life in my hand, and I clenched it, ready to make this fucker pay for his sins.

Colin's eyebrows lifted with a look of amusement. "I'd heard you gained that unique side effect. I look forward to gaining it myself when I take Veronica as my bride. She's a queen far worthier to be by my side, wouldn't you agree?"

A vise gripped my heart and lungs as he confessed that his obsession had moved from Fiadh to Veronica. But even if I couldn't stop him here and now, Veronica would never let him touch her. He was in for a rude awakening.

I smirked, enjoying the way it made him shift his weight with unease. "You have no idea how much I'd enjoy watching you say that to her."

"Such a pity you won't be there." Colin switched his attention to Angela and the staff. "I hear you're the bearer of Abaddon's Last Hope, which is rightfully mine."

"Rightfully?" I repeated with a laugh.

"As the most powerful fae necromancer of this time, yes, rightfully." He snapped his fingers, and an inhuman groan came from Fiadh's mouth.

The dead queen's body twitched and spasmed, her mouth opening and closing. With growing horror, I watched as Fiadh pushed herself upright with jerky movements and stood on wobbly legs. Black stains streaked down her chin, and her glossy black eyes stared forward.

My palms grew clammy, and I gripped my scythe tighter. At the snap of Colin's fingers, she'd become one of the Risen.

How in God's name was that possible?

"As I said, the Last Hope belongs to me." Colin held out his hand toward Angela. "Surely you don't want me to pry it from your cold, dead hands."

There was no more time to waste. I ran at Colin with a roar, swinging my scythe at his neck.

He flicked his wrist, and my stomach dropped to my feet as I went flying. I slammed into a wall, and the back of my head hit hard enough to shake debris loose from the ceiling. My vision spun and blurred as I collapsed in a heap.

Angela raised the staff to deflect a spell from Colin. Shadowy tendrils slithered from the steel and snatched the spell from the air, swallowing it whole. As the shadows retracted into the weapon and disappeared, I stared, bewildered.

The Last Hope hadn't done *that* trick during training.

The witch shrieked my name, stirring me from my trance. More like a concussion but still healing faster than a human. I grunted as I got back to my feet, shaking my head to stabilize my vision.

Fiadh shuffled toward Angela, who backed away and stumbled into a bedpost. I had to trust that she could handle a walking corpse.

The guards took a step toward me, but Colin held up a hand and smiled. "Oh no. This one is mine."

I went for him again.

Over and over, he knocked me aside like I was little more than a pesky fly. It was infuriating and demeaning, fueling my limbs with rage and hatred as my body dragged from fatigue. Slowly healing broken bones screamed in agony, but I refused to give up until he or I was dead.

Unfortunately, it was looking more likely that it would be me dying first. If that was the case, then I would deplete his magic, or come as close to it as possible, so that Angela could finish the job.

Somehow harnessing Winter Court magic, Colin's warped spell crushed against the scales covering my chest, coating them with a stream of frost. As my boots slid across the floor from the constant force, I gritted my teeth and raised my scythe, hoping to slice through the spell.

Angela rushed toward Colin, releasing an eardrum-shattering scream. Holding the staff like a baseball bat, she smacked him hard across the head, then gripped the weapon in both hands. She followed up with a jab beneath his chin, knocking him backward.

As his magic attack on me ceased, I stumbled forward

off-balance and grabbed the vanity to stop my fall.

Nearby, the dead queen lay on her back, contorting her limbs as she struggled to get back on her feet. Her robe had fallen open, revealing a necromancer's unmistakable enchantment etched into her chest. The swooping scabs were red and raised, recently carved.

Bile rushed up my throat, and I swallowed hard against the burn. That poor woman had suffered such brutal atrocities before dying a horrible death. He didn't even give her a chance to rest in peace.

As I raised my scythe, ready to put her out of her misery, Colin grabbed the staff on Angela's next jab. He swung her around until she crashed into a bedpost. Her head smacked against it with a loud crack, and her hands slipped off the staff.

Groaning, she slumped to the floor.

My heart—and hopes for victory—grew heavy with dread, and my shoulders dropped.

We'd failed.

Colin's eyes widened as he held up Abaddon's Last Hope. The staff shimmered and warped in his hand, contracting as it returned to its original shape. The sigils etched along the sword's steel blade and hilt pulsed once with a soft white holy light before it faded away.

Shadowy tendrils rose from the sword, looping their way up his arms and lying across his shoulders. Spectral whispers teased me from where I stood, too soft for me to understand. Colin's grip on the hilt tightened, his eyes shining with excitement. Almost rapturous.

Testing the sword's balance, he twisted it in his wrist. A giddy smile tugged at his lips. "So much hunger, such *power,* and it's all mine." He raised his gaze to mine, and I knew I faced my death yet again. Except this time would be the last. "Let's see what it can do."

He swung at me with a snarl.

I raised my arm, deflecting his blow with my dragon scales. The blade slid along my protected skin with a high-pitched squeal until the sword's magic washed over me and nullified mine. My scales retracted, leaving me as vulnerable as a human.

With a maniacal gleam in his eyes, Colin laughed and swung again, slicing across my ribs before I could knock the blade aside with my scythe. The gash stung, but I leaped to the side as he came at me again.

I faced his next lunge full-on without thinking, expecting my scales to protect me as I'd become so accustomed. My eyes widened, realizing my mistake too late.

The sword slid through my stomach like a knife through butter until the hilt hit my skin, and I stood toe-to-toe with Colin. My breaths came out hard and fast, but shock numbed the truth of the wound.

Smiling maliciously, he twisted the blade.

Excruciating pain ripped through my middle, and I grunted and stumbled back. He withdrew the sword, only to plunge it through and out my back once more. Warmth gushed down my legs. I reached up to stop the flow, but it was pointless.

I staggered to my knees, my body tingling as my strength fled.

Colin rested his boot against my chest and pushed, toppling me onto my back. It had taken little force, and I hardly felt the floor beneath me.

"I'll tell her you said goodbye." He positioned the sword over my heart. "Right before I claim her as my queen and fuck her so hard, she forgets your name."

The glass wall overlooking the city below shattered and exploded inward from the force of a deafening screech. Shards of razor-sharp glass flew in all directions, embedding in walls and furniture and raining down over me.

As my vision blurred and darkened, I was sure I was dreaming. Wings of fire beat against the wind outside the palace, and an angel of death landed gracefully on the floor. Her features contorted with lethal fury, but nothing could take away her beauty.

My mate.

Listening to her negotiate with Xavier the day before and witnessing her growth firsthand, I'd finally accepted she didn't need me—or anyone else—to defend her. She was a force to be reckoned with and more than capable of protecting herself.

Our love and commitment to each other surpassed any perceived faults or weaknesses. We complemented each other perfectly.

Had this day gone differently, we would have lived a wonderful life and grown old together, dealing with obstacles as they came *together*. I loved her with every ounce of my being, and I urged all my love through our bond.

Death had come for me today, but she would live knowing how much I loved her and always would. Someday, I would see her again.

Ready to meet my maker, I exhaled and let the impending darkness overtake me.

CHAPTER 28

Wednesday Midday

Thane exhaled, and our soul link pulsed with an intense love that nearly brought me to my knees. The link vanished, leaving behind a gaping hole in my heart. I was too late.

Blind rage, unlike anything I'd ever known, flooded through me and numbed the intense pain burning my blackened arm. The anger strengthened my flames, which searched hungrily for anything they could devour. I set my sights on Colin and the familiar sword in his grip.

Grief would have to wait.

The fae necromancer who had just killed my flame's mate stared at me with something like awe and lust, unaware he was about to die. A mistake I was happy to correct.

Two guards ran toward me. Without a drop of leniency, I threw my hand up and directed fireballs straight for them. Their uniforms caught fire at once. They yelled and fell to the floor, trying to extinguish the flames. Their screams faded away, replaced by the sounds of a crackling blaze.

"You're spectacular." Colin's gaze swept over me, enraptured. "A true queen fit to rule by my side, my true mate."

My mind reeled. How this idiot came to that conclusion was beyond me. After everything we'd been through to be together, my true mate was dead, and soon, Colin would find his place in Hell.

Gripping Lisa in both hands, I stalked toward him. He might have the Last Hope, but that detail didn't matter anymore; it had become insignificant.

Because I would end him no matter what it took or what it cost me. I would sell my soul to whatever devil wanted it if it meant vengeance would be mine.

He grinned and raised his sword in a casual yet defensive stance. "You want me to prove my dominance over you, is that it? With pleasure, my love."

Proving his dominance over me? Talk about gross. My fire snapped out, clawing at him as I closed in, only to be snuffed out as his sword swept through the flames.

"He has the Last Hope, V. I'm so sorry," Angela's voice called out weakly.

I hadn't even noticed her before now. She sat beside the bed, holding a dagger in her limp hand. Blood oozed down her face from a deep gash on her forehead.

A really disgusting-looking Fiadh was in pieces around the witch, the limbless torso lifting as she attempted to move. Her blackened mouth and eyes opened and closed, and I shuddered.

I already knew Colin had the weapon. It wasn't Angela's fault. None of this was. It wasn't anyone's fault except his. He caused all this death and destruction, and today, he would finally face the consequences of his actions.

Except my magic didn't work against him now. I would need to beat him without it.

Extinguishing my flames and wings, I held Lisa loosely by my side.

His eyebrows raised in a look of surprise. "Giving up so soon?"

I stared at the man who had forced my parents to flee their home and return to the sun far before their time, requiring that I care for Maddox alone. I stared at the man who'd had my brother's murder staged as a suicide, rendering me guilt- and grief-ridden for years.

I stared at the man who'd taken my mate's life, leaving me with nothing left to lose. He had no fucking clue he'd fucked with the wrong woman for the last time.

As I stared, Colin's gaze flicked around the room as if not understanding why I'd dropped my fire and hadn't attacked him yet.

My lips curled up into some sort of grotesque smile. "Do you still feel them?"

He frowned. "Feel who?"

"Not who, what." I circled him slowly, my steps light. "Your wings." His expression darkened with understanding, but I kept going. "She took them from you, stripped away your fae essence. *Rejected* you as a man and a worthy mate."

I enjoyed a sick sense of satisfaction watching his anger rise, and I added a taunting, sultry lilt to my words. "So I ask you again, do you still feel them? Do you go to spread them wide only to realize once again that they're gone? Do you feel them aching against your back, phantom limbs that reduce you to little more than a human?"

Angela's tired chuckle added fuel to the fire building within him.

Not that I had anything against humans, especially after befriending Angela, but it would be a low blow to him. One more jab should make him combust.

"You're so weak and pitiful, you can't even beat me without that sword's magic."

I loved being right.

His face transformed and reddened with rage, and he charged at me, raising the sword to strike me down. I parried and twirled, kicking him hard in the knee as I danced away.

He grunted and stumbled but blocked my next jab. "You're right about Fiadh. She ruined me, ruined my life. My family and friends—the entire Spring Court—wouldn't take me back. They ridiculed me, made me an outcast."

Spotting an opening as he rambled on, I lunged.

He caught and twisted my blade, knocking it aside. We circled each other, lunging and parrying.

Adrenaline would only keep me upright for so long, especially if the toxin eating my arm continued to spread. Good thing I had a host of anger issues to back me up.

"Who else could I turn to but the Winter Court?" he continued. "As all proud seelie do, I'd derided them my entire life only to discover they weren't the monsters everyone claimed them to be. No, the monsters were everyone else."

Oh, yeah. I was *sure* Colin wasn't to blame for his banishment. It must have been someone else's fault.

He launched into a series of attacks, forcing me into purely defensive moves. "They taught me how to harness magic thought long gone from the world. I was a quick study with necromancy, earning their respect, moving up in their ranks."

Gods, he sure loved hearing himself talk. My breath was getting raspier without saying a word. With any luck, he'd talk himself to death.

Sweat glistened on his forehead as we backed away, eyeing each other's movements. "I befriended the unseelie clans next and learned to control more of their shadow and ice magic. I united them with a singular goal. Then I met William and Galina and encouraged their grand plans until they blossomed. Manipulated them into doing exactly what I needed to enact my revenge."

A growl rumbled from my throat. "So you *encouraged* them to murder my family?"

His gaze raked over me, lust clouding his eyes. "Had I known you would grow up to be the perfect queen at my side, I would've convinced them that your parents' fleeing was enough."

"How very noble of you," I spat out.

"It all came together perfectly when I heard a rumor that changed everything. I discovered *this.*" He twirled the sword in his hand. "Abaddon's Last Hope. *My* last hope."

I rolled my eyes. "You know, I didn't ask for your

pathetic life story."

"Still so impatient, I see." He chuckled and shook his head, not taking my bait to rile him up. "Sophia was eager to please, believing she'd enjoy life as an angel rather than become the instrument that would form the greatest weapon of all time. She and Emilia turned out to be colossal disappointments."

Hoping to catch him off guard as he babbled, I feinted a lunge, then swung Lisa at his legs. As he attempted to deflect my swing, I drew a knife behind my back.

His sword struck against mine at the last moment, but I thrust upward with the knife. The blade sank into his side, and he bellowed in pain and anger.

I dodged his counterattack and spun away. "Let me guess where you're going with this long-winded rambling: I fucked everything up for you. Boo-fucking-hoo."

Snarling, Colin grabbed the knife's hilt and pulled it out, then tossed it to the side, where it clattered against the floor near Angela.

As if I didn't have plenty more where that came from.

Her arm lifted feebly toward the blade before dropping back to her lap, empty.

At least I knew she was still awake, still holding on.

A thunderous explosion shook the castle, and shards of broken glass clinked against the marble floor. I sent a quick prayer to Dazhbog, Ognebog, and sweet Mother Mokosh that everyone else was holding on, too. The longer this idiot delayed his inevitable death, the more others would die.

"I thought so at first," he said, his wound already healing thanks to his fae genetics. "You and Xavier. At each step, you two thwarted my plans. Xavier needed to die, but the more I studied *you*, the more I came to admire you. Your bravery and impulsive selflessness, your determination to succeed, no matter the odds stacked against you."

Remembering the vampire's sacrifice and dying words, I gripped Lisa tighter. This needed to end, and this traitorous, narcissistic fae needed to die.

If he got in a lucky strike with that sword, my soul would shatter into oblivion. Not that it mattered anymore— my heart had already fractured beyond repair.

Why not shatter my soul, too?

My legs quivered, and I almost crumbled to the floor. A trickle of overwhelming agony had slipped through my mental wall before I closed it up tight again. I needed to ensure his end before I joined my mate in death.

Tensing my muscles to pounce, I arched an eyebrow. "Your admiration is not a compliment."

"It should be. For thirty years, I've fooled everyone, including that ancient archangel and your precious ex-reaper." His lip curled into a vicious snarl. "Whatever you think you feel, Thane is—*was* not your mate."

My heart stuttered to a stop, and the distant sounds of battle faded away.

"In the end, you left me no choice," he said with a sad shake of his head. "You forced me to break the bond between you two and claim you as mine, proving to you once and for all that *I* am your true mate."

No more lies, no more caution, no more fucks.

I switched to the offense, bombarding him with everything I had, using every move in the book and several that weren't. I thrust and swiped—hell, I even bit him.

Nothing was beneath me.

Then I saw it—my opening.

After I struck his forehead with another knife's hilt, he stumbled, and I kicked. Not at him, but at the sword.

The blade flew from his hands, clattering to the floor and sliding toward Angela.

As he dove for the weapon, I jumped onto his back and drove Lisa deep into his side.

He pitched forward with a grunt. Looking down at the blade piercing him, he laughed.

Only I wasn't dumb enough to think I'd killed him. I just wanted to distract him. "Angela, now!"

With one eyelid caked shut from drying blood, the witch's hand closed on the sword's grip. She raised it in trembling hands, pointing the blade's tip at Colin. Her expression turned dark and stormy as she harnessed the sword's magic.

She screamed out her hatred for the fae man, and a flash of black lightning blasted from the sword. I ducked behind Colin, letting him take the brunt of it.

His body shook violently beneath my hands as the magic grabbed on and ripped into him. His skin warmed beneath my hold, and while it didn't hurt, I didn't want to get caught in the crossfire. Yanking Lisa free as I rolled away, I crouched a short distance away.

When Angela's scream died out, she dropped her arms with a sob, and the sword's magic released him.

Colin fell to his knees, breathing heavily. With a look of horror, he held his hands before his face. Steam rose from his clothes and hair, but he didn't appear injured. "No, this can't be possible."

I glanced at Angela, not sure what she'd done to him. I'd kind of expected him to be dead, and I was even okay not being the one to kill him. She glared at him with her good eye, a fierce stare that clearly said she wanted him dead, too.

The queen's torso slumped to the ground with a thud, lifeless.

My head jerked back as the realization hit me.

Colin's magic was gone.

The fae man—or I guess, basically human now—glared at Angela, savage cruelty twisting his once handsome features into that of a monster. "You can't do this to me." Staggering to his feet, he leaped for her with his hands outstretched.

Only I got there first.

I dropped Lisa and grabbed him by the throat, using my inhuman strength to lift him to his toes. His eyes watered as he tugged at my hand, but my grip was ironclad. I carried him to the now open window and stepped over the debris to the very edge, glass crunching beneath my boots.

Fierce winds snagged at my clothes and hair. The city lay several hundred feet below us, and this fae fuck didn't have magic or wings.

A steady thrum beating against the air signaled a winged creature's arrival right before Adam touched down, avoiding the glass littering the floor. He folded his wings and quickly surveyed the scene, glancing from Angela to Thane to the queen and prince's bodies, then to Colin and me.

Nathan and Jessa landed next to him, and Jessa rushed inside.

"Ms. Neill, let us take it from here." Adam's voice was calm as he looked from me to Colin, whose feet still dangled over nothing but air.

The fae man's eyes rolled wildly with fear, and he clutched my arm for dear life.

Good.

I wanted him to feel absolute terror before he plummeted to his death. He deserved nothing less.

"Veronica, please. Let me take him," Adam urged.

I waited for Colin to meet my gaze. His blue-green eyes pleaded with me, but I had no mercy to give. "Like I've always said, I'm not a fucking hero."

Then I let him go, and his screams faded away.

CHAPTER 29

Wednesday Midday

Unfortunately, my bliss at hearing Colin's screams was short-lived. Nathan tucked his blue-tinged wings close to his body as he dove to catch the fae man who'd ruined my life and so many others'. The angel grabbed him by the ankle, and I sighed.

Well, I tried. At least Colin thought he was going to die.

I stood there, my chest heaving and my arm throbbing, afraid to turn around. I wasn't ready to face the truth, to admit that I'd lost everything. My parents, my brother—

Oh, gods…

My legs buckled beneath me, and I collapsed. Glass dug through my pants and into my palms, but the only thing I felt was debilitating grief. I freed the violent sob I'd held back since our link vanished.

Behind me, a wild blast of heat and light nearly toppled Adam and me off the ledge after Nathan, and Angela screamed. The archangel spread his wings to keep his balance and shield me, his wide-eyed expression mirroring mine.

Raising my good arm against the settling debris, I stood and pushed past Adam's feathers to find out what had just happened.

Dark smoke and ash choked the room, concealing almost everything within. A pinkish sparkle appeared through the drifting haze by the bed, revealing Jessa's pearlescent wings curled around Angela. As the dust settled, the red-headed angel spread her wings and beat them against the air, clearing out some of the smoke.

Dried blood still covered Angela's face, but the wound in her hairline had sealed shut under angelic care. Her eyes were opened wide, and she seemed more alert than when she'd turned Colin into a magical eunuch.

A thick layer of smoke and settling debris floated where Thane had fallen and obscured his form. My breath caught in my throat.

In my rush to kill Colin, had I missed a bomb he'd planted?

Had he destroyed Thane's body as a final guarantee to keep us apart?

As my heart beat furiously, demanding to be free of my chest, I hurried over and fell to my knees beside Thane. I reached out to touch his body.

Except partway there, I froze, and everything went numb.

Thane blinked in confusion and sat up, unharmed and completely naked. Fresh as a newly hatched chick.

Afraid I was hallucinating, I ran my fingers over his unbroken skin, covered only by a layer of ash and dust. I didn't understand what I was seeing.

"What just happened?" he asked, glancing down at his body.

"You just resurrected," I whispered, hardly able to take a breath, "like a phoenix."

His eyebrows drew together. "What? How?"

Shoes crunched over the glass, and I glanced up at Adam with wide eyes. "Did you do this?"

Slowly, the archangel shook his head, his expression incredulous.

A loud gasp rang out from where Angela and Jessa had been, but I was too stunned to differentiate who'd made the sound.

"You've done well, my daughter," a woman said. Her pleasant voice chimed like a dozen tiny bells.

A figure emerged from a sudden blaze that blinded me with its intensity. The fire's heat warmed my skin, then disappeared altogether.

I blinked away the spots in my vision and focused on the woman standing beside Adam, who had bowed his head.

Long, strawberry-blonde hair fell in gentle waves to the woman's waist, and a simple white dress covered her body. A wreath of flowers adorned her head like a crown, and rainbow-hued eyes like Pietr's, shifting colors as quickly as the ocean, regarded me.

She smiled, and everything was right in the world. "I am so proud of you, Veronica. We all are."

"Who are you?" I asked, hardly able to breathe as I stared up at a deity. There was no other explanation. "Who's *we*?"

Thane's hand slipped into mine and squeezed.

"Who I am depends on several factors, as I am the mother goddess of all living creatures." She clasped her hands in front of her. "You know me as Mokosh, while our brave witch over there calls me Diana. Dazhbog, Ognebog, and many others send their blessings and heartfelt thanks. To all of you."

A goddess was thanking me? Was this a dream?

Had I died?

I blinked. "How are you here? Why? What's going on?"

Mokosh laughed, the contagious sound brightening my soul. "Dazhbog was right—you do ask many questions." Heat rose in my cheeks, but she shook her head softly. "Never stop, my darling. Questions produce knowledge, and knowledge is the greatest weapon of all. The answer to all your questions is simple: I am worshipped in every realm. Therefore, I may go wherever I wish.

"As a token of my gratitude for what you have accomplished here today, I bestowed the gift of a phoenix lifetime upon your mate. Your one *true* mate and a union blessed by the gods." She winked as if sharing a joke among friends.

Pressing a hand to my lips, I laughed. Or maybe I sobbed. I didn't even know anymore, but I threw myself at Thane, knocking him flat on the floor again, and kissed him hard.

After a moment of surprise, he wrapped his arms around me, holding me close as he kissed me back. As our tongues met in a familiar dance, I felt whole again. Heat swirled around us, and love pulsed between our renewed soul link.

Something else pulsed against me, too.

Thane groaned and broke the kiss. His deep blue gaze searched mine, ravenous with desire. "Let's finish this moment later, or everyone here will become a voyeur, including a goddess."

I laughed and kissed him again without a care in the world.

Adam cleared his throat. "Many thanks to you and the others, Mother Mokosh."

Somehow finding the strength to extract my limbs from Thane's, I stood and helped him to his feet while eyeing his sizable erection in appreciation.

Shooting me an exasperated look, he spun me around by the shoulders. He held my body in front of his and wrapped his arms around me.

His goal was probably to hide his obvious state of arousal, but all he did was rub it against my butt, which only made him—and me—pulse harder.

Grinning, I met Mokosh's sparkling gaze. "I don't know what to say except thank you, sincerely. From the bottom of my no-longer-shattered heart."

She lowered her chin in acknowledgment, then looked at Angela. "Come here, my child."

The witch thought she'd seen it all when she met Imos and Tundreg. Now she could add meeting a goddess to her list of firsts, a feat most Community members could only dream about.

Angela's thick curls were grey from soot, her black beanie nowhere in sight, and so much dried blood and ash covered her skin that she was almost unrecognizable. Dropping her gaze, she gulped as she approached.

Mokosh placed her hand beneath Angela's chin and lifted it until the witch looked at her. "A blessing upon you as well, dear one. May you enjoy several centuries of love and laughter with your Katherine."

My mouth dropped open, and I gripped Thane's arms.

Angela's face crumpled as she burst into tears. She threw her arms around Mokosh and hugged her tight.

The goddess let out a surprised laugh and returned the embrace.

I tilted my head to smile at Thane. The nightmare was over, and we could finally go home.

He pressed his lips against mine, but even that soft touch was enough to ignite a passion so deep, I thought I'd combust on the spot. I pulled away to thank Mokosh once again for her gift.

Except when I looked back, the goddess was gone.

Shortly after we met Mokosh, the war was over. When Colin had lost his magic—no, when Angela stripped that motherfucker of his ability to ruin people's lives like the fucking badass she turned out to be—the dome covering the city had popped like a bubble.

All the magic stripping the capital of its beauty

dissipated, and the grey clouds that loomed overhead broke apart and drifted away. The sun shone down, reflecting off the golden hue of the cobblestone roads and the lake's crystal-blue water as gentle waves lapped against the city docks.

We found Thane some clothes, then stood at the open ledge of the queen's quarters and stared out over the city, watching as it regained its crystalline glimmer.

After Jessa had healed my arm and lectured me for being near death yet again, she and Adam had flown down to meet with our troops and end any further fighting. Lena had flown up to squawk at me for my reckless endangerment. When she failed to get a rise out of me and eventually given up, she'd moved on to enjoying Angela's dramatic reenactment of the ordeal with Colin.

Without Colin's abomination of blended magics strengthening and urging them on, the unseelie who'd enjoyed life under his brief reign fled back into the forests. Seelie fae and the Guardians chased after them, striking down and stomping the stragglers without mercy.

Before leaving the queen's destroyed room, Adam had informed us that Nathan had taken Colin back to the human world and straight to the maximum-security prison. It wasn't the outcome I wanted for the bastard, but I would have to accept it—for now. He would still have a sentencing that would most likely result in his death.

If not, I could always plan a breakout and kill him myself.

Time would tell how merciful I would be because I wasn't feeling it right now.

While our casualties were more significant than I'd

hoped for, they gave their lives to free us—to free the *world*. We would honor their sacrifice forever, and I would make sure the Community never forgot.

When Angela's tale ended, she and Lena joined us on the room's ledge. The phoenix woman had no risk of falling, but it surprised me how fearless Angela was, holding the staff upright and standing with her toes right up to the edge.

This day had changed us all.

"Ready?" Thane asked.

"Not yet." I walked back to Fiadh's broken body and knelt beside her. After closing her eyes, I took her hand. "I'm so sorry you didn't live to see this, but your kingdom is free. *You're* free, and so is your son. Rest in peace."

Thane's warm presence neared as he crouched beside me. Except he pressed his lips together tight. He flicked her golden robe to the side by her neck, just enough to reveal scarred skin beneath.

My inner flame shrunk to a pinprick, realizing what that monster had done. I hadn't even thought about the fact that necromancers had to carve symbols into their target's flesh. And since Colin hadn't done it after he'd killed her, he had cut into her while she was still alive.

I closed my eyes and shuddered, allowing Thane to draw me away.

By the time we realm walked to the castle's lower level, a small contingent of Summer Court fae and angels had gathered together in the front entryway. Pietr, Imos, and a handful of others had joined them.

As we approached the group, I narrowed my eyes at the fae. Where the fuck had these assholes been this whole time? As far as I was concerned, they'd enabled this shitshow.

I strode right up to the fae like I owned the place. Not that I wanted to rule the Otherworld—I didn't even want to oversee my own world, for flame's sake—but if we followed conquering rules, this palace was mine.

Adam spoke up before I could utter a word, "Ms. Neill, I would like to introduce you to Méabh Fagan, next in line for the royal crown. Colin has held her and the others captive in the dungeons for eighteen years."

Holding back my accusation, I nearly choked on my spit.

Eighteen *years* held as prisoners?

Now that I took a good look, the five fae gathered were like walking corpses. Dirt and other stains I didn't want to know the origins of covered their bodies and clothes, which were filled with holes and barely clinging to their skeletal forms.

The woman Adam introduced was beyond frail, and her long stringy hair was dark with grime and missing in patches from her scalp. I couldn't even tell what color it had been.

The saddest part was that fae didn't age like humans did, which meant Colin's magic had been draining her life force much like Octavia's had done to Angela. Except he had drained theirs for eighteen godsdamn years.

Sweet Mokosh, Colin's depravity knew no bounds.

The fae held themselves tall and proud despite their poor health, though two cast nervous glances around the area. I could only imagine what horrors they had faced as Colin's prisoners, and they would no doubt look over their shoulders in fear for the rest of their lives.

"I'm so sorry for everything that's happened to you and your people, Queen Méabh," I said, meeting her lilac gaze.

"We'll help you rebuild the Summerlands, whatever you need, and reestablish trust between our realms."

Her eyes glistened with tears, but not a single drop spilled over. She gave a quick nod. "Thank you, tsarina. We welcome your help."

I held up my hands and laughed. "Just don't call me that. We agreed to dissolve the phoenix monarchy and form a council instead. I hope we can be friends. You can call me Veronica."

She smiled. "It would honor me to have you as a friend."

After a round of introductions followed by gushing thanks and pleasantries, Angela and I were itching to escape. I wasn't one for political anything, and Angela wanted to check on Kit and announce the good news.

Méabh tasked two of her fae with opening a new portal once Kit released hers. Then we would begin the slow process of getting everyone home, either to the human realm or beyond. This wasn't my mess to clean up, and I was glad of it.

Well, it kind of was my mess, but more organized people were managing it.

Thane jumped us back to the human hotel where Kit waited. A group of reapers stood around the chalk circle, prepared to defend the witch in case of an attack. Their faces lit up with excitement when we arrived and shared our victory.

As expected, Kit was beyond exhausted, her legs wobbling. She released the portal, which swirled into a pinprick of light before disappearing altogether.

Angela ran to her, holding her upright before she could collapse.

"It's really over?" Kit asked, her voice hoarse from all the chanting over the last few days.

"It's really over." I smiled. "But I'm sad I didn't get to kill Colin."

Her face darkened as she leaned on Angela. "You and me both. He'll be dead soon enough, mark my words."

Her words carried a note of premonition, and I prayed she was right.

CHAPTER 30

Wednesday Night

Back at my penthouse, Thane and I took the longest, steamiest shower of our lives, reuniting in the best way possible. When I finally dressed in a silk nightgown that barely covered my butt, I joined Thane on the terrace. We were completely alone for the first time in *months.*

Ivan had jumped Lena home to Mirfeniksa to check on her twin sister Liz, who'd stayed behind with Oleg to monitor things. Lena warned me they wouldn't be gone long, even though I'd reminded her I wasn't royalty and didn't need a bodyguard.

Unfortunately, she didn't seem to care. Whether I was royalty, a council member, or just plain Veronica, she would be by my side forever.

According to her, I was too chaotic and impulsive not to have a full-time bodyguard, but I was almost positive she thought her sword would get more use if she stuck with me. She probably wasn't wrong.

I approached the chaise where Thane sat, and he drew me onto his lap. I laid my head against his chest, listening to the steady rhythm of his heartbeat as he stroked my hair. The moon was only a sliver in the clear night sky, but the city provided more than enough light to see the cresting waves.

With the battle in the morning and all the time we spent in the shower this evening, I would have thought I'd be too exhausted for any more action.

Turned out I was wrong.

Thane's grip tightened in my hair, tilting my head back. Raw hunger lit his blue eyes from within, lightening the hue to sapphire. My body wasted no time reacting in kind.

Our mouths crashed together in our urgency. Without breaking the kiss, I moved up to kneel on the chaise and straddle his lap. Our tongues danced together as his straining erection pressed into me through our clothes.

His hands slid up my thighs and under my nightgown, his touch scorching my skin as he continued upward. His thumbs brushed against my bare breasts, and I moaned into his mouth before breaking the kiss and removing the dress altogether.

It disappeared into the terrace shadows or fell over the edge. Those details didn't matter right now.

I tugged his shirt over his head and raked my nails down his bare chest, leaving red marks and earning a deep growl from him. He grabbed my lacy thong in one hand and yanked hard, ripping it from my body, then slipped his fingers inside me.

My head fell back as he thrust and stroked, until he gripped my neck in his free hand and drew my mouth to his. His tongue devoured mine as his thumb circled my clit. I moaned again, deeper, and rolled my hips in time with his fingers.

As my movements grew more frenzied, the need to release rose, and so did my internal heat. Knowing I was close, I panted against his mouth and stopped moving against him. "I want you inside me when I come. *All* of you."

Faster than most humans would be capable, Thane's shorts were off, and his unrestrained cock glistened with his readiness. I slid onto his length and pressed my forehead against his. I whimpered in pleasure as he stretched and filled me.

"God, you feel perfect," Thane groaned and dug his hands into my hips, holding me firmly against him. "So fucking warm and wet for me."

We moved slower than before, my hips rolling against his and our gazes locked together. My love for this man knew no end, and his matching emotions resonated through our soul link. He completed me, and not in a sad, codependent way. We were fine on our own.

But together, we brought out the best in each other.

Thane's strokes grew faster, more urgent, building our need to claim each other fully. As the intense heat rose within me, I sat back and rode him hard. My fingernails dug into his shoulders.

His hand moved off my hip and rubbed my clit with his thumb, while the other rose to cup my breast and lightly pinch my nipple. His gaze penetrated mine, fucking me with his eyes as much as his hands and cock.

As I panted, about to release, my fiery wings unfurled. I cried out, and fireworks exploded behind my eyes. A raging fire overtook my senses as my orgasm consumed me.

Gripping my hips again, Thane thrust fast and deep until he released inside me with a groan. Pleasure unlike anything I'd ever known spread through me, electrifying and igniting my entire body.

Something new had happened, something beautiful and powerful.

Gasping, I opened my eyes. Flames engulfed us. My legs were wrapped around his black-scaled waist, my arms around his neck. We were suspended above the chaise as my wings beat against the night air.

I met Thane's shocked gaze and slowly returned us to the singed and smoking chaise. "Well, that was a new one."

He grinned as I doused my flames. "Time for some sturdier chairs."

I laughed as he scooped me up and carried me into the bedroom.

CHAPTER 31

Three Months Later

othing in my life had ever been easy—until now. In fact, life was just about perfect these days. No more wars, no more subterfuge (other than my own making, of course).

Thane and I finally had our chance to enjoy life as a couple, spending every night together while resuming normal activities during the day.

Semi-normal, anyway.

It had taken a month to clean up Colin's mess and bury or burn the dead in the Otherworld. We worked non-stop to erect funeral pyres, rebuild the capital, and remove the last traces of Colin's contaminated magic.

Likely because of their guilt for siding with William initially, Rico's shifters had volunteered to lead the infantry's charge, which resulted in most of the clan's deaths. But Luka had kept his promise and then some to the survivors. Instead of forming an alliance, he'd invited the few remaining shifters, including his brother, to join his pack.

Sure, Tabitha had grumbled a bit, but she wasted no time feeding them and finding them places to stay. A true momma wolf and alpha's mate.

Once we'd returned home for good, Thane had given in to Adam's incessant requests to work for the DEA. I'd just smiled when he told me, knowing he wouldn't last as a kept man. Thane needed to stay busy as much as I did and loved his job at the DEA. For now, he would train new grim reapers.

Adam had surprised us all when he turned down a promotion. Not just any promotion, mind you—his fucking retirement. As in everlasting peace in his god's heaven.

And why would he do such a nonsensical thing? Because he claimed to love Earth too damn much.

Fucking crazy if you asked me.

His newest mission was persuading the upper levels of the DEA to change the agency's rules about not getting involved with other realm affairs. Had we had other branches' help from the beginning, we would have squashed Colin like the cockroach he was long before my parents fled Mirognya.

Too many lives were lost or destroyed because of a stupid, out-of-date rule. Well, to be fair, it was all Colin's fault for not accepting his role in life, but I hoped Adam's mission would be successful.

Speaking of Mirognya, I'd spent a week helping the phoenixes and dragons set up their new council governing the three territories. I'd even met the merfolk of Mirvody, and I was sure I made a fool of myself over their tails.

The merfolk I'd met in the human realm walked on two legs and didn't like it when I'd asked for a glimpse of their tails. In fact, they'd found it downright offensive, but how was I supposed to know they considered it rude?

Anyway, I'd turned down all attempts at making me a permanent part of the council. I was one of the worst people for the job; I just needed to convince everyone else of that fact.

Seriously, wasn't my track record proof enough?

Yeesh.

In other good news, Jackson was back in prison with beefed-up security. While I wished he'd died a horrible death, I was okay with this outcome. Plus, Lisa and I would happily hunt him down if he escaped again.

Even better? I'd discovered a passion for wedding planning. We were only a few short weeks away from Kit and Angela's big day, and I couldn't be happier for my best friends.

Since Kit had inherited Parker House, and I'd lived up to my promise of a deep cleaning—physical *and* psychic—it had turned out to be the perfect venue. Especially because her mother couldn't crash the party, what with her several life sentences.

My maid of honor dress was stunning—a first in modern history—and I couldn't wait to show it off on that dance floor.

Angela had no desire to keep Abaddon's Last Hope,

proving once again that she was the right person to wield it. Thankfully, Adam had discovered how to break the bond fusing the three daggers together. With the help of a demon who'd befriended Kit and Dr. Owen Cooper, the DEA's resident mortician and part-time necromancer, they destroyed the daggers forever.

I didn't understand their newfound friendship with a *demon* of all things, but who was I to judge?

But the best news of all?

Colin was dead. For real dead, not like Xavier-faked-his-death dead, before he actually ended up dead-dead.

Along with a multitude of eager Community members, I watched the fae man's execution. When his heartbeat flatlined, and his body burned to ashes on the pyre (*way* too nice of a gesture, if you asked me), a weight lifted from my shoulders.

There would be no Rising in his future.

I'd avenged my family at last, and I could finally move past all that anger and grief.

So what was a girl to do with her time?

Well, I still had a shitton of money, so I did what any sane, no-longer-royal woman would do—I bought the Morning Grind.

That's right, I was Isaac's boss now. Too bad I didn't get to rub it in his face. The man's personality had done a one-eighty after meeting his so-called soulmate.

No, I wasn't being judgy—humans didn't really have soulmates. Only those with special abilities like mages, witches, or the rare case of realm walkers. Regardless, I wished Isaac nothing but the best.

Besides, I'd fire his ass so fast if he ever returned to

being an ungrateful shithead.

I broke down the last few cardboard boxes from the daily supply order, stacking them next to the trash can, and headed out of the coffee shop's backroom. Smiling, I stood with my hands on my hips and surveyed my newest adventure.

Three baristas worked behind the counter, restocking low supplies and whipping up caffeinated masterpieces while they chatted and laughed. Joe sat on his usual stool, sipping his espresso and scrolling through his phone. College students with laptops and stacks of books and a group of moms with strollers occupied the remaining tables.

The front door opened, and Thane walked in. Even though he still wore dark sunglasses, I felt his gaze land on me. His love radiated through our bond, and I practically swooned where I stood.

And here I thought I wasn't the swooning type of girl.

Guess it just took the right guy.

"Ivan, I'm going to lunch," I called over to where he stood behind the counter.

Yep, the young phoenix who reminded me so much of my little brother worked for me. He loved the human world and all the perks that came with it, mainly the video games, nightlife, and, of course, Morning Grind coffee.

Deep in a conversation with another barista about some new game release, he waved over his shoulder as I removed my apron and tucked it under the counter. He might have been new at the human job gig, but I trusted him with my life. I knew he could manage the shop.

After grabbing my purse, I met Thane by the door and looped my arm through his. We'd made plans for lunch down the street at a new Cuban restaurant I'd been dying to try out. These days, I was absolutely ravenous by lunchtime.

We walked in silence for a bit, enjoying each other's company. The sun was shining in a bright blue sky, and seagulls cawed overhead as they soared toward the ocean. Dazhbog had blessed us with this gorgeous day like he knew what I'd planned.

Judging by his past comments about my life, he probably did.

As usual, Lena watched over us from above, drawing lazy circles in the air as she enjoyed the cool breeze. Not long after returning from Mirognya, I'd somehow convinced her to take a trip to Italy to visit Holly.

She hadn't come back for almost a month, and when she did, it was with the best news—Holly was her flame's mate. She was beyond smitten. In fact, I was close to convincing her I no longer needed a bodyguard. So close.

"I heard the news," Thane said.

I repressed the urge to pout. It wasn't a pretty look on a grown woman. "Who told you?"

Shooting me a curious look, he waited to answer until we passed a busy bus stop. "Adam. I'm pretty sure he's keeping it a secret from most of the Community for now."

I was also pretty sure we were thinking about different news. "Right…what secret is this?"

"A new Keeper of the Forest was born," he said.

My loud gasp caused a few passing humans to glance over in suspicion. I squeezed his hand. "Isn't it so exciting? I hadn't even thought about how that worked."

He grinned. "Thought he had just appeared one day?"

"I'm sure I'm not the only one." I gave a teasing huff. "So what happens next?"

We stopped at a red light, waiting to cross the street.

"The little guy will grow up, then do exactly what his predecessor did," he explained.

The light changed to green, and we crossed to the next sidewalk. The new restaurant was only a block away, and my pulse thundered in my ears. It was almost go-time.

Thane glanced down at me. "I can feel your tension. What's wrong?"

"I wouldn't call it *wrong*," I said with a coy smile.

He smirked, sending tingles through my body. "Don't be a tease."

I laughed. "You should know better than to ask an impossible thing like that."

"Okay, then what's going on in that beautiful head of yours?"

Removing my hand from his, I stopped and took out the small gift box hiding in my purse. I'd thought about giving it to him over lunch, but I hadn't planned on him sensing something off so soon.

Plus, I was too damn excited to wait any longer.

I handed him the box, grinning at the surprised look on his face.

"Did I forget an anniversary or something?" he asked, grimacing.

I nudged him. "Just open it."

He untied the ribbon and removed the top. A tiny ceramic bird's nest and egg sat snugly within, and he frowned in confusion. When he read the date painted on the egg, almost nine months from now, sudden realization registered on his face.

His sapphire gaze snapped up to meet mine. "Is this real?"

"It's real." Smiling, I took his free hand and rested it on my stomach. "We're having a baby."

He slammed the cover back over the bird's nest and egg and swooped me up into his arms, spinning us around. "I'm going to be a dad!" he yelled out, earning smiles and even a few cheers from pedestrians nearby.

Life would be easy for a few more months, then it was on to our next chaotic adventure.

I'd finally gotten my happy fucking ending.

No pun intended.

That's a lie—pun *totally* intended.

THE END

GLOSSARY

Adam Larue – Archangel of the Miami DEA branch

Adrik – phoenix; rebel leader

Albert Renauldo, Dr. – human plastic surgeon; owns Star Island mansion

Anastasia – phoenix; captive

Annika – phoenix; high priestess

Anthony "Tony" – piano shop owner; friend of Veronica

Becca – grim reaper; Adam's receptionist

Bianca D'Angelo – vampire; Queen of the European Vampire Association

Bolgar – Mirfeniksan city where Zasha lives

Brandon – grim reaper trainee of the DEA

Broderick Ó Faoláin – fae duke; *deceased*

Colin Ó Broin – Spring Court fae

Charlotte Blanchet – Master Vampiress in the European Vampire Association

chort – "shit"

Dazhbog – Mirognyan sun god; primary deity and known as the Father

Death Enforcement Agency – also known as the DEA; agency of the human world that keeps the Community safe

Drystan Neill – phoenix; Veronica's father; real name Dmitrei Vasiliev; *deceased*

durak – "fool"

Edric – fae prince; Fiadh's son

El Sombra Mercado – also known as the Shadow Market; safe haven for Community members

Emilia Delacroix – Master Vampiress of Miami; *deceased*

Enrique Alvarez – human street musician

Federico Russo – natural born warlock; *deceased*

Feodora – phoenix; rebel leader

Fiadh – fae queen; Edric's mother

Fortunato – vampire; one of the *veteres*, the originals; *deceased*

Frank Turner – human mage; ex-necromancer

Gabriel – Master Vampire in the European Vampire Association

Galina Volkov – grim reaper; usurper; *deceased*

Gavan (Haven) – phoenix rebel hideout; also known as Haven

Giovanni "Joe" Facchini – fae regular of The Morning Grind

Holly – natural born witch; Kit's friend

Imos, the Great – dragon; alpha

Inessa – phoenix; Pietr's mother, Tundreg's mate

Isaac Davidson – human manager of The Morning Grind; Veronica's ex-boss

Ivan – phoenix; rebel

izbrannyy – "Chosen One"

Jackson Reed – realm walker

Jessa – angel; healer

Julian – werewolf cub; Tabitha's son

Katherine "Kit" Parker – natural born witch; Veronica's best friend

Katya – phoenix; Haven birdkeeper

Kira – phoenix; captive

Lizabeta "Liz" – phoenix; healer

Luciana Pérez – natural born witch; owner of The Witch's Brew shop in *el Sombra Mercado*

Luka Navarro – werewolf; alpha of the Miami pack; Tabitha's mate

Maddox "Mad" Neill – phoenix; Veronica's brother; *deceased*

Mama Anya – phoenix; midwife

Manuel – warlock; owner of food truck in *el Sombra Mercado*

Méabh Fagan – fae prisoner

Mila – phoenix; rebel leader

Mirdrakona – dragon lands within Mirognya

Mirfeniksa – phoenix lands within Mirognya

Mirognya – "world of the sun"

Mirvody – merfolk waters within Mirognya

Mokosh – Mirognyan earth goddess; known as the Mother

moya koroleva – "my queen"

Myldrur, the Patient – dragon; Imos's son

Nathan – angel; fighter

neamh-mairbh – unseelie fae; means "walking dead" but similar to vampires

Octavia Parker – natural born witch; Kit's mother

Officer Harris – receptionist at prison; species unknown but most likely a troll

Ognebog – Mirognyan god of fire

Oleg – phoenix; rebel fire communicator

Owen Cooper, Dr. – head mortician and grim reaper at the DEA

Papa Boris – phoenix

Pavel – phoenix; rebel; *deceased*

Philip – Master Vampire in the European Vampire Association

Pietr – phoenix; rebel leader; Inessa's son

Rhiannon Neill – phoenix; Veronica's mother and previous tsarina; real name Mirilla Vasiliev; *deceased*

Rico – werewolf; leader of the Hollow Hounds rogue pack; Luka's brother

Rogelio Diaz – natural born warlock; deep in his cup somewhere

Romid, the Bold – dragon; Imos's son

Rozanica – Mirognyan three goddesses of fate

Shirley – vampire; Octavia's maid

Sokol – Mirfeniksa's capital city

Sophia Clark – grim reaper agent of the DEA

Suzdal – small town in Mirfeniksa

Tabitha Delgado – werewolf; Luka's mate, Julian's mother

Taisiya – phoenix; rebel leader

Thane Munro – ex-grim reaper; Veronica's mate

The Morning Grind – a DC-based coffee shop in Miami

Tsitadel – griffin stronghold in Vechnyy Mountains

Tundreg, He Who Sees – dragon; seer; Inessa's mate

Vechnyy Mountains – mountain range in Mirdrakona

Veronica "V" Neill – no longer the last phoenix

veteres – original kings and queens of the vampires

Viktor – phoenix; rebel spy

Vincenzo Morelli – vampire; King of the European Vampire Association

Vladimir – phoenix; palace guard

Walter Whitmore – human; Octavia Parker's butler

William Caomhánach – Winter Court fae and unseelie; *deceased*

Xavier Garcia – Master Vampire of Miami

Yazyk – phoenix language

Yelena "Lena" – phoenix; rebel

Yury – phoenix; rebel scout

Zasha – phoenix; Veronica's aunt

Zastava – phoenix outpost at the base of the Vechnyy Mountains

ACKNOWLEDGEMENTS

I feel like the luckiest girl in the world because I get to do what I love every single day, all because of the unbelievable and ongoing support I receive. This series wouldn't exist without my husband, mother-in-law, and my entire amazing family, who believe in me no matter how difficult the road is/has been.

I can't thank my beta readers enough for sticking with me through the entire series: Marty, Tom, Kimmie, Jessica, Alisha, Rachel, and Erica. Amazingly, they all signed up to beta read my next books, too! You guys rock!

Once again, Claire Holt designed a cover I fell in love with to complete the series epically, and I hope you feel the same.

Thank you to all my friends, family, and fans, who show their support in many different ways and motivate me to keep going. I've formed some awesome new friendships with readers because of this series, and I can't wait to get to know even more of you. <3

ABOUT THE
AUTHOR

Stephanie Mirro is an Amazon Charts bestselling author with a lifelong love of ancient mythology. That love led to a college major in the Classics, which wasn't as much fun as writing her own fantastical mythology stories. But her education combined with an overactive imagination and a love for all things fantasy resulted in a writing career.

Although born and raised in Southern Arizona, Stephanie now resides in Georgia with her husband, two kids, and two furbabies. This thing called "seasons" is still magical.

Interested in the longer, more entertaining story? Visit stephaniemirro.com/about